# SHE SAYS SHE'S MY DAUGHTER

# BOOKS BY LAUREN NORTH

*My Word Against His*

*All the Wicked Games*

*Safe at Home*

*One Step Behind*

*The Perfect Betrayal*

# SHE SAYS SHE'S MY DAUGHTER

## LAUREN NORTH

*bookouture*

Published by Bookouture in 2023

An imprint of Storyfire Ltd.
Carmelite House
50 Victoria Embankment
London EC4Y 0DZ

www.bookouture.com

ISBN: 978-1-83790-662-8
eBook ISBN: 978-1-83790-655-0

*For Andy*

*

*Before you read this story – my story – there are three things I want you to know:*

*1. Only I know what really happened to Abigail fourteen years ago, and only I know why she came back when she did.*

*2. There were no accidents. Everything I did, I did with intent.*

*3. I never meant for any of this to happen.*

*If you think these last two points contradict each other, that I'm somehow confused or sick like some of the papers are calling me; if you think it's not possible to have intent and not mean it, then turn the page. Read on, read every word right to the end and you'll see just like I did that everything you think you know, everything you believe, can change in the blink of an eye.*

# PART I

# PROLOGUE

## SARAH

Peals of giggling, childish delight carry in the salty sea air. Screeching and laughter and 'Hey, look at me'. It lights a warmth in the pit of my stomach that radiates through my body all the way to the tips of my toes, now buried in the cool sand.

'What are you thinking about?' Michael asks, turning on the blanket and kissing my neck. His hand brushes against my thigh, flooding my thoughts with images of last night and the heat of our bodies.

I prop myself onto my elbows and feel the shift of sand and pebbles beneath the picnic blanket. I smile at Rebecca, sat propped up against a towel by my feet, babbling to herself as she plays with a collection of colourful stacking pots.

I nod to Daniel and Abigail by the shoreline. A barefooted Daniel, six now, and full of the importance of a big brother, is crouching in the shallows of the North Sea on the coast of Suffolk, filling a yellow bucket with water and sludgy sand while four-year-old Abigail waits nearby, dancing from foot to foot as the waves hit the sand and run closer and closer.

'I'm thinking how nice it is to see them playing together. And how I don't want to go back to the real world tomorrow.'

We're only an hour from our home in the Essex countryside, but it feels like a different world here. A different pace.

'I thought you might be thinking up new ways to bribe Abigail into taking her shoes off before bed tonight,' Michael says, pushing a hand through his dark-blond hair before shielding his eyes from the afternoon sun to watch too.

'And that.' My laugh is easy and light. A holiday laugh. I draw in a deep breath of fresh air and lean my head against Michael's chest. I don't want this feeling to end but already to-do lists and schedules are creeping into my thoughts, a tide moving ever closer.

'Those shoes will probably fall apart when we get home, considering how many times they've been in the sea this week.'

I watch now as Abigail takes the yellow bucket from Daniel and carries it, water sloshing, up the beach a little to three huge rocks – boulders really – that sit a metre from the shore. She is wearing a pink summer dress underneath an old *Thomas the Tank Engine* jumper of Daniel's that she loves just as much as the garish red supermarket trainers Daniel chose for her birthday last month.

'What time is Janie getting here?' Michael asks.

I can tell from his tone that he'd rather not spend the last night of our holiday with my best friend.

I check my phone. 'In an hour. And before you say anything, she was visiting her parents just up the coast and she's the kids' godmother. She's been going through a tough time with Phil and I know she'd appreciate an evening with us. Phil might drive up too and join us for dinner.'

'No luck with IVF then?' Michael asks.

I shake my head. 'Which is why she needs distracting. You know how much she dotes on the kids.'

My eyes stray back to Daniel and Abigail, and I feel another burst of warmth for how lucky we are. I watch Abigail, brown hair straggly and wild, her face set in concentration as she places the bucket on one of the lower rocks before Daniel tips the contents out and they giggle as gloopy wet sand splats onto the rock.

I laugh too. The sound of it fills my ears and then my head and then suddenly the sound is all wrong. It's a ringing in my own head. Distant and strange.

The sun pulls away. The sand disappears from between my toes. I don't know what's happening but instinctively I fight it.

'Mummy.' Abigail is calling me from the rocks, beckoning me to join her. Every cell in my body wants to leap up and run to her, to sweep her into my arms and hold her tight. Safe. Forever.

\*

FRIDAY

# ONE

## SARAH

Friday, 5 a.m.

I wake with a start, eyes flying open, breath catching in my lungs. For one glorious second, the warmth in the pit of my stomach remains. Then it's gone – grains of sand washed away by the reality now crashing through me.

My chest tightens and my first breath is shallow against the hollow pain.

Thirteen years, ten months and nine days.

I repeat the numbers in my head another three times. Thirteen years, ten months and nine days since I last saw Abigail – my beautiful daughter with her wild brown hair and mischievous smile.

In the early days, I counted the hours too.

Three.

Ten.

Twenty-four.

Forty-eight.

Seventy-two.

On and on and on as we waited for news that never came. Words never spoken.

*Found. Safe. Unharmed.*

For a moment the pain is a knife wound in my heart threatening to engulf me, but I grit my teeth and force it back into its box. It doesn't want to go; it never does, like a toddler bucking against the pushchair, refusing to be strapped in. But I am stronger than this pain and I will not allow it to beat me today.

I throw back the covers and pull on yesterday's discarded jeans and an old green jumper, out of shape but too warm and familiar to ever throw away. Every night when I close my eyes, I will the dream to come, desperately longing to see Abigail, to be back in that moment, but when it does, the day that follows is so much harder.

*Escape.* The word whispers in my thoughts. I need to get out.

'Barley,' I whisper, glancing at the digital clock on the nightstand. It's only a few minutes past five.

His long floppy ears twitch, but he doesn't move from the bottom of the bed.

'Barley,' I say again.

My voice seems loud in the silence. Not even the boiler is humming into life. It will be 8 a.m. before Michael emerges from our bedroom – his bedroom now I suppose. Rebecca will be up in an hour, allowing herself time to do her hair just so and rehearse for the school play before Michael drives her to school. Fifteen years old and one year away from her exams.

As for Daniel, he'll swing out of bed when it suits him. I try to remember if he has lectures today but the timetable always seems to change. When he's not studying computer science at the local uni, he's picking up shifts at the bar in town, coming home at all hours. Sometimes days will pass without me seeing him.

I feel a pang for the gaps in his life he doesn't share with me. The friends and relationships, the life he has outside of this house. I know all of Rebecca's friends. I know where she goes and when she'll be home. But Daniel, at twenty, shares little of his life with us. It's normal. I understand, but still there's an ache for how it used to be when he'd tell me all about his day at school and the lessons he liked. When he'd sit in bed with me and show me the sketches he'd done of a bird that had caught his eye or a car he liked.

I shake the thought away and turn to Barley. 'I know it's early.'

Barley stretches his front paws but refuses to open his eyes. His soft apricot fur is brown in the dim light of the bedroom.

'Walkies.'

The word cattle-prods him to life. He whips around, half tumbling, half leaping from the bed and beats me to the door.

*One, two, three, four...* Barley's small body whips around my heels as I count the steps along the hallway and down the staircase, all the way to the kitchen and the mudroom beyond it. Fifty-five.

Sometimes counting helps to fill the silence, to keep the thoughts I dare not think at bay. I wonder how many steps I'll count today, how many blocks of time, how many tiles on bathroom walls, and a hundred other nonsense things. Sometimes it helps, sometimes it doesn't, but either way it's a habit now.

By the time I open the back door and step into the darkness of the morning, the box in my mind is shut tight and my thoughts are my own again. I draw in the first deep breath of cold spring air blowing across the Essex countryside and feel ready to face whatever the day will throw at me.

A laughable thought in hindsight. I could live a thousand lifetimes and nothing could've prepared me for what was coming.

# TWO

## ABI

Friday, 2 p.m.

Abi grips the dark-blue railing and stops halfway up the four concrete steps that lead to her new life. Her real life. The rumble of engines carries from the road behind her – London buses, delivery trucks, black cabs, cars and bikes all weaving around each other; the noise a constant hum.

She moves. Another step up. Then stops. The enormity of what she's about to do suddenly feels like a brick wall, a locked door. No way to continue. He made it all sound so easy. This is what she deserves. This is where she belongs. She wants to believe it, but if her real life is ahead of her, then what does that mean for her past? If she isn't the person she thought she was, then who is she?

An icy wind hits her face and lifts up the brown waves of her hair, landing it in a tangle on top of the small black backpack sitting on her shoulders. The wind sweeps through the loose knits of her jumper, the cold pushing just as easily into her mind, blowing away the questions like it blows the empty crisp packet on the pavement, chasing it away to rest somewhere else.

Abi shivers, wiggling toes that feel so cold they could snap right off in the once-white trainers she's had since forever. According to the fuzzy image of the blonde weather woman she watched on the tiny TV in her hotel room this morning, it's the coldest spring in England since records began. Abi can believe it. Why the hell hadn't he given her a coat?

She pulls the straps of her rucksack tighter and stares at the glass door and the silver lettering bolted to the brickwork above it: Bethnal Green Police Station. It's now or never. There's no more time to be sure. She's out of money and out of options.

Abi takes the final step, pushing open the door and stepping inside. A moment later, the door closes behind her with a swoosh, cutting off the wind and the hum of traffic. Her fingers throb with the sudden warmth of the empty waiting area.

To either side of her sit two rows of blue plastic chairs, bolted to a metal beam that runs the length of the wall, leading down to a high front desk. There are no pens on the desk, no leaflets. Nothing that could be picked up and flung in a heated moment.

There's a movement in front of her. The creak of a chair and then a police officer standing and clearing his throat. He has grey thinning hair next to wisps of faded orange sideburns that curl and poke in different directions. The collar of his shirt shines a bright white next to the black of his jumper.

'Good afternoon,' he says, his voice deep and scratchy. 'Can I help you?'

The question sends a bullet of fear through her. Her body freezes. Her lungs, her heart, her mind – they are now locked behind the unmovable door. From somewhere deep inside her, a distant alarm starts to ring.

Is she sure about this?

The moment passes and she moves again, walking the final paces to the desk, her legs shaking beneath her. Sure or not, this is her life, Abi reminds herself. Her real life.

The policeman smiles as she approaches. A well-practised smile – friendly but standoffish. Business-like. Abi wonders how many years that smile has taken to perfect, how many victims and criminals and everyone in between he's greeted to get it just right.

'Is there anything you need?' The officer raises eyebrows the same colour as his sideburns.

*Out of money, out of options*, Abi reminds herself.

The words rise inside her. She's said them a hundred times or more to her reflection in the rusted hotel mirror, but still they feel clunky in her mouth. 'I... I'm Abigail Wick.' The words come out fast, as though she's speaking in her Spanish tongue, the rush of sentences pushed together.

Silence. The stunned kind that no words can fill.

Abi watches the officer's lips part, mouth gaping. She sees his eyes widen and wonders if goosebumps are prickling along his arms and marching like ants across his body in the same way they are hers.

How long, Abi wonders as the silence draws from one beat to the next, will it be before speaking her own name doesn't cause a flutter in her chest and her breath to snag in her throat? *Hi, I'm Jane Smith, Elizabeth Jones, Katy Tomlin, Abigail Wick.* It's just a name. Except, of course, it's not. Everyone in the world knows it, knows her, and saying her own name to someone else for the first time is dropping the mother of all bombshells.

The officer coughs. 'Excuse me?' he says.

'My name...' Abi slows down now, her accent softening as she makes an effort to pronounce the words clearly. And even though she's just as terrified, a small part of her relishes the look of piss-your-pants disbelief on the officer's face. Or maybe she's just delaying the detonation of the bomb, the inevitability of what will come next when her words sink in. 'I'm Abigail Rose

Wick. My parents are Sarah and Michael Wick, and I've been missing for fourteen years.'

Her heart drums against her chest. 'Inhale, blink, exhale. Don't look away,' he'd told her. She pictures his face now; his dark eyes alight with something – desperation, love, fear – burning into her own as he spoke. Always repeating himself and demanding she say it back. 'You can do this. You have to do this. Not just for yourself or for me, but for them – your family. Make them believe you.'

Abi watches the colour of the officer's face change from pasty white to puce and imagines a button under the desk, and fingers, out of sight, jabbing. A silent alert flashing somewhere in the building: *Help needed at the front desk.*

She turns, glancing back to the glass entrance. Does it have a locking mechanism controlled by the same button? Is she trapped?

It's a stupid thought. Too many American action movies growing up, fuelling the active imagination of a lonely child. It was Caroline, her mother's, fault – if Abi can even call her that now. A blonde American living in the suburbs of shitsville, with Jhon away on business, or wherever, so much of the time. Caroline devoured cheesy American movies and TV shows from the eighties and nineties. *Lethal Weapon, Beverly Hills Cop, Columbo* reruns, and anything with Harrison Ford.

Abi shuts down the thought. Just thinking about those films, that time, her mother, brings back the cloying, inescapable heat and the smell of body odour and stale food. The feeling of suffocation that comes from being trapped inside the same four walls day after day, month after month.

The policeman's mouth opens then closes again, then opens, then closes, like the gimmicky singing fish on the wall at the café she'd worked in up until last summer. Up until the moment she'd read Jhon's letter.

Staring at the officer, Abi can hear the grating sound of the fish's song as it turned its head and opened its mouth anytime a customer decided to press its button. And they all liked to press that stupid button.

The officer moves a hand to his mouth, wiping a finger over the edges. One side, then the other. 'Would you mind taking a seat for a moment while I call one of my colleagues to assist you?'

Abi nods, edging backwards towards the row of chairs, her gaze fixing once again on the glass doors. She wonders if he's still out there. Watching her. She wants to tell him that she did it. She wants to see his smile and hear the praise he so rarely gives.

'On second thought,' the officer says, 'perhaps you'd be more comfortable in one of our interview rooms while you wait.' He disappears and a moment later the door beside the desk opens and he's beckoning her forward.

Does he think she's likely to run away? A bubble of nervous laughter fizzes up Abi's body, catching in her chest, making her lips twitch. She has nowhere to go. Everything she owns is in her backpack. £89.61 – all the money she has, all that's left of what he gave her – is hidden beneath a single change of clothes and the Colombian passport she'll never use again.

If she turns now, if she runs out the glass door, back to the biting wind and the exhaust fumes, where would she go? She has no home. £89.61 won't go far. Not even one more night in the grubby hotel three streets away with walls so thin that she can hear the guest in the next room watching porn long into the night.

No. They've both come too far to turn back now. And so Abi clutches the straps of her backpack and follows the officer deeper into the police station, her trainers squeaking with each step across the grey linoleum floor.

For the first time since entering the police station, Abi thinks of Sarah and Michael – her parents. How long until they're told? Her throat clenches like a fist, cutting off her airway for several beats as a deep, wrenching fear charges bull-like through her mind, and with it comes the questions she cannot answer. Will they love her? Will they accept her? Will they believe her?

# THREE

## ABI

The officer leads her to a room with a table and four chairs. 'Someone will be with you in a moment,' he says, staring at her face for another long second before closing the door and hurrying back to his desk to make the call.

No windows. No one-way glass mirror. Just four cement-grey walls that feel like they're closing in around her as she slides into the seat opposite the door. The enclosed space makes her skin itch and prickle, reminding her of a childhood spent in locked rooms.

Two fluorescent tubes on the ceiling emit a harsh light that makes the skin on her hands look dirty. Less than a week without sun and already her tan has faded.

'It's good to be pale,' he told her yesterday, but she didn't like the washed-out, frightened face that stared back at her from the rusty mirror this morning.

The hard plastic of the chair digs into her spine as Abi waits. She can feel the edges of her mobile digging into her from the back pocket of her jeans, urging her to retrieve it, tap out the number she's memorised but not stored, and reassure him she's OK. She's done it. She's in.

But in the top corner of the room, above the door, is a discreet black dome, and somewhere in the building, at the end of one of the grey corridors with the squeaky floors, is a room filled with recording equipment. And somewhere in a computer system, her every move is being recorded, logged and stored away. So instead, she waits.

It takes twenty minutes for the door to open.

Something Caroline used to say pops into Abi's head as two women step into the room: 'Out of the frying pan and into the fire.' Abi can hear Caroline's nasal American accent in her mind. Only now does she grasp the full meaning of those words.

'Hello,' the first woman says, greeting Abi with a confident smile. She's tall and angular with tight blonde curls cropped close to her head. No uniform. Instead, she's wearing a lilac cotton shirt and black fitted trousers. There's a notebook tucked under one arm and a pen pushed behind her ear. 'I'm DC Cara Swain.'

'Hi,' Abi replies, her voice lost to the scraping of chairs as the officers sit down.

'And this,' DC Swain continues, motioning a hand to the woman now sat beside her, 'is PC Robertson.'

The smile feels tight on Abi's face. It's a fight to keep her gaze up, her head held high, the kind of posture a person who's done nothing wrong would have.

'Can I get you some water?' PC Robertson asks. She is younger than DC Swain, her petite frame hidden beneath a shapeless white shirt and black uniform.

Abi shakes her head, allowing locks of her hair to fall forward. 'No, thank you.'

'I'm so sorry for keeping you waiting,' DC Swain says, elongating the 'so' as though to prove she means it. 'We needed to determine if a guardian should be present before we spoke to you and that took a bit of back and forth.'

'Oh... right. Why?' Abi asks, using the same one-syllable

word that drove Caroline crazy. Why can't we go out today? Why can't I go to school like the other children? *Por qué?* Asking and whining until the palm of Caroline's hand smacked her cheek.

'Just because, Abelia. Just because,' Caroline always replied.

Sometimes Abi pushed and pushed just to get that slap, just to feel the tingling sting on her skin, to break up the day, the week, the month, the boredom.

'Legally speaking,' DC Swain says, opening the notebook and flicking to a clear page, 'anyone under the age of eighteen should have a parent or guardian present during police interviews. Something which is difficult in your case, because we think the next step here is to speak to you before notifying Mr and Mrs Wick.

'So, before we begin, I must explain that this is an informal discussion. No recordings are being made. However, you do have the right to a police-appointed appropriate adult, should you want one.'

Abi shakes her head again, feeling stupid. How could she forget she's only seventeen? Panic rears up, wild, untamed, shrinking the walls of the room around her. What else has she forgotten?

'Would you like someone to sit beside you and help you?' PC Robertson asks.

'I'm fine,' Abi replies. 'But thank you,' she adds, remembering at the last moment to be polite. It's not natural for her like it is for some people. Too much time spent alone. It's not like she's ever had to remember to say please to herself.

There's a pause. The only noise is the creak of PC Robertson's chair and the drumming of Abi's heartbeat in her ears.

'I'm sure you can appreciate that this will be a huge shock for Mr and Mrs Wick,' DC Swain continues, her tone sympathetic. Soothing. And yet it rattles Abi a little. Why doesn't the detective call them her parents? 'And while we don't want to delay the news for any longer than necessary, we have a duty to verify your information first, in case we can save them from any undue distress.'

'In case I'm lying, you mean?' The words rush out, feeling hot on Abi's lips. Her accent sounds suddenly stronger. Less Colombian, more LA twang like Caroline's, with a hint of something else just underneath.

'That's an interesting accent you have,' DC Swain says. 'I'm terrible with accents. Is it Spanish?'

'Colombian,' Abi replies, forcing herself to calm down. They haven't even started asking her questions yet. She knew this wouldn't be easy. He made her practise every answer she'd need to give. Not just the words but the tone too, so it lands just right. 'It's where I grew up. In Buenaventura.'

Abi lifts her face and stares into the eyes of the detective. They're the same pale-grey colour as the walls. 'What else would you like to know?'

DC Swain taps her pen on the notebook but, before she can reply, the door opens and the officer with the orange sideburns appears, carrying a tray with three cups on it. He slides it onto the table and retreats without a word.

'Thanks, Jim,' DC Swain calls after him as PC Robertson passes a cup to Abi.

It's tea. Milky and weak. Abi would've preferred coffee. Not the instant crusty granules in the little brown packet she's been drinking in the hotel room, but the rich earthy powder Jhon used to bring back from his long trips away and drank as if it were water.

'This is a rather unprecedented situation,' DC Swain says, taking a sip of tea. There's a slight pause, a grimace, and then she places the cup back on the tray. 'But right now there are three things of critical importance that we – the police – need to determine.'

Another tap of the pen on the blank page of the notebook.

'Firstly, we need to make sure you are who you say you are. Secondly, if you are Abigail Wick, then you've been the victim of a heinous crime and we have a duty to make sure you are well, both psychologically and physically. And finally, of great importance, is that the Abigail Wick disappearance is an open child-abduction case. We need to find the perpetrators, and we'll need lots of information from you to help us with all three of these things. Does that sound OK?'

Abi nods and moves the cup to her lips. Scalding liquid fills her mouth. It tastes as good as it looks, but she has to do something to break the piercing glare of the detective. The alarm is ringing in her head again. Less than an hour in and there it is – the whopping great hole in their plan they hadn't seen coming. Of course the police will want to find the perpetrators. It isn't as if Abi wandered off and has been lost for fourteen years, is it? Why hadn't she realised this? Why hadn't he?

Her mouth turns dry. Thoughts and questions swarm in dizzying circles around her head.

'Perhaps the best place to start is just to tell us a little about yourself. Fourteen years is a long time. Abigail Wick was four when she was taken. Not many people remember much that far back into their childhoods. What makes you think you're Abigail?'

There is so much Abi could say right now. She could launch into the whole story of her childhood, her life. But already she's tired of this room, and time is marching on and right now she has nowhere to sleep tonight. So she gives them what they want. Proof she is Abigail.

'I... I have a chicken-pox scar on my right breast.'

'Excuse me?' DC Swain's eyes widen a little but then she seems to gather herself. 'A chicken-pox scar?'

Abi nods, her confidence returning. This is right. She is right. 'You want to make sure I'm Abigail Wick, right? So I'm telling you I have a chicken-pox scar on my right breast, an inch below my nipple. I don't remember having chicken pox, so I'm guessing I was really young and that maybe I had it before I was taken.'

The grey eyes of the detective bore into Abi for a long moment, and then, as though deciding something, she scrawls a line of words on the notepad.

Abi glances at the scribble of the detective's handwriting. She has no idea what it says. Even if it was inches from her face and the right way round, Abi still isn't sure she could read it, but PC Robertson must decipher it because she stands and, after shooting Abi another smile, leaves the room.

Abi wonders for a moment if the detective will ask to see the scar. The thought of the white circular indent makes her stomach turn. She doesn't want to think about it. What she wants, really wants, right now, is to go home. But Abi doesn't know what that word means anymore, or if she'll ever find out.

# FOUR

## ABI

### Then

Abelia's stomach gurgled as she hovered in the living-room doorway. A streak of afternoon sunlight peeked through the faded floral curtains and landed in a stripe on the back of the red sofa. A stinky kind of smell hung in the air, like her bedcovers smelled sometimes after a nightmare when she'd wake to find her skin damp and her hair stuck to her head.

A sudden spatter of gunfire from the TV bounced around the small room.

Abelia glanced at her mom. She was doing the sleep thing she did – awake but not awake; sat upright on the sofa, eyes open but glassy. Her mom's face was puffy from crying, and tears sat on her cheeks.

'Momma?' Abelia said when the *pop-pop* of the guns stopped. It was the first word she'd said all day and her voice was too quiet, as if she'd forgotten how to use it.

'I'm hungry, Momma,' she said, a little louder this time.

She watched her mom, waiting for the words to register in

her ears and wake her up. Sometimes it worked, and sometimes Abelia could push her face right up to her mom's ear and shout, and still she wouldn't wake up.

Her mom didn't blink or move or show any sign she'd heard Abelia.

Abelia sighed and walked around the back of the sofa, keeping her eyes away from the TV in case she saw a dead body that would float in her nightmares for weeks. She didn't care about the noises anymore. She was seven now, and seven-year-olds didn't need to cover their ears, but she hated the dead bodies.

Her bare feet scuffed the dirty floors as she moved noiselessly past the front door, towards the kitchen. But at the window, she paused. She could hear the children shouting. School had finished, she guessed, as the pain of hunger became a stab of something else she didn't understand.

She longed to throw open the curtains, press her face to the glass and watch the children play. She imagined two girls swinging a jump rope high in the air and singing a rhyme as another girl jumped in the middle. She imagined the boys too; charging after an old ball, their T-shirts discarded in the dust.

Abelia's fingers brushed the coarse fabric of the curtains. She flicked a look back at her mom, still staring at the TV, before inching herself closer to the window. She desperately wanted to be out there with them, to be the one jumping in the centre of the rope. What harm could watching do? No one would see her.

In one movement, Abelia ducked down and sprang up between the curtains and the window. Her eyes stung against the piercing daylight. She blinked, a smile touching her face as she waited for her eyes to adjust and the children to come into view.

'Get away from the window.' Her mom's voice was hoarse

and scratchy and laced with fear that made Abelia's legs buckle. She dropped to the floor and back to the dimness.

'It isn't safe,' her mom said.

Abelia hugged her legs closer to her body and sighed. At least she'd woken her mom up. 'I'm hungry, Momma,' she said, placing a lock of hair in her mouth and sucking on the end.

'Oh, Abelia, please, Momma is so sad today. You can make yourself something, can't you? There's some bread still.'

Abelia didn't bother to tell her mom that she'd finished the bread yesterday when she'd chewed on the last stale crust for dinner. Instead, she pulled herself up and moved into the kitchen. She stood on her tiptoes and stretched until the tips of her fingers touched a plate. She scooched it closer until she could grip it enough to pick up.

The cheese was hard and smelled funny, like the living room, like her bedcovers, but Abelia was too hungry to care.

'Come sit with me, Abelia. Make me happy with a cuddle,' her mom called from the living room.

Abelia's heart sank but she did as she was told. If she could make her mom happy, then maybe she'd go out to get food.

She sat down beside her mom and allowed herself to be pulled closer until her head rested on her mom's chest. The stink was worse now. Abelia could taste it lining the roof of her mouth.

When the credits ran in lines up the screen, Abelia raised her head, hoping to see a smile on her mom's face, but she was sleeping with her eyes open again.

Abelia pushed her mom's arm away and went to lie down on the cool covers of her bed. All of a sudden, she felt tired and sick.

*What are you so afraid of, Momma?*

*Why can't we go out?*

*Why can't I go to school like the other children?*

Abelia pushed the questions away. She'd asked them so

many times, but not once had she had an answer. She closed her eyes and wished Jhon would hurry up and come back. She hated that he travelled so much, only staying for one night every two weeks, bringing shopping bags filled with food and more schoolwork for her. Maybe if she got all the sums right this time, he'd stay longer; maybe he'd take her with him next time.

# FIVE

## ABI

Friday, 3 p.m.

The mention of the scar has changed the atmosphere in the room. Abi senses the caution still there, coated in a friendly professionalism – like the sugary sweetness of the cocadas she loves so much. But there's an excitement now too. A maybe. A what-if.

DC Swain's pen stops tapping and she tilts her head a fraction as her gaze fixes on Abi. 'Would you mind telling me a little about your childhood? If it's not too upsetting. Do you remember anything from the abduction?' Her questions are tentative now, her tone softer.

Abi wants to ask the detective if she believes her, but she keeps the question in and fiddles with the ends of her hair instead. 'No,' she says. 'I don't remember my real parents – or at least I don't think I do. I've always had dreams of a place I've never been and building sandcastles on a beach with people I've never met. I don't remember ever being scared or alone,' she lies. 'Or missing anyone when I was very young, although I'm sure I must have done because Buenaventura is nothing like here, but I don't remember.'

DC Swain's pen scratches on the notebook for another few seconds before she looks up. 'What about the person or people who raised you?'

'A couple. The woman I thought was my mother, her name was Caroline Pérez. Pérez is her married name. I don't know her maiden name. She never told me. She was an American. From Los Angeles, I think, although I can't remember her ever telling me that. She didn't speak about her past, but I always had the sense that something happened in America and she couldn't go back, even though I think she wanted to. She died of breast cancer when I was twelve.'

'And her husband?'

'Jhon Pérez. He worked for a coffee-bean export company in Buenaventura. He died of bowel cancer last year.'

Despite everything she now knows about the man who raised her, an ache still balloons in her throat at the mention of his name. But Abi doesn't stop. It feels good to talk. Not just because her only contact with anyone for months now has been him, and he isn't exactly the chatty type, but because it's a relief to tell her story at last.

'They were kind parents,' she continues, 'if that's what you were going to ask me next. I wasn't locked in a dungeon or made to do horrible things. I was a normal child. We lived in a house with high walls and a gate that was always locked.' Abi stares straight into DC Swain's eyes as she retells the story they've practised so many times it feels almost real. 'I wasn't allowed out at all when I was younger. I was told, and had always believed, it was because the city wasn't safe. It still isn't. Buenaventura is one of the biggest ports in Colombia. Drug trafficking and violence are part of everyday life. It's easy to get caught in the crossfire, especially if you look like my— if you look like Caroline, I mean. She was blonde and her skin was fair. She stood out. I did too but not as much, and Jhon worried something might happen to us.'

'When did you discover you might be Abigail Wick?'

'When Jhon died,' Abi says.

Inhale, blink, exhale. Don't look away. Truth, lie, truth, lie, truth – like the spinning of a roulette wheel.

'He was ill for a long time beforehand,' Abi continues. 'Afterwards, I was going through a stack of papers and there was a letter addressed to me. I opened the letter and it was all there. The truth.' Tears pool in Abi's eyes; for Jhon, or for the truth inside that letter, she isn't sure.

'Have you got the letter with you?' DC Swain raises her eyebrows and glances to the floor, where Abi's backpack sits.

'No.' She shakes her head and resists the urge to pull her bag closer to her feet. 'I was angry. I didn't believe it. Not at first anyway. I didn't want to believe it. I ripped it up and threw it away. But then I guess it started to make sense. How I wasn't allowed out, how there weren't any photos of me as a baby or growing up. It was in Spanish anyway. I can tell you what it said if you like?'

'Yes please.' DC Swain tilts her head a fraction, her pen poised on the notebook.

'It said: "My dearest Abelia"—'

'Abelia? Is that a Colombian name?'

'It's actually American. They always called me Abi, which up until last month didn't really make sense. I thought it was a nickname that stuck. But I also thought that I was their child. I thought I was Colombian – half Colombian anyway – that my birthday was in October and that I was eighteen.'

Inside Abi's head, the roulette wheel continues its clicking spin – black, red, black, red, truth, lie, truth, lie.

DC Swain scribbles another note before nodding at Abi.

'"My dearest Abelia",' Abi begins again, '"I'm sorry to be writing this letter, sorrier still for the sadness it will cause you. I must start by telling you how much you mean to me, and how much joy you've brought me and your mother from the first day we set eyes on you. Your mother and I longed for a child for many years, but we met late in our lives and God was not kind to us. Your mother became depressed. Whilst my love for her was enough for me, I knew she needed more. She needed a child, but things in her past, which are not important now, made legal adoption impossible."'

She pauses, hurt stinging at the edges of her eyes. It doesn't matter how many times she thinks of the letter Jhon gave her, how many times she searches between the words for answers, it still causes a stab of pain to her chest.

'Take your time,' DI Swain says, her face softening.

'Then it said, "I had to go away on business to England. I hated leaving your mother alone and worried constantly for her. I knew we wouldn't be able to continue as we were. I was on the east coast when I saw you walking alone on an empty beach. I watched you for some time. I wanted to make sure you didn't fall in the sea before your parents realised you were lost, but after a while, when no one came, I realised you weren't lost but found. God had smiled down on us.

'"What I did has rotted our insides. Your mother paid her price, and I am paying mine. Your real name is Abigail Wick and you have a family in England. I am sorry for the hurt I've caused your family, and will now cause you, but you were loved by us as much as it is possible for any parent to love a child. Your adoring father, Jhon."'

Abi draws in a shaky breath. *Loved by us.* She wishes it was true.

'Eventually the truth sank in and I searched the internet. I even saw the image. The stranger on the boat was Jhon.'

DC Swain drops her gaze to her notebook again before focusing back on Abi, and just for a second there's a flicker of something behind the sympathy and the kindness. A steely glance, a suspicion that shoots a bolt of ice through Abi's veins.

'How did you get to London?' DC Swain asks.

Abi fiddles with the ends of her hair before dropping her hands and squashing them between her thighs. He's always telling her not to fidget so much. 'I sold Jhon's car and used the money to get a plane ticket. It took a few weeks.'

'Do you remember the flight number?'

She shrugs. 'No.' Abi wants to ask, *Who does?*, but keeps it in. 'It landed on Sunday morning at London Airport.'

'Which one?'

'Sorry?'

'Which London Airport? There are several,' the detective explained.

'Oh, I see. It was called He-something.'

'Heathrow.' DC Swain writes another line in her notebook. 'Today is Friday. Why did you wait five days before coming here? And why here?'

'I... I was scared,' Abi says. 'I didn't know how to do it. I didn't know if I should try and find them myself or come here. I wasn't sure anyone would believe me. I've been Abi Pérez for as long as I can remember. It's not easy to find out your whole life is a lie,' she whispers. Black, red, black, red, truth, lie, truth.

The door opens again and PC Robertson takes her seat as before, her cheeks slightly flushed, eyes bright, alert. Abi wonders where's she been and what that look means.

DC Swain closes her notebook, tucking the pen back behind her ear. 'Thank you, Abi. I'm sure it wasn't easy to tell me all of that. PC Robertson is going to stay with you now, and I'm going to call Essex Police and have a car sent to Mr and Mrs Wick's house.'

'You believe me?' The words tumble out of Abi before she can stop them.

DC Swain stands, pulling at the bottom of her shirt where it's risen up. Her eyes seem to assess Abi as she scoops up her notebook, flipping it to an empty page. 'I believe that the next step is to inform Mr and Mrs Wick. At a later date, you'll need to tell us all of this information again in a formal capacity and go into as much detail as you remember about your time in Colombia. There may have been more people involved in the abduction that just the couple who took care of you. We'll need to reach out to the Colombian authorities to verify the details you've given.'

Abi nods. Relief floods through her. She's done it. DC Swain can plan all she wants now, but Abi won't be speaking to her again. He promised her that.

DC Swain steps around the table towards Abi and, for a moment, she thinks the detective will offer a handshake or a reassuring shoulder pat, but neither come.

'Just one more thing,' DC Swain says, placing the notebook and pen in front of Abi. 'Would you mind writing down your address for us please?'

The relief twists into a knot of dread. She stares up at the detective, powerless to stop the sudden shift in emotion from playing on her face. 'You mean, the hotel I've been staying at?'

'Yes, and the address of your home in Colombia too. It will help us with our enquiries; nothing to worry about.'

Abi drops her head, allowing her hair to cover her face again. The plastic of the biro feels slick against the sweat forming on her palms as she thinks of the *Columbo* episodes Caroline forced her to watch every afternoon. Abi can't remember a single storyline, but she remembers the brown flapping raincoat and the hard-boiled eggs, and the way Columbo waited until he was just about to leave before delivering his final question to the suspect; the question that would blow the whole case open.

Is this what DC Swain is doing? What does she suspect?

Abi wills the pen to stop shaking in her hand as it touches the paper.

---

*I watch from across the road, half hidden by the bus stop and the two lines of steady traffic. A stranger. A nobody.*

*Abigail reaches the steps and my heart rattles in my chest like the idling engine of the bus now blocking my view.*

*It pulls away and I expect to see the door to the police station swinging closed, Abigail a silhouette inside.*

*But she is still on the steps. Hunched over with cold, frozen with indecision.*

*The fury comes instead. How can she not be sure? After all these months of coaxing and guiding.*

*I've told her over and over that she deserves this. That she must take what is rightfully hers. She has no idea how much I mean those words.*

*But still she hesitates.*

*Stupid little girl.*

*It's an effort not to rush at her, to push her the final steps through that door and into her new life.*

*There is nothing to lose and everything to gain. Why can't she see that?*

*I take a step closer to the road, ready to intercept if she turns and flees. I check the time, aware that I need to get going if I'm to be ready for the next part of the plan.*

*Then Abigail looks up at the doors and starts to move, disappearing a moment later.*

*Yes, Abigail!*

*Good girl.*

*You deserve this life.*

*But of course, it's not just Abigail whose world is about to change. There are her parents too.*

*What do they deserve?*

*The answer – everything. They deserve everything that's coming to them.*

# SIX

## SARAH

Friday, 4 p.m.

My fingers drum against the steering wheel as I watch the dark wooden gates shudder slowly into life. I know it's pointless, but I punch the black clicker beside my seat one, two, three more times, just as I always do. The gates ignore me, just as they always do, and continue at their designated speed.

A foot of my driveway is visible now and a familiar urge tugs at my insides, willing me to charge through the gap, to scrape the paintwork of my black Audi, just to hear the crunch of the wheels on the gravel drive. That noise, the rolling grind of a thousand pebbles, triggers something inside me. A Pavlovian response that signals the unbuckling of the invisible armour bolted so tight that I wonder sometimes in the small hours of the night if it's protecting me or killing me.

It's the noise that signals I'm home. The noise I hear when I vow never to leave again. Knowing even as I whisper the promise to myself, even as I shower off the layers of make-up from my day at the studio, how foolish I sound. In a day or two,

I'll be back in my car, willing the gates to hurry up and open so I can escape.

I breathe in, catching the pungent smell of perfume and hairspray, taking me back to the debate we shared on *Loose Women* today over Prince's Harry's right to royal security on UK visits. It feels so meaningless sometimes – most of the time. When you've lived through the worst thing imaginable, when you continue to live through it every day, it's impossible to get worked up about much else.

I do my weekly cookery segment and whatever other scraps of presenting are tossed my way. I should've given up after Abigail's abduction. I was no longer the sparkling TV presenter, a celebrity on the rise, hosting Britain's most popular daytime TV show.

I was toxic. I didn't need my agent, Don, to tell me that, although he did, multiple times. Nobody wanted to watch the tragic woman whose child had been abducted. And yet I stayed, I fought, I took whatever I was given, ignoring the critics and the suggestions of something in production. Janie was in production over with the BBC and I knew the kind of work she did, and I knew it wasn't for me.

Besides, I couldn't quit. I needed the familiar, the routine. Presenting was all I knew how to do. It was all I wanted to do after my dreams of being a newsreader went out the window early in the audition process.

'You're too pretty to read the news,' Don told me. 'Men will be thinking of sleeping with you; women will hate you. They'll turn over. You'll have to do something lighter if you want to be on TV.'

So I had. Starting with a daytime quiz and then a remake of *Blind Date*, then *Big Brother*. And after Daniel was born in my mid-twenties, and I'd gone from 'sexy to mumsy', as Don had so kindly put it, I'd landed co-host on *This Morning*.

After Abigail's abduction, it felt like I'd failed so spectacularly at being a mother and protecting my children, that presenting was all I had left that I was good at. And Michael had sold his business to throw himself into finding Abigail and later running her charity, so we'd needed the money. A whisper of another reason I'd stayed in TV enters my thoughts, but I snap open my eyes and continue to count.

It takes sixty seconds for the churning motor to pull the gates open. I've counted it a thousand times, maybe more. Today I counted how many steps it took from the car park to the studio: 250. I counted how many seconds it took Laura, the make-up girl, to make me presentable: 2,566. I counted the steps from my dressing room to my stool behind the *Loose Women* desk: fifty. And the time it took for the audience to stop clapping so the show could begin: twenty seconds. I continue to count and wonder if pulling into our wide sweeping driveway would feel as good with the grey rectangular paving slabs Michael had asked for one afternoon last summer.

'I've had a brilliant idea,' he'd said, leaning against the black granite island in the centre of the kitchen and waiting for me to ask what it was.

*Another one?* I'd wanted to say instead as I'd glanced at the modern monstrosity that was our new kitchen. Shiny black worktops and high-gloss white cupboards without handles – Michael's idea, along with the low glass conservatory on the side of the kitchen, overlooking the garden. Another room, another dining-room table and chairs that we really don't need. But I hadn't said it. I hadn't said anything. I'd just turned and raised my eyebrows.

'Daniel's driving now, and Rebecca will be too in a few years. We should get the driveway paved. We could get rid of the flower beds and that ridiculous patch of grass. It's an arse to cut, you know?'

I'd thought about my precious gravel and known I couldn't allow it. 'Why don't you dig the grass over and buy another bag of gravel then? It's not as if you don't have the time to do it.'

I'd clamped my mouth shut, but it was too late. It had been a stupid remark. Too harsh. It had hurt him; I could tell by the way his eyes had darkened a shade. I never knew eyes could do that until I met Michael. Way back when we were both young and full of passion and love, long before either of us knew what real pain felt like, his eyes had been one of the things I'd fallen in love with. They're a startling sky blue, but like the mood ring I had as a teenager, they change with his emotions – passion, anger, excitement, hurt and they darken to the colour of the deep-blue sea.

Michael had huffed and dropped to a crouch, yanking open the wine fridge underneath the island, hiding his hurt in the search for a bottle of Chablis. I hadn't bothered to glance at the red lines of the digital clock on the oven to check if it was even mid-afternoon. One argument at a time. Though the truth is, I'd stopped caring about his drinking a while ago – after the affairs had become public and we'd had to face up to the carcass of our marriage.

'It's not just the space, it's that bloody gravel,' he'd said with his head still buried in the fridge. Bottles had clinked and knocked against each other. He'd pulled one out to examine before swapping it for another, as if the vintage and the year made any difference – all he really wanted was the numbness alcohol could provide. 'You and Daniel drive off like you've committed a prison break, none the wiser to the stones that fly up and chip my windscreen. I had to call the windscreen repair service twice last month.'

'The gravel is staying.' I'd shaken my head, even though he wasn't looking. 'I like it, and anyway, we have a double garage full of junk, mostly stuff of your mother's. Clear it out and leave your car in there.'

So he had.

It was one of those mundane and utterly pointless arguments that I hate. The art of survival is all about knowing which parts of ordinary life to accept and which to avoid. Getting out of bed each morning, eating, going to work: these are crucial to my survival. Bickering with Michael, going to support groups, having friends are not. I could write a book about the art of survival. The ways I've learned to cope. The things that matter and the things that don't. But then, that's another thing about surviving – I have to focus on the day in front of me. Dwelling on the why or the how just won't do.

*Fifty-eight.*

*Fifty-nine.*

*Sixty.*

I open my eyes. The gates are wide now, revealing the bare yellow walls of Rose House, no longer covered in the pink climbing roses I'd fallen in love with. The roses I can no longer bear. My patience has worn thin, so when I tap my foot to the accelerator, the car lurches forward too fast. The sound of the tiny stones crunching and sliding underneath my wheels fills my ears, unwinding the outer edges of tension that have been throbbing in my head since I left the studio.

Without thinking, I swing the car around to the right, past the stone steps and white columns of the entrance porch, past the long flat window with the white wood moulding that looks into our living room, and the patch of grass beneath it that Michael hates to mow.

It's only then that I realise the space to the left of the garage where I park is taken. I stomp my foot to the brake and jolt to a stop half a metre behind a red Ford Focus. Sitting beside it is another car I don't recognise: a dark-blue saloon.

*Dammit!*

The tension in my head returns, like fingers under my skull, pressing into my brain. It has to be Michael's support group.

The women and men with watery eyes and shaking voices who retell the same story over and over. Who untuck the raggedy ends of toilet tissue from the sleeves of their jumpers, dab their eyes and help themselves to another slice of cake.

'What does it achieve?' I'd hissed at Michael a few months back, after another meeting had run on and pots of tea had been replaced with bottles of wine, and four women and three men had taken over my kitchen for the evening, talking over each other to be heard.

'We can't all be like you, Sarah,' Michael had replied. 'Some of us need to talk about it. These people need—' He'd stopped himself then, but I knew what he'd been about to say: *me*. They needed him, and I didn't. Michael was a man who needed to be needed. It was in his DNA, and I didn't need him anymore.

Stay or go? The question plays a tug of war in my head.

I twist in my seat and glance up at the house. And then behind me to the gates. They're still open. I can reverse back into the road and go for a drive. Wander the aisles of Waitrose and kill time. But I promised Rebecca I'd help her with her lines for the school play.

I think of her flopped on her bed, mouthing the words of her script for *Fame*, and my desire to flee evaporates. I thrust the gear stick into reverse and manoeuvre my car to the other side of the red Focus.

On the driveway, a bitter wind billows through my blouse, carrying with it the smell of burning cherry wood drifting from our red-brick chimney. The gates are already closing, shutting me in.

I turn to glance at the two cars and that's when I notice the sticker in the back window. Sudden panic sweeps through me. My armour, my outer shell, splinters as if it's made from the flimsy plastic of a cheap toy rather than the steel I imagine it to be.

The sticker is black with two words written in bold white writing: Essex Police. I turn towards the house and even though my heart feels like it's stopped, I run. Please not again. Please don't let anything have happened to Daniel or Rebecca.

# SEVEN

## SARAH

My hands shake as I thrust the key into the lock on the front door. It crashes open, banging against the wall hard enough to leave a dent, but I don't care.

*Please not Daniel or Rebecca. Please not again.*

'Michael?' My voice is loud. Shrill. 'Michael?'

'I'm here.' He appears in the doorway from the kitchen. A tuft of grey-blond hair is sticking out at an odd angle where he's run his hands through it and forgotten to flatten it back. 'I've been calling your mobile,' he says, already moving towards me.

Barley bounds towards me. He waits for me to stroke him, tail wagging, paws dancing on the wooden floor, but I'm too distracted to give him more than a brief pat. 'I... was driving. What's going on? Is—'

'The police are here to talk to us,' he cuts in.

My gaze flicks past Michael to the kitchen beyond and an unfamiliar black suit jacket hung over the back of a chair.

'Is it... Daniel? Has he done something stupid?'

I don't know why I say it. Daniel doesn't do stupid things. At least, I don't think he does, but maybe in the storm raging in my thoughts, that scenario is the only one I can process. An unpaid speeding fine or some other misdemeanour.

'Everyone's OK,' Michael says.

Our eyes connect and that one look conveys a thousand unspoken truths between us.

'They arrived twenty minutes ago and they want to talk to both of us.'

There's a flash of something unfamiliar in his blue eyes. Hope, I realise.

*Oh, Michael,* I want to say, *after all this time, surely even you're not that deluded?*

'There's someone else here too,' he adds.

'Who?'

A movement in the kitchen doorway catches my eye. Barley spins around, rushing at the man already crouching down to stroke him.

'Hi, Sarah.' Ryan smiles as he rubs Barley's fur.

Memories I've forced myself to forget thrust themselves to the surface, bringing with them a torrent of pain that hits my chest and punches the breath out of my lungs. I gasp for air, but it doesn't help.

All of a sudden I'm slipping, like I'm on the muddy banks of the river in winter, sliding my feet out from under me. The salty smell of the sea and the screech of seagulls fills my senses.

Another kitchen, almost fourteen years ago. When the denial stopped and the real pain started. When it was no longer about a four-year-old who'd wandered too far from the garden of a holiday cottage to be found at any moment.

Endless days of waiting for more news, more sightings that never came. I remember six-year-old Daniel, sullen and mute, colouring on the floor beside my feet, and Rebecca fidgeting on my lap, babbling and oblivious, banging a plastic rattle against the table. I remember the echo of Michael's voice in the next room as he made phone call after phone call.

And the young family liaison officer in a cheap suit and creased shirt on his first assignment, making cups of tea and cheese sandwiches that nobody touched, his large frame dwarfing the cottage kitchen just as it dwarfs my kitchen doorway now.

I stare at him, wading through the memories and the pain of the past until I can find my voice. 'Ryan, what are you doing here? Where's Becca?' My heart thunders in my chest as new fears propel through my mind.

'I'm right here, Mum.' Rebecca's white-blonde hair and grinning face appear beside Ryan; he's still squatting so the two appear almost the same height.

I rush towards her, ignoring the unsteadiness of my legs.

One, two, three, four strides and I'm beside my daughter, pulling her into a tight embrace and breathing in the smell of her deodorant – sweet, candy-like. 'How was school today? Are you OK?'

'It was fine, Mum,' Rebecca says, stepping out of my arms and leaving a cold void in her wake. 'I'm fine.'

'What's going on?' I look at Michael now. Properly look, for the first time in years it feels, catching a tiny glimpse of the man I married, the man I was so very happy with, laughed with, joked we'd take over the world with – me in TV and him in marketing. Oh, how we'd thought we could have it all. Careers, money, a family, love, happiness, the world.

'I don't know,' Michael says, and the glimmer is gone, and he's just the man I share a house and the care of our children with once more. A partnership of some sort that I wonder sometimes if I'll ever have the courage to end. It's then that I catch the excitement in his voice. It turns my stomach. He can't really think—

'Mr and Mrs Wick,' another voice calls from the extension at the side of the kitchen. 'Perhaps you'd like to take a seat?'

Ryan stands up, the tips of his dark hair skimming the top of the door frame. I take him in. He has aged well, in the way that men do, better looking in his late thirties than he was in his twenties. The extra weight is gone, as are the cheap suits, and he has a short, dark beard that shapes his face.

'I'm making tea,' Ryan says as if it's the most normal thing in the world to walk into someone else's house, put their kettle on to boil and rifle through their cupboards for teabags.

The air smells of herbs and Michael's beef stew bubbling gently in the slow cooker as I follow Ryan into the kitchen. My body feels weak and yet, at the same time, full of lead. Michael's hand touches my back, guiding me through the kitchen, past the island with the four high stools we never sit on and the wine fridge only Michael uses.

I step through the wide arch into the rectangular glass extension that overlooks the garden. A man is standing by the long dining table, a notebook and phone beside him. He holds out a hand for me to shake.

'Mrs Wick, I'm Detective Sergeant Howard from Essex Police. I believe you've already met Ryan Goodchild, our head of family liaison.'

I nod at the police officer as he grasps my hand. He's a similar age to me, mid-forties, maybe older, with a bald head and a demeanour that rings of competence and calm. He's not a young PC chasing up on a missed stop sign or a recent spate of burglaries in the village. And that alone makes me want to shout the words raging in my mind.

*Why are you here?*

DS Howard sits down and motions for us to do the same. Time slows, as if Michael and I are contestants on one of the reality singing shows that Rebecca loves to watch, and we're waiting for the presenter to announce the losers.

I slide into a chair beside Michael and a moment later feel Barley's warm body flop onto my feet. Above our heads, dark clouds roll across the sky.

'I'm sorry for intruding on you like this' – DS Howard looks between us as he speaks – 'but I need to ask you a question about Abigail.'

Ice fills my blood, pumping around my veins and causing my whole body to shiver. Thirteen years, ten months and nine days. The time is fluid, water running through my fingers.

Raindrops begin to drum on the glass above our heads, running in lines down the French doors that open onto the patio and the square lawn and neat shrub borders beyond it.

Under the table, Michael's hand covers my own. It's been five years since we touched each other with any kind of intent, and his hand over mine feels both alien and familiar.

'You've found some remains?' I ask, my voice a shaking whisper I don't recognise.

Michael's hand tightens around mine. It's not comfort that makes him do this but a middle place between hate and hurt that we don't speak about.

I feel DS Howard's eyes assessing me as he speaks. 'Do you recall if Abigail had any distinguishing features? In particular, a chicken-pox scar?'

My heart pounds with renewed fury, and the pain in my chest intensifies. I want to ask this DS Howard if he has any idea what his presence in our home is doing to us – if he realises the damage he's causing by asking me to remember what I've worked so hard to forget.

'Mrs Wick?'

A rock swells in my throat, the pain enough to cause a sob to escape. Tears blur my vision as memories of sparkling eyes and squealing laughter fill my head. A trickle of something foreign winds its way through my body. It's been so long since I've felt it that it takes me a moment to place it: hope. And now it's me that hates. I hate the man opposite me for making me feel it.

I close my eyes, blocking out the faces of Michael and the

DS waiting for me to answer. I don't want to remember, but it's too late.

We're in the main bathroom upstairs. I know it can't have been long after we moved, because the bathroom suite is still a salmon pink, offset against peach wall tiles. The memory is so clear, so vivid – a home movie playing just for me. Daniel is in the bath, washing his plastic dinosaurs. His pale face is a constellation of red dots, and no part of his body has been spared. All but a few have cracked and scabbed. The worst of it is over for him.

I see myself kneeling on the bath mat, when my hair was still long and fell in auburn waves down my back. I'm wrapping Abigail's chubby toddler body in a fluffy white towel and kissing her wet hair as she wriggles and squirms against the cotton. Abigail has fewer spots than Daniel, only five or six, but they've been irritating and itching her into frenzied sobs all day.

'No, no, honey – they'll scar if you itch them,' I hear myself coo.

'Itchy,' Abigail wails. Fat tears drop from her deep-brown eyes.

'We'll put some calamine lotion on them; it'll help them feel better, I promise.'

I dab the cool, creamy liquid onto each spot and sing a silly song that makes her giggle. That's when I see the dot of blood, bright red against the white of the towel, where she's rubbed and knocked the top off one of the spots. A smudge of red smears Abigail's chest.

I open my eyes and stare at DS Howard. 'She had chicken pox when she was two. We fastened those scratch mitts to her hands at night, but one still scarred. On her chest, just above her ribs.'

He nods, checking something on the screen of his phone. 'Do you remember which side?'

'Excuse me?'

'Which side was the scar on – left or right?'

'What's this all about?' Michael croaks, his voice a mix of impatience and desperation.

I close my eyes again and force myself to the bathroom once more. 'The right side. Her right.'

More memories are escaping from their hiding place. They swirl around my head like ghosts. I can almost hear Abigail's laughter from the beach that day, drifting on the wind, just out of reach in my memories.

I blink as tears sting the backs of my eyes.

'Was the scar ever made public knowledge during any of the appeals, do you remember?' DS Howard asks, his gazing moving between us.

I turn to Michael. The campaigns were his domain not mine, but he shakes his head.

'No. I don't think I even knew about the scar.' He frowns, rifling through his own memories.

'Are you sure?' DS Howard asks.

Michael looks at me and shrugs. 'If I knew at some point, then I'd forgotten.'

He turns back to DS Howard, a sad expression forming on his face. 'When Abigail was little, I started my own business – a commercial marketing company. I was working all hours, so I wasn't home for bath times and that kind of thing. A lot of the early childhood stuff passed me by. Something I deeply regret now of course. It's why I like to be home for Rebecca.'

DS Howard nods, accepting Michael's excuses.

Michael is right. He wasn't around much when the kids were very little and I'm not surprised he doesn't remember Abigail's chicken-pox scar, but tacking on the regret – the need to be home for Rebecca – is a step too far. I bite back a cruel barb.

Michael is home now because he disgraced Abigail's Angels

– the charity he built in our daughter's name. He's home because he drinks too much to ever settle into a normal job.

'I'm writing a book about Abigail's abduction,' Michael continues. 'I'd have mentioned the scar if I'd known, and I didn't.'

The mention of Michael's book causes my muscles to tense. I hate the idea of our tragedy being given to the world to fawn over like celebrity gossip. All those naive parents who'll tell themselves it couldn't happen to them, that they'd never have done what we did. But I keep it to myself. Now isn't the time, and really, Michael saying he's writing a book and him actually doing it, finishing it, are two different things.

'Thank you, Mrs Wick, Mr Wick.'

DS Howard nods at each of us in turn and shifts in his seat. My heart leaps into my mouth, and for a moment I think he's going to stand up and leave us without an explanation, but instead he leans forward.

'The reason I asked you about the chicken-pox scar is because, earlier this afternoon, a girl claiming to be your daughter walked into a police station in East London.'

'What? Oh God,' Michael's voice drifts to my ears. The sound is distant, oceans apart from where I sit.

I scrunch my eyes shut tight and fight the urge to shake my head, to scream.

It's not possible.

# EIGHT

## SARAH

Thirteen years, ten months and nine days without a single trace of my daughter or the dark-haired man who took her – the stranger on the boat, as the papers called him. I remember the call to the detective's phone and him sitting us down to tell us that a woman had reported seeing a little girl with red shoes in a pushchair, being rushed towards a ferry an hour away in Felixstowe, and Ryan bending down to pass through the front doorway and introduce himself just as the bottom fell out of our world.

'They're treating the case as an abduction,' the detective said. 'We're redirecting the local officers now.'

Abduction.

Someone had taken my baby girl.

We waited after that. Sitting in the poky kitchen of the holiday cottage. Hour after hour. Day after day. Weeks went by, but we stayed. We waited. The silence driving us half crazy.

There were a few possible sightings – Michael's constant appeals and calls to the media made certain of that. Abigail's face and the image of the stranger on the boat were on the front page of every UK newspaper, and many others across the Western world for weeks.

The first sighting was from a British man on holiday in Spain. He called the hotline number after he saw a girl being pulled along the beach by a Spanish woman. Then a group of travellers in Sydney reported seeing a girl who looked like Abigail on a local bus. And so it continued. Every sighting was investigated by the police, and by Michael's private investigator, as well as being publicised in the tabloids and discussed in detail on *Sky News*.

It was never Abigail.

With each new sighting, the delicate new existence I was building around myself, around Daniel and Rebecca, crumbled. In thirteen years, ten months and nine days, Michael never stopped believing, hoping, and searching for Abigail. But I did.

'Is she...' Michael trails off, clearing his throat and pulling my thoughts back to the present. His shoulders start to shudder. His breathing becomes short, hissing gasps, and when I turn to look at him, I see two wet lines streaming down his face.

A flash of irritation scorches my cheeks before morphing quickly into guilt. This is the moment Michael has waited all these years for. Of course he's emotional. I know I should be too, but the panic I felt rushing into the house earlier has settled. Congealed. A thick, numbing sludge.

'Michael' – I touch his arm – 'we don't know it's her.' This is a false alarm, I want to tell him. A wild and painful goose chase, which will end in hurt and disappointment like all those early sightings, except worse this time. It's been so long, and yet beneath the bandage that DS Howard's words have ripped off, the wound is still so very raw.

'I know.' He nods, wiping his hands across his face. 'It's such a shock though. Is she OK?' he asks. 'Has she been hurt?'

'I'm afraid I don't have all the details, but it doesn't sound as though she's been harmed,' DS Howard replies.

I notice two cups of tea have appeared. I look up and find Ryan has joined us, sitting beside DS Howard. Our eyes meet. I see concern, his 'Are you all right?' question. His 'What can I do?' expression. I lift my shoulders in a small shrug.

I look away and watch the ghostly tendrils of steam drift up from the mug of tea and then I gather my strength, scooping up the shattered pieces like the hundreds of tiny Lego bricks Daniel used to leave scattered across the living-room floor.

When I draw in a breath, it feels like the first in minutes. I have so many questions. Who is this girl? Why is she doing this? What does she want from us? But DS Howard can't answer these, so I settle for something I think he can answer. 'What do you know about this girl and her background?'

'She's been living in a city in the west of Colombia with a Colombian man and an American woman she thought were her parents. The DC in Bethnal Green said that she found a written confession from the man she thought was her father after he died, telling her she was Abigail Wick and that he'd abducted her. She flew to London earlier this week.'

'Do you have a picture of her?' Michael asks.

DS Howard taps on the screen of his phone. 'This is a still from the CCTV camera outside Bethnal Green Police Station.' He places his phone on the table and slides it to a space between Michael and me.

The image is as clear as a photograph, and I can't help but think about the last CCTV image I saw of Abigail from the dock at Felixstowe, all blurred – the square pixels making up a mosaic of the image. In this one, though, I can see a teenage girl. Her long brown hair has been lifted by a gust of wind and is frozen mid-flight. She's wearing a pair of tight jeans and a loose jumper, and appears to be staring straight at the camera.

Michael gasps, a hand flying to his mouth.

'What?' I ask.

'She... Don't you think she looks... she looks like you. She looks just like you, Sarah.'

'Does she?' I frown and enlarge the image so the girl's face fills the screen.

'Trust me,' Michael continues, his voice a little too high. 'In those headshot photos you had taken after your degree.'

The excitement in his voice stabs at my chest, because I know the photos Michael is referring to, and he is wrong. While some parents claim never to see the similarities between themselves and their children, I'm not one of them. In Daniel, I see the Michael I met when I was twenty – all long limbs and floppy hair. Daniel has my dark eyes and hair, and Michael's slim physique. It's Rebecca that's inherited Michael's fair skin and straight blonde hair. She's still growing, but even at fifteen I can see my own slight curves forming on her. The fifty-fifty of our genetics is startlingly clear in both Rebecca and Daniel, but I can't see the same in this girl.

I continue to stare though, pushing aside my doubts and trying to convince myself. Maybe she has a similar colouring to me: skin that tans a golden brown after minutes in the sun, and auburn-brown hair, before mine was cropped and dyed blonde to hide the streaks of grey. But her figure... even in her loose jumper, I can see more curves on her than I ever had, even before my weight loss.

It could be nurture, a voice inside of me reasons. An upbringing in a different culture with a different diet. Do I really believe that?

My gaze moves to the almond-shaped eyes of the girl in the photograph. Could it be the black smudges of eyeliner disguising the two perfect Os of the little girl who used to tug on my arm in the middle of the night and whisper in tearful hiccups about her bad dreams?

The whispers of hope return. Eyes change, faces change, especially in those fourteen years between young child and adult. It could be.

'When will we know if it's really Abigail?' I ask, blocking out the voices in my head.

Michael tenses beside me, but he says nothing. Michael might have allowed hope to push through whatever barriers he's constructed to get by over the years, but even he knows this could be a mistake, the cruellest kind.

'We can arrange for a DNA test,' DS Howard says. 'But the labs are pretty backed up. It could be a while. Even with a rush on it, it's likely to take a few weeks.'

A few weeks? It's a lifetime. A lifetime I don't want to live.

'You can pay for a private company to do it,' Ryan says. 'Essex Police have worked with one before. They're very efficient. I can make a call. I don't know the costs, but the quicker you want it, the higher the price, I imagine.'

'What's the soonest we can get the results?' I ask.

'Seventy-two hours is the fastest I've heard of a straightforward DNA comparison test being done.'

'Thank you, Ryan. Please make the call. I don't care about the cost. I want the results as quickly as possible.'

'What about the scar?' Michael runs his fingers through his hair in one terse movement. 'She's got the chicken-pox scar,' he says, his voice low as though he's talking to himself, convincing himself. 'How could she have known about it if it isn't her? I didn't even know about it.'

The lump returns to my throat. I want to believe. I really do. I want to break down into a deluge of sobs for all that I've lost and now, it seems, have found. But I can't.

'What do we do now? Do we go visit her in London? Where is she staying, do you know?' Michael asks.

My thoughts jump ahead to tomorrow and a journey to London. Awkward and emotional on more levels than I can process. I'm about to say that we should wait for the DNA test results before meeting her, but DS Howard gets there first.

'The detective in Bethnal Green is trying to find Abi a

hostel for tonight. She's travelled from South America and apparently has limited money. I'm sure they'll find somewhere, but after tonight, I'm not sure what will happen.'

'She could stay here,' Michael says. 'Is that an option?'

I shake my head. 'Or we could pay for a hotel in London.'

'Sarah,' Ryan says, his tone tentative, 'perhaps having her here would be better than a hotel. I'm only thinking of making it easier and quicker to get the DNA test, and of course there's less chance of the newspapers hearing about it.'

Michael is already nodding beside me. 'Good point, Ryan. We don't want this getting out until we know one way or another.'

'I'm sure someone from Bethnal Green can drive her here,' DS Howard says, his gaze moving to me. 'If that is something you were prepared to do, and it would save the question of where she'll stay after tonight. And as Ryan says, it would also make things easier for getting the DNA test completed.'

'I'm not sure if it's the best decision.' I think of Daniel and Rebecca and the fragility of our family.

'Always so practical,' Michael mutters in a voice so quiet only I hear it. 'I need a drink.'

*Of course you do.*

'Fine, bring her here,' I sigh, rubbing a hand across my forehead and trying to focus on the DNA test. The sooner we have the results, the better. That's all that matters. 'I'll need to sort out the spare room.'

Ryan is right about the reason to have her here, and yet I know it's a mistake. I can feel it hammering down into my core. But I say nothing because, however small, there is a part of me who wants to meet this girl, just to confirm what I already know – that it's not Abigail. Even if she does look a little like me, and even if she does have the same chicken-pox scar that Abigail had, this girl, whoever she is, is not my daughter.

Abigail is dead.

# NINE

## SARAH

The freezer door opens and the sound of ice clinking into a glass carries across the room. I stare at the mug of tea growing cold on the table. Wholly inadequate. 'I'll have one too,' I call to Michael.

'What do you want?' he asks.

'Whatever you're having.'

'I'm having a gin and tonic.'

'That's fine.'

'With the gin?' he asks.

'Yes, Michael, with gin,' I sigh.

'Right.' Michael pulls open the fridge with enough force to cause the bottles and jars in the door to rattle and clang. 'It's just that you don't normally drink.'

He's right. For all of the reasons Michael likes to drink more than he should – the escape it offers him, the numbing of his thoughts – I don't. I can't afford to lose control, but right now, I don't care. Right now, I crave the nothingness too.

DS Howard rises to his feet. 'If you'll excuse me one minute, I'll go into the next room and call the DC at Bethnal Green. They can ask Abigail what she'd like to do.'

'Thank you,' I say.

'Mum.'

The word jolts me. I spin around to find Rebecca, standing in the archway between the kitchen and the extension, arms hugging her body.

I leap to my feet, upending Barley in the process. He skitters around my feet before trotting over to Ryan. I fold Rebecca into my arms and run my hand down her smooth hair. I'd been thinking about myself right up until this moment. My thoughts, my hurt, my fears. I'd forgotten Rebecca was standing behind us the entire time.

'How are you feeling about this?' I ask.

'I'm fine, Mum. This is... strange, but good, right?' She leans her head back, grinning up at me before returning to our embrace. 'You can put one of my Harry Styles posters up in the spare room,' she says.

The urge to pull back takes hold of me. How do I tell my daughter not to get excited? That the sister who's cast a dark shadow over her entire life isn't actually about to return? I want to tell her not to expect a happy ending here. There isn't one to have.

'We need to take things slow, Becca. We don't know anything about this girl yet, or what's true.'

'I know,' she says. 'But, like, why would she say she was Abigail if she wasn't? Who would do that?'

I shake my head. 'I don't know, but that's my point. We don't know anything.'

'It's going to be fine, Mum.'

I hug her tighter and wish I could believe it.

My sweet Rebecca. Thick, spidery eyelashes – the result of too much mascara – against her porcelain skin and long white-blonde hair create a doll-like effect on my daughter. She is beautiful. The type of person, even at fifteen, that men and women alike take a second glance at. She is sweet and kind too. Each year her school reports read the same: *Rebecca is always smiling and willing to help her fellow pupils. Her never-ending happiness lights up the classroom.*

Rebecca has nice friends, she goes to sleepovers, she works hard at school. She never complains when her curfew is two hours before all of her friends', or when I insist that Michael or I collect her rather than trusting a friend's parent to do it.

But when she thinks no one is looking I see strain lurking behind her pale-blue eyes. I see the physical exhaustion that knots on her face when she sleeps. Rebecca may have been too young to remember Abigail and the holiday cottage, but it has still left its scars. Despite how hard I've tried to create a normal family feel, Rebecca has grown up in a thick cloud of grief, and I'm sure that's why she tries so hard to be happy, to lift us up, as though she feels it's her job.

I sometimes wonder if we were wrong not to send Rebecca to Dr Hall even once. The therapist worked wonders for Daniel when he stopped speaking after Abigail's abduction. A six-year-old boy who missed his sister so much, who was so confused and so sad that he lost the ability to speak for an entire year. But what would I have said to the therapist? My daughter is too happy...

Rebecca's hands move from my back and I follow her gaze to the neon-blue mobile in her hand. A new wave of anxiety swells inside me.

'Becca?'

My words fail to penetrate Rebecca's focus.

'Rebecca?' I place my hand over hers.

'Yeah.' She looks up.

'Who are you messaging?'

'Daniel. I've just told him to come home.'

'Oh.' I move my hand away, noticing for the first time that it's shaking, a little like Michael's do in the morning when he thinks we don't notice. 'Has he replied?'

She shows me a screen of green and white speech bubbles. There's a scroll line on the right of the screen showing a conversation spanning beyond the last few minutes. Despite everything that's happened in the past twenty minutes, a whisper of relief floats somewhere inside me. It's the same feeling I get when I catch Daniel lurking in Rebecca's doorway, talking to her about the teachers at her school.

I love that they're close. That, despite what this family has been through, they have each other. Something normal amidst the darkness and grief we pretend isn't there. One day soon, I expect Daniel will move out and I'll see less of him. I hope his relationship with Becca continues. He shares so much more with her, a side I'm not privy to.

A new message appears as I'm staring at the screen. Daniel's reply is three letters. *FML*.

'Does that mean he's coming home?'

Rebecca laughs and rolls her eyes. 'Yeah.'

'Thank you, sweetheart. But, Becca' – I touch my fingers to her chin and guide her face up to look at me – 'you know you can't tell anyone about this?'

Rebecca's gaze drops to her phone before lifting back to mine. 'Not even Ellie? She's my best friend – she wouldn't tell anyone.'

'No.' I shake my head and bite down on my lip, fighting to keep the urgency and panic out of my voice. 'Let's wait until we know more.'

Rebecca nods. 'OK, I get it,' she says. 'We don't want the papers to find out too soon. We want to control the story, which means we share the information when we want to, when we're ready.'

I nod and wonder when my daughter became so media savvy? I think back to my own life at fifteen. I read Marian Keyes novels and had a secret crush on a boy in my class, and in the summers I went crabbing with my dad. I knew nothing of politics or the media. I knew very little outside of the things we learned at school, or I'd picked up from conversations between my parents.

Would I have been as clued up as Rebecca if I'd lived her life, seen the heartache of her parents and lived through her father's scandal? Not just lived through it but survived the teasing taunts from her classmates and the headlines splashed across every tabloid. Five years on, and I remember them all.

EMBEZZLEMENT CHARGES FOR ABIGAIL WICK CHARITY

MISSING GIRL CHARITY A SHAM

MICHAEL PRICK

FATHER OF MISSING ABIGAIL IN HOTEL ROMP

ABIGAIL WICK CHARITY PAYING FOR DAD'S AFFAIR

Another shadow over our lives we don't talk about. The affairs were bad enough, but the coverage of them was another level of humiliation, as much for me having to show my face on TV every week as for Rebecca and for Daniel, who was three months away from taking his GCSEs at the time.

I couldn't leave and rip our home apart with Daniel's exams so close. And so I stayed and waited for the time to feel right to break our family apart. I'm still waiting.

Michael pats Rebecca's shoulder and presses a heavy crystal tumbler into my hands; the liquid inside fizzes and spits tiny dots over my skin.

I draw in a long mouthful. The bitter fizz of tonic and lime dances on my taste buds, whilst the strong tang of gin seems to cloak my thoughts before I've even swallowed.

'Mr Wick, Mrs Wick.' DS Howard steps back into the kitchen. 'I've spoken to the detective at Bethnal Green. They're happy to have a car drive Abi here. By the sounds of it, she's happy to stay here.'

'Thank you.' Michael raises his glass. 'Will you stay for a drink, Detective?'

'Thank you, but I'm needed back at the station. I'll see myself out,' he adds as Ryan steps back into the kitchen.

'I've put in a call to the private DNA processing lab I've worked with before,' Ryan says. 'They'll send a technician here first thing tomorrow with the DNA testing kits.'

'Thanks, Ryan.' I meet his gaze and he smiles, asking me again with just a raise of an eyebrow if I need anything.

Michael lifts the glass to his lips and gulps down a large mouthful. 'You'll have a drink, will you, Ryan?' he asks, already reaching for the fridge.

'I've just made myself a cup of tea, but thank you,' Ryan replies. He turns back to the sink and the mugs he's halfway through cleaning. I think about pointing out the dishwasher but stop myself. He told me the first time we met – the first time he bent his head under the low beams of the holiday cottage and shook my hand – that his role as a family liaison officer is to support without intrusion. He's better at it now.

'Sarah?' Ryan says.

'Um?' I look up and meet his eyes. A flash of memory: standing in the gloom of the cottage kitchen, long after I stopped jumping up each time the phone rang. Allowing myself to fall into Ryan's arms, allowing myself to feel the heat of his body, allowing myself to forget, just for one moment, that I was living in a nightmare.

I drop my eyes and push the memory away. *Look forward not back.*

'Shall I help you prepare the spare room?' Ryan asks. 'If it's anything like mine, it'll be filled with boxes and tat.'

'I'll help too,' Rebecca chips in.

'Er... yes, thanks.'

I regret my words the instant they leave my mouth. The spare room isn't filled with boxes or tat. It's filled with my belongings. I'll need to move my things back into the main bedroom. Move back in with Michael.

I lead the way up the stairs, my legs weak from drinking on an empty stomach.

It doesn't feel real.

Rebecca's words circle my head as I dig out clean bedding and move armfuls of my clothes out of the drawers. Why would she say she is Abigail if she isn't? Why would someone do that?

I don't know the answer, but I'm going to find out.

# TEN

## ABI

Friday, 5 p.m.

Adrenaline pumps through Abi's veins as she follows DC Swain along a grey corridor leading deeper into the police station. Finally, they're moving. Finally, she's out of here.

It's been hours since she walked through the glass doors and dropped her bombshell. Too many hours. It's made her nervous. Skittish.

Why has it taken so much longer than he said?

The seeds of doubt she felt in the interview have grown into gnarling thick vines that wrap around her every thought. They were so focused on getting ready, building up to the moment she said those words: 'I'm Abigail Rose Wick and I've been missing for fourteen years.' Then seeing Sarah and Michael— Abi stops, correcting herself just like he has done so many times – seeing her parents. They hadn't taken a moment to consider that the police would still want to investigate what happened all those years ago. And he didn't tell her they'd want her address in Buenaventura. And now Abi worries that there is more he hasn't thought of, more questions, more trouble she alone will have to face.

'All anyone will care about is that you're home,' he told her more than once. 'Back where you belong. It's the feel-good story of the century. Nothing else will matter.'

And yet it was Abi in that interview room, a thin film of sweat cloaking her skin. Hot at first, then cold, evaporating to leave a clammy feel to her clothes, already in their third day of wear, already in desperate need of detergent and a washing machine – or, better yet, a bin.

She should have asked him more questions. Not that he ever answered the ones she did ask. Everything was always, 'We'll cross that bridge when we come to it... if we come to it.' But it's not *we*, is it? It's just her. Why did she not realise how alone she would be? No different from that room, that dusty heat. Hours of watching daytime soaps broken only by the occasional shouts of a driver on the road outside the barred windows.

'*Salid del camino!*'

'*Mira por dónde vas!*'

They reach a thick grey door at the end of the corridor. DC Swain taps a pass against a square pad and shoves her shoulder to the door. A moment later, the last dregs of dusky daylight fill Abi's vision.

The temperature has dropped another few degrees in the time she was inside, the sun dipping below the building, casting one large shadow over the rows of cars in front of them. The cold whips through her, but she's grateful for it now. Anything to be away from the four grey walls.

DC Swain motions to a small flight of steps and, as Abi steps forward, she feels the detective's hand on her elbow. Habit, Abi tells herself, from the number of times the detective has escorted handcuffed criminals to their prison transport. And yet, in that moment, DC Swain's touch feels like an iron grip as one thought rushes through her mind. Lying to the police is a criminal offence. She's a criminal now.

Abi's feet falter. There's a car just ahead of them, engine running. The rear passenger door is already open, and Abi can see two officers in the front seats. The car, like half a dozen others in the lot, is silver with a blue-and-yellow chequerboard stripe, and a rectangular siren on top.

Criminals sit in the backs of police cars, she thinks.

'Everything OK?' DC Swain asks, dropping her hand from Abi's elbow and resting it on the top of the open car door as her eyes assess Abi once more.

Abi nods, willing herself to get it together. She drops her rucksack into the footwell before slipping her body across the leather seats.

'You know PC Robertson,' DC Swain continues, bending down and poking her head in after Abi. 'And this,' she adds, moving her gaze to the driver, 'is PC Matthews. She'll be driving you to Essex.'

'Thank you.' Abi forces her mouth into a smile.

There's a pause. A silence. The vines of doubt tighten around Abi's thoughts once more. What are they waiting for?

DC Swain moves a fraction, and for a moment Abi thinks she'll slide into the seat beside her, travel with them to the Wick house, carry on with her questions. Her mouth dries at the thought.

Only a few hours in, and she's already exhausted from the scrutiny. That spinning roulette wheel. Truths and lies. He told her to stick close to the truth. Easier that way to remember. Easier to lie too. And so she created a parallel life in her head, one with clean floors and fresh white walls. A proper house with a place for her to ride her bike outside. One with a mother who played board games with her in the afternoons and read her bedtime stories. Only Jhon remained unchanged.

Another beat passes before DC Swain speaks again. 'Don't

forget what I said earlier – we will need to see you again with a guardian or appropriate adult so you can give a formal statement on what we've talked about this afternoon.'

'Thank you. I'll see you soon,' Abi says as DC Swain steps back and closes the passenger door. And then they're moving, joining a line of traffic crawling slowly down the road. Only then does DC Swain's comment sink in. Guardian or appropriate adult. The detective could've said her parents, but she didn't. And Abi wonders what exactly it was that she said or didn't say, what facial expression or hand gesture of Abi's caused the seeds of doubt to plant in DC Swain's mind too.

'It would usually take us about an hour and a half this time of day to get to the Essex borders,' PC Matthews says, smiling at Abi in the rear-view mirror. 'But what with it being Friday, it might be closer to two hours.'

'We can always switch on the siren if we get really stuck,' PC Robertson says with a grin.

'Thanks,' Abi replies, settling into her seat, content to stare out of the window. As far as she can tell, rush hour is the same as every other hour. The traffic in London never seems to stop. Even in the dead of night, buses rushed past the second-floor window of her hotel room, rattling the single pane of glass against the rotting wood frame with enough force to jolt her from the shallows of her fitful sleep.

Abi's stomach growls, a hollow rumble lost in the purr of the engine. Apart from a chocolate bar and a can of Sprite PC Robertson gave her an hour ago, she hasn't eaten anything since the stale pastry she bought from a convenience store that morning. The familiarity of the hunger unleashes a grating hatred inside her.

He promised, 'No more dirty floors, no more hunger.' He promised her money too, and yet she's felt poorer since landing in England than she's ever felt before.

At least she had the income from the waitressing job in her

old life, which is more than she can say about her current situation. But she doesn't want her old life. She wants the life she's owed. She wants to be part of a real family. Her family. She wants to be loved. Only now she's on her way, the vines of doubt are coiling tighter and tighter, and it feels as though the lies she's told are written on her face, there for everyone to see.

# ELEVEN

## ABI

Friday, 7 p.m.

He told her they had money, but it isn't until the large black gates open into a sweeping driveway that Abi realises how much. Even in the dark, she can tell the house is huge. A goddamn mansion compared to the square block she grew up in. Something stabs her stomach – the same silent pain that drove her here, she thinks.

She steps out of the car with stiff limbs. The air smells like bonfires but with a sweetness she doesn't recognise. She stretches, aching from the long journey, and waits for PC Robertson to get out too. Abi doesn't know how long they'll stay for or if they'll drive off right now and leave her to knock alone, and even though she couldn't wait to be away from DC Swain, she wants PC Robertson to stand beside her.

'We'll make sure you get in all right and then we'll head off,' PC Robertson says, hiding a yawn behind her hand.

'Thank you for coming with me,' Abi says, noticing the wobble in her voice. The uncertainty. She didn't think it would be like this. Scary. Lonely.

'Are you OK?' the officer asks, patting her arm.

Abi nods. She pulls in a deep lungful of air and watches it float away into the darkness like the plume of smoke from the chimney on the side of the house.

Light shines from the windows, illuminating the pale-yellow two-storey property. One-storey rooms with their own sloping tiled roofs stretch along either side of the house, as though they were added as an afterthought.

'Ready then, Abigail?' PC Robertson asks.

The name hangs in the air, adding to the enormity of what she's about to do and causing a shiver to race down her spine. She is the long-lost daughter returning home. It isn't just her life that was stolen – theirs has been robbed too. She must remember that.

As Abi pulls her backpack onto her shoulders and takes a step towards the front door, it flies open and a girl with hair and skin that glows white in the darkness flies towards her.

'Oh my God, I can't believe you're here.' She bounces forward and wraps her thin arms around Abi, squeezing her tight.

'You must be Rebecca.' Abi smiles, swept up in the younger girl's energy.

'Where's your stuff?' Rebecca asks, glancing back towards the police car.

'This is it.' Abi lifts one shoulder to show the backpack she filled in Buenaventura.

'Really, that's all you have? Guess we'll be doing some shopping then.' She laughs and grabs Abi's arm before dragging her towards the house. 'Everyone's inside. They thought they'd scare you if they all came running out, but I didn't care. I knew you wouldn't be scared of us; we're your family.'

Abi swallows the emotion building inside her as their feet crunch on the gravel driveway. Her family. Hers. This is home.

'I'll leave you to it then,' PC Robertson calls from behind

her, already moving back to the car. 'If there's anything you need, there's a family liaison officer inside who can help you.'

Abi turns, unsure what to say now. 'Thank you,' is all she can manage, and then Rebecca's hand is in hers and she's pulling her up the steps and through a wooden front door and into a large hall with a ceiling that seems to go on forever.

To one side, a young man sits on the bottom step of a wide staircase. Dark hair droops over his face, and his black combats hang from his body like clothes on a skeleton. He's tapping on a phone cupped in his hands, but he looks up and smiles at her, giving a salute-type wave. 'I'm Daniel,' he says.

His greeting is so easy, so simple, that Abi has a sudden desire to step towards him, to sit down on that bottom step, but she can't. There are two people standing before her. Staring.

Michael and Sarah, side by side. Michael is an older version of Daniel, with grey-blonde hair. His eyes are pale blue and watery. He has the look of a man in shock. A man who's seen a ghost.

Abi moves her gaze to Sarah. She's familiar in that way people are when you've seen photos of them before you've ever met them, and Abi has seen so many photos. She's watched hours of clips on YouTube from cookery segments and a talk show about women that Caroline would've loved. And yet, Sarah is nothing like Abi expected. She is smaller, half a foot shorter than Abi, and her face is gaunt. But it's the look in her eyes that unnerves Abi the most – a cool intensity more terrifying than any of DC Swain's questions.

'This is very strange for us,' Michael says. 'I'm sure it is for you.' His voice breaks a little at the end. 'But we're glad you're here.'

It isn't quite the tight hug, the 'our Abigail, home at last' sentiment she was hoping for, or even Rebecca's bouncing acceptance, but it's a start.

Abi opens her mouth to reply, but something in Sarah's

expression changes. The woman's eyes narrow, her jaw clenches. Abi takes an involuntary step back, knocking into Rebecca as she moves.

'I don't know who you are,' Sarah says, her finger lifting, pointing at Abi and shaking as much as her voice, 'or why you've decided to come here, but you're not my daughter. You're not Abigail.'

# TWELVE

## SARAH

Hope is a horrible thing. A monstrous disease of a thing.

When had it hooked its claws into me? Had it been when DS Howard first uttered Abigail's name? No. It was before that even, when I'd seen it glinting in Michael's eyes. That's what most people don't realise about hope – it's contagious. Highly contagious. It jumps from one person to the next, infecting them, deluding them, deluding me.

I tried to keep the whispers of it at bay. I questioned the resemblance of the photo that Michael had been so sure of. I pushed for the DNA test, but somewhere between scooping up my nightdress, clothes and creams from the spare room, and muttering something to Ryan about Michael's snoring, hope had dug its claws into me, wrapping me in its deluded warmth. And I let it. Then she stepped into the hall and I asked myself how I, of all people, could let that madness into my thoughts.

A delusion. No different from Rebecca watching *Supergirl* as a child and wishing she could fly. An impossible wish.

There's no amount of wishing that can undo the past and change the events of that Friday in May when everything fell apart. But this girl, whoever she is, whatever she's doing here, she isn't my daughter, and there is nothing I can do to stop the words from leaving my mouth as a shaking takes hold of my body.

'I don't know who you are, or why you've decided to come here, but you're not my daughter. You're not Abigail.'

My remark lands like a slap on her face. Her eyes – almond in shape; there can be no mistaking that now – widen and her cheeks redden.

And when I glance to the faces of my family – Rebecca, standing with an arm around the girl; Daniel on the stairs, already halfway to standing; and Michael beside me – I see it has had the same effect on them.

I clamp my mouth shut, pushing my teeth together to stop the chattering. I try to breathe, but the cold, hard hollowness in my chest makes each breath a shallow gasp.

A tense silence ripples around the hallway. The girl looks over her shoulder to the closed front door and then drops her gaze to the floor.

'What the hell, Mum?' Daniel's voice bounces off the walls, loud, affronted.

Out the corner of my eye, I see Michael's mouth drooping open and the shock of my words creasing his forehead, and then he, too, recovers.

'Sarah.' His voice is a whispering hiss. 'What's wrong with you? We don't know anything yet.'

He steps away from me, moving closer to her. 'I'm so sorry.'

*What's wrong with me?* I want to scream. *Look at her. What's wrong with* you? I'm desperate to shout. *Our daughter is dead.*

'It's fine,' she says in a quiet voice, an unfamiliar accent carrying around the hall. Sort of Spanish but not quite.

'No, it's not,' I say, shaking my head. Nothing about this is fine. I look to Michael, then Daniel, who has moved to stand beside him. And finally to Rebecca. My precious Becca. Tears glisten like a wall of water in my daughter's eyes.

The hurt on Rebecca's face – the hurt I've caused – breaks me, and I realise my mistake.

It was always going to be awkward – her and us. But in one flash of hurt, I've changed the dynamic. It's not her and us. Michael, Rebecca and Daniel now feel sorry for this girl. It is them and me. My family and the girl who isn't part of it.

'I... I'm...'

Words fail to form. A silence descends upon us. They're waiting for me to say something, but my voice is no longer under my control.

No one speaks. No one moves.

I can't say how much time is passing, seconds or minutes, but we're all frozen. Paused in time.

The harsh *beep-beep-beep* of the slow-cooker alarm startles us all back to life. Rebecca dabs her fingers to her eyelids, and all at once my strength returns. One emotion consumes the rest. The hurt, the sadness, the confusion is gone, smothered by one all-encompassing feeling: anger. It scorches through my thoughts and my body.

Only one thing has truly mattered to me in my life – protecting my children, shielding them from harm. It is both spectacular and epic how badly I've failed in this one task. I've shouldered the blame for what happened to Abigail, and the damage it's done to Rebecca and Daniel. What mother wouldn't? I blame Michael just as much as I blame myself, sometimes more. But right now, it is this girl trying to hurt my family, and that makes a rage burn in my blood.

The beeping stops and then Ryan steps to my side, a firm hand touching my shoulder.

'Why don't we all have something to eat?' he says. 'This is a huge shock for everyone. Michael, I think your stew is ready.'

Michael nods, slowly at first, then quicker. 'Yes, good idea, thank you, Ryan. Are you hungry, er...'

'Abelia,' she says. 'Everyone calls me Abi.'

I'm grateful Michael didn't call her Abigail, but Abi – Abelia – it's so close. Too close.

'You're not a vegetarian, are you, Abi?'

A slight smile touches her lips. 'No.'

I stare at them. Four pairs of eyes stare back, but I am focused on only one. *Did you not hear what I said?* I want to scream at her. *Get out. Get out. Get out.*

But I don't scream. I'm angry, angrier than I've ever been, but I'm also Rebecca and Daniel's mother, and I can't bear to watch the hurt contorting Rebecca's face and know that I'm the cause. And Daniel might be an adult now, but he's still my child and this will affect him more than he'll ever tell me.

'I need some fresh air,' is all I can say before turning on my heels and striding through the kitchen to the mudroom.

Barley shoots out from under the table and skitters around my feet. He had the good sense to hide from whatever that was in the hall just now, but he can never resist a walk, even if it's dark outside.

I shut the mudroom door behind us and force myself to count.

One. I kick off my heels, unzip my skirt and let it fall to the floor.

Two. I pull on my walking trousers.

Three. I shove my feet into my boots.

Four. I grab Barley's lead.

Five. A blast of bitter air smacks my face as I throw open the back door and step into the darkness of the garden. It isn't raining, but drops carry in the wind, as if it's just about to start or has just stopped. The droplets kiss my face like icy tears, soothing the heat burning in my cheeks.

Six. I breathe.

The counting is working. My mind begins to focus. The anger starts to shift. Not disappear. Oh no, I'm still angry, but I can't allow it to cloud my judgement, not if I'm going to protect my family from this girl and get her out of our lives as soon as possible.

# THIRTEEN

## SARAH

I find the concrete slabs that wind along the edge of the lawn. If there is a moon out tonight, it's hidden behind the clouds. It's dark, pitch-black beyond the light from the house, but I don't care. I need the air and I need the distance, but the light I can take or leave.

I hear the back door slam behind me, and I wonder in my haste to escape whether I forgot to shut it properly. Then a second later, I hear Ryan call my name.

'Sarah, hold up.' His voice grows closer. 'You'll need a torch.'

I stop and turn, but it's not Ryan's silhouette that my eyes are pulled to; it's my house. I can see them all in the extension as clear as if my nose is pressed to the glass. Rebecca is laughing at something the girl is saying. It seems she's ignored my warnings about taking it slow and has accepted this girl into our lives in the same way she does everything – with boundless energy and grace.

I worry again for my daughter and how important it is to her to please people, to smooth over awkward moments and make everyone happy. She has yet to learn how impossible that task is.

It's my fault, I'm sure. All the years of pretending we're fine – a normal family – have taken their toll.

My gaze moves to Daniel. He's setting the table, his back to me so I can't see if he too is smiling, accepting this as Rebecca is. Michael's head pokes into view from the kitchen. He says something to the girl and she nods. I watch him watch her; his expression is cautious, I think. Is he wondering like I am who this girl really is and why she's come here?

She sweeps her hair away from her back and lets it drop over one shoulder. She's fidgeting, nervous. I study her face and wait for even the faintest whisper of familiarity. It doesn't come. All I see is a stranger. More than a stranger: an imposter.

An orange glow appears on the ground by my feet, illuminating a small circle of my garden. Ryan holds out a torch – the fat orange one I keep by the back door in case of a power cut – but I don't take it. Ahead of us, Barley voices his impatience with two swift barks and spurs me forward. The bouncing glow of the torch follows.

'Sarah, can you wait a moment please?'

I reach the gate and fiddle in the darkness for the bolts. They clonk open, causing another whimper from Barley. I run my fingers along the wood until I feel the iron handle in my hands and twist it.

Barley's body whips around my legs before shooting out into the night. From beside me, Ryan touches my elbow. 'It's too dark. You'll slip and fall.'

'I need to get out.' I glance ahead into the nothingness. 'Give me the torch if you want and go back inside.'

'No.' He moves the torch out of my reach and shines it ahead of us. 'I'm coming with you.'

'I don't need a babysitter.' The earlier anger still carries in my voice.

'I didn't say that you did.' His voice is calm next to mine.

'Why are you here, Ryan?'

'I thought I could help.'

'No, I mean here, in Essex. You worked for Suffolk Police before...' My voice trails off. I don't want to think about that time. The cottage. The desperation. The heartbreak.

'I moved for a promotion and because I knew the head of family liaison at Essex at the time and she was a good person. Really smart and a great mentor. When she retired, I stepped into her role. I'm good at what I do now, Sarah.'

I shrug and say nothing. I don't have the strength to argue, to push him away like I normally would when someone offers to help me. The sad truth of it is that I'm better on my own. There is no space in my life for friends anymore. I simply don't need to share my problems, and I certainly don't have the capacity to listen to someone's insignificant ramblings about their failed diet or marital issues.

All the friends I had before Abigail – the ones I made during my studies and the local mums I met after Daniel was born – I let go. Most were happy to step away; I could see it in their faces. It wasn't just pity but fear. *It happened to you, so it could happen to me.*

Even Janie, my best friend, the godmother to all three of my children, couldn't handle what happened to Abigail. Janie was there that day at the holiday cottage. She saw the devastation unfolding, and yet the moment the police had finished questioning her, she left. Ran away. She never called to ask how I was, and in all the years since, I've never understood or forgiven that.

After a few metres, we find the well-trodden footpath that loops around the fields and back to the village or carries straight on to the old mill at Flatford. The path is slick with mud from the recent downpour. My gaze drops to the ground and Ryan's feet. In the torchlight, I can just make out the shape of his office shoes, no doubt already caked in mud, socks soaked through.

A gust of wind roars in my ears and, just a few paces to my left, the River Stour, high from a long winter of rain, gushes by.

In the daylight it is beautiful. Constable Country. Lush green grass and willows leaning lazily into the river, but in the daylight it is also busy with walkers and rowing boats, families, dogs and runners. This path is only empty at night, and I'm grateful for that.

As the wind dies, Ryan takes my arm and pulls me to a stop. 'Sarah, talk to me for a minute. Just you and me. Tell me, what are you thinking? What makes you so sure it isn't Abigail? Michael said the photo of Abi looks just like you when you were younger. What is it you see that he doesn't?'

A dozen wasp stings pierce my heart. 'If you're trying to imply that I didn't want that girl to be Abigail, then you have no idea what you're talking about. Of course I wanted it to be her. I want my daughter back more than anything else in this world, but that girl in there' – I throw a hand into the darkness in the direction of the house – 'isn't her.'

I start to walk again, the anger forcing me to keep moving across the slippery ground.

'It's always been different for Michael,' I say as Ryan walks beside me. 'I had to think about Daniel and Rebecca, but Michael... well, you saw him in that first week. He was a man possessed. He even managed to speak to the PM.

'I spent most of the time rocking Rebecca to sleep and trying to comfort Daniel as best I could. The police were chasing down every whisper of a lead and you were there telling us there was nothing new. But Michael was in our bedroom making phone call after phone call. To the press, to our MP. Everyone he could think to call. It went on like that for weeks.

'And then you left. No new leads, nothing to go on. Other families needed you more than us. The daily updates became weekly and eventually we had to go home. Daniel had school and Rebecca needed a routine. It felt like admitting defeat.'

'It wasn't—'

'I know. It wasn't like Abigail was going to wander up from playing on the beach at that point and ask where we were, but it was still hard.

'When we got home, Michael didn't even consider returning to his business. He sold it. Just threw away all his hard work. That holiday was the first we'd taken in two years. I'd had to force him to take the time off. Nothing else mattered to him except finding Abigail, like he alone could do what the police couldn't.'

I stop talking before pain overwhelms me. *Look forward not back.*

'Sarah?' Ryan's voice cuts through the memory. 'How many other people knew about the chicken-pox scar?'

'I thought Michael knew, but he says he didn't. He wasn't around in the evenings for bath time, and it was just a little scar. He probably wouldn't have noticed.' I don't know if it's the wind, or memories of the past still running in my head, but my voice sounds distant.

'Let's say for a minute then that it isn't Abigail—'

'It isn't,' I cut in. 'I won't pretend.'

'How do you think Abelia Pérez came to have the scar?'

'I don't know.'

'Her father was Jhon Pérez, and her mother was called Caroline Pérez. They're both dead now. She left her home in Colombia and everything she knew to come here. Regardless of who she is, in your house is a teenage girl in need of support with no other family in the world.'

Pressure pushes down on me and a noise escapes my throat. Then another. My legs give way and all of a sudden, I'm falling. Ryan's body is sturdy and strong. I allow myself to sink into his embrace and cry until I have nothing left, just as I did all those years ago in the kitchen of the holiday cottage. The thought of that moment and what came next makes me pull back, step away.

'She's not Abigail,' I say when I can talk again, my voice raspy from crying.

'How can you be so sure?'

I bite down on the inside of my lip, keeping the truth in. If I tell Ryan that I know Abigail is dead, he'll want to know how I'm so sure and I can't tell him that. I've lived with this secret for so long now, I can never break it.

'Because...' I say, 'because I'm Abigail's mother. I would know if she was my daughter.' I shiver and, for the first time since leaving the house, the cold stings my face and bites at my skin, and I realise what madness it is to be out by the river in the dark like this.

My eyes scan the black nothingness for Barley. I take the torch from Ryan and shine it into the distance ahead of us, before sweeping it in a full circle until I see the bright reflections of two eyes already waiting by the gate back into the garden.

'And whatever her intentions are, whatever she believes, that girl is a storm about to hit and destroy my family.' Tears prick my eyes. 'I should never have let her come here.'

We turn back and reach the gate, then step into the garden. My eyes are drawn instantly to the extension where my family are sitting down to eat.

'Maybe,' Ryan says, 'you're scared to believe it could be Abigail.'

I think about that for a moment. Am I scared?

*Yes*, is the answer. I'm scared of many things, but mostly I'm scared of what this will do to the tentative existence of our family – built and crafted so carefully out of delicate china that could crash to the ground any moment. I'm scared that if I accept this girl into our lives, she'll end up destroying us. But I also know that if I walk back into my house right now and demand that she leaves before the DNA test is taken, before we learn the truth we'll inevitably learn from the results, then I could lose Michael, Daniel and Rebecca forever. And that's a risk I'm not prepared to take.

I wipe my fingers under my eyes and look at Ryan. I'm glad he followed me. I'm glad he's here. 'What do I do now? I can hardly go back in there, apologise and sit down to eat with them.'

'That's exactly what you do, Sarah.'

I feel a pressure in me again, this one building up not down. I glance back into the black night and want to scream and rage into it. The injustice of what happened to Abigail, to all of us, is as raw as if I'm back in the cottage waiting and desperate for news. But I don't scream. Instead, I close my eyes and nod. What good would screaming do me anyway? The days of allowing that injustice to take over are gone. I have to stay in control, now more than ever.

The wind rustles through the apple tree above me, causing raindrops to patter my hair as we make our way to the back door. 'Give me a minute, OK?'

Ryan looks at me for a long moment before nodding and disappearing into the house.

I close my eyes and count to ten, focusing on each number, rolling it around in my head until it's all there is. Then I open my eyes and watch my family from the darkness of the garden, feeling more alone than I've ever felt before.

I think of Janie again, and even though it's been thirteen years, ten months and nine days since we spoke, I pull out my phone from my pocket and find her number. I don't know what I'll say yet, or why I'm calling, except that Janie knew Abigail too. She loved Abigail. Doted on her. Michael might already be on his way to being convinced that our daughter is home, but I'm not.

One of us is wrong, and right now I want to speak to

someone else who knew Abigail. I want to show Janie the photo and share my thoughts. My fears.

It rings three times before a man answers with a muffled, 'Hello?'

'Hi,' I say. 'Erm... is this Janie's phone?'

'Who's asking?'

'It's Sarah. Phil? Is that you?'

There's a rustle on the line and then nothing. He's hung up.

I pull the phone away from my ear and stare at the home screen, half expecting a call to come in, an apology. The phone dropped. Fat fingers pressing the wrong button, but there's nothing.

It's probably not even Janie's number anymore. I didn't recognise the voice. It was probably a stranger. I'm not even sure Janie and Phil are still married. They were going through such a rough patch after the third round of IVF failed, a few months before the holiday to the Suffolk Coast.

I slip the phone back into my pocket and step through the back door. Calling Janie was stupid anyway. What can she possibly say to me that I don't already know?

Maybe this girl believes she is Abigail. Or maybe she has another reason to be here. Either way, the only way to handle this situation is to stay in control of it. I will do anything to protect my family. I've proven that already and I'll do it again now.

---

*And so, at last, she's in.*

*I stay on the outside, hiding in the shadows, the darkness, watching as she walks into the house, Rebecca bouncing around her like an excited puppy.*

*Abigail's smile is tentative, but she's relaxing. I can see it in* the way her shoulders pull back, body shifting to stand a little straighter.

A giddy excitement unleashes inside me. It wasn't easy to pull this off, to line up all the dominoes. Days and weeks and months of planning and bending someone to my will. But I did it. And now it's up to Abigail to do the rest. I have to trust that she remembers the plan, and all that I've taught her.

But what is this?

Sarah leaving already. Storming out in a temper tantrum.

Tut tut.

She didn't even try.

Oh, Sarah. Don't you see? There is no running from this. I've only just begun.

You have no idea what's coming for you next!

One way or another, we'll face the truth together. One way or another, we'll all pay.

The phone in my hand buzzes. I look at the screen and smile. Everything is ready for the next part of my plan.

# FOURTEEN

## ABI

*You're not my daughter.* Sarah's words spin in Abi's head as a chunk of soft beef melts in her mouth and slides down her throat, making her stomach ache for more. It's an effort not to gorge on the rich flavours of wine and herbs, and the soft texture of juicy meat, but to eat slowly, one mouthful at a time, as if this is the kind of meal she eats every damn day of the week.

She can't believe they're even sitting here eating like this after Sarah's reaction, no one saying a word about it. Not even Michael offered Abi a reassuring 'Don't worry about that'. Abi clearly has a lot to learn in the art of pretence.

She looks around the glass room that's stuck onto the side of the kitchen. The rectangular table in the centre is wooden. It's thick and dark with pale knots and the swirling of the grain inching across each plank. *Oak*, Abi thinks although she doesn't know why. *Expensive.*

'Tell us what it was like in Colombia, Abi,' Michael asks from his place at one end of the table, pausing to take a sip of dark-red wine. 'If you can. If it's not too upsetting,' he adds, his voice quick and uncertain.

Abi can tell by the way he keeps looking at her that he

hasn't accepted her like Rebecca has. She senses a wariness in Daniel too, but at least Michael's behaviour isn't the outright hostility Sarah showed her.

'They'll welcome you with open arms,' he said. Yeah, right. Another thing he was wrong about.

She realises they're staring now, waiting for a reply. She tries to smile. 'I don't know where to start.'

'Is it super hot there right now?' Rebecca chips in from beside her. 'I'm so sick of this cold weather.'

An image of the ground-floor apartment springs into her head: sticky heat fogging the empty rooms; metal grilles over windows casting square shadow patterns on the dirty floors; the isolation and loneliness that threatened, and almost succeeded, to send her half mad. She pushes the image aside and remembers what he told her. 'The truth won't do them any good. Why make it harder on them?'

She nods. 'It's very warm right now. I lived in a city called Buenaventura. It's the biggest shipping port in the country, which made it quite a violent city, but we lived in a house out of the way of the harbour and the really bad areas. It wasn't very big, nothing like this' – she gestures to their surroundings – 'but it had its own courtyard where I could ride my bike. There were no other kids about, but it was OK, I guess, better than most childhoods there. Caroline – the person I thought was my mum – she kept me busy.'

An ache weighs on Abi's chest as she watches them absorbing the half-lies, half-truths, of her story. She wishes it was all true with the same guttural longing she feels for this life – the one she should have been living all these years. A home with a kitchen bigger than her entire apartment; a proper family; siblings that laugh and tease; money and food. Finally, it's hers for the taking – isn't it?

'So, you know,' Rebecca says, tilting her head and grinning at Abi, 'you're, like, bilingual and everything?'

'Yes.' Abi smiles, feeling the infectious energy that radiates out of Rebecca ignite inside her. She likes Rebecca already. An ally. A friend. A sister. 'Caroline was American. She liked to speak English.'

'So when you think about things in your head, do you think in English or Colombian?'

Daniel makes a noise from across the table, laughing and choking on a mouthful of food. 'Sis.' He smirks, shaking his head. 'What kind of question is that? Anyway, it's Spanish. Colombian isn't a language.'

Rebecca shrugs, clearly unfazed by her brother's scathing remark. 'She knows what I mean, don't you, Abi?'

From somewhere in the house, a door bangs shut and a blast of cold blows over their heads, like a ghost searching for someone to haunt. The tentative joviality of the dinner slips away from them.

'Er...' Abi tries to continue, 'I'm not sure how to explain it. Both I guess. Some words are easier in one language than another.'

Abi's pulse quickens. She's still hungry, her dinner only half eaten and yet she's not sure she can swallow any more. What will she do if Sarah forces her to leave right now? She doesn't have a clue where she is. It's not a town though, she knows that much. The view outside the window of the police car was black. An endless darkness of countryside not a town. £89.61. She has to make this work somehow.

A silence fills the room. The only noise is the clink of cutlery on plates – and the glug of wine as Michael refills his glass.

It doesn't take long for Sarah to appear in the archway from the kitchen. There's a smear of mud on one of her cheeks, and her short blonde hair clings to her head in damp streaks. Her eyes are puffy and rimmed with red. She looks closer to fifty-four than the forty-four *Wikipedia* reports.

Abi swallows hard, sympathy and pity slicing through her. Beyond the outburst and the cutting edge of Sarah's words earlier is a woman struggling. And yet the set of Sarah's face is not one of apology or sadness now – it's resolve, Abi thinks. She looks ready.

For what though? Abi isn't sure.

Fear curls its fingers around Abi. She suddenly understands the pressure on a wild animal in that split-second where it stands frozen making the choice between fight or flight. She wishes she could ask him what to do right now. But she knows he'd tell her to fight. To stand her ground. To do whatever it takes.

She is Abigail Rose Wick and this is her home. She has to make them see that.

She places her knife and fork carefully onto her plate and slowly she stands up, the chair scraping on the tiled floor. She turns to face Sarah, and with her head down, hair falling across her view of those once-white trainers she's had since forever, she forces herself to speak. 'I... I can go.'

It's a gamble. A bluff. Pathetic. She doesn't mean it. She waits – hopes – for Michael or Daniel or even Rebecca to leap up and stand beside her, but no one moves. She stands alone and waits – a criminal waiting for the judge's verdict.

# FIFTEEN

## ABI

When Abi can't stand the silence for another second, she steps away from the table and, keeping her head down, walks towards the archway leading from the dining room into the wide expanse of the Wicks' gleaming kitchen. Sudden tears build in her eyes. It was stupid to bluff, and now it has failed. Hurt and humiliation battle for space in her body, and alongside it is a slippery fear she's tried to ignore for months now.

What will he do if she messes this up? He'll be angry. Furious. His plan only works if she's living in this house with them. And she's failed before she's even started.

Another thought occurs to her and she can't believe it's taken her until this moment to realise it: if she can't fix it, then she's useless to him. Surplus to requirements, a dead weight he'll set free. Except he'll never let her walk away. She knows too much. The thought curdles with the food she's eaten until she feels sick.

He was so kind to her at first, so understanding. It was all about how much she deserved this life, how wronged she'd been as a child to have what should have been hers snatched away from her. But then it became about something else that she still doesn't understand. There were so many lies she had to remember, hours of going over and over it together. She remembers the flashes of rage in that hotel room when she got the answer wrong, stumbling over the roulette wheel of truth and lies.

By the time Abi realised this was about more than her going home, she was in too deep – a pawn in a game she can't see. But Abi knows one thing. If she walks out of this house right now, if she fails, he'll kill her.

From the corner of her eye, Abi sees Ryan standing by the sink, watching her. His feet are bare and the bottom of his suit trousers are rolled up after his walk with Sarah. What did they talk about? she wonders. What did he say to bring her back? She has a sudden urge to shout at him to help her. Why else is he here if not to help?

Abi makes it all the way to the archway before Sarah stops her with a firm, 'No. Stay. I'm sorry for what I said. It was the shock. I...'

Sarah's words trail off and Abi lifts her head to see she's crying again.

The sympathy returns. It occurs to Abi in that moment, as their eyes meet, that it took her weeks to process the truth of Jhon's letter, to accept that everything she thought about her life was wrong. It's been over a year since she prised open the lip of the envelope and found her life forever changed, and yet Jhon's words still haunt her dreams.

*I'm not your father.*

Can Abi really blame Sarah for not welcoming her with open arms less than an hour after meeting her?

'I'm glad you're here.' Sarah nods as though trying to convince herself or maybe the rest of the family. 'And I'd like it if you stayed for now.'

Instantly, the air in the room changes. The bubble of tension pops. Abi draws in a long breath and exhales slowly, allowing the fear to loosen its clutches on her. She's staying where she belongs. She's safe.

Rebecca moves first, jumping up and throwing her arms around her mum, guiding her to the seat opposite Abi's. Michael tops up his glass and pours another for Sarah while Daniel plates up some stew and hands it to his mum.

'The rehearsals went well today,' Rebecca says as they all take their seats again.

She looks from Sarah to Michael, and Abi thinks she sees a strain lurking behind the bright smile lighting Rebecca's face, betraying the chatty tone.

'I'm in the school play,' she says to Abi before delving into a world of school and rehearsals that Abi didn't know existed outside of TV shows.

Abi loves Rebecca for the effort she's making, the rambling details, the smiling face. She's doing everything she can to keep the atmosphere light, but Abi is only half listening. Sarah's final two words of apology run on repeat in Abi's mind, like a scratched CD stuck in the same place. *I'd like it if you stayed for now.*

For now.

She's safe for now.

All of a sudden, Sarah's apology seems cloaked in a warning. However heartfelt she sounded, she hasn't changed her mind about Abi at all.

'Where did you go to school?' Sarah asks after the last of the food had been eaten.

Images of the grey-walled police interview room fill Abi's head, but she forces a smile. 'To start with, nowhere. I was home-schooled by the woman I thought was my mum, Caroline. She died when I was twelve. That's when I went to school.'

The truth feels good. Easy. Even if it's just a splinter. Abi doesn't mention that it was Jhon who set her lessons before he left each time. She doesn't tell them about the endless weeks where Caroline lay immobile on the couch, watching one stupid action film after another, crying softly and muttering to herself.

'Is home-schooling the norm in Colombia?' Sarah's next question breaks into Abi's thoughts; so does the next, and the next.

Abi pictures the story in her mind, the parallel life he told her to build. She answers every one of Sarah's questions without hesitation, without looking down or left, just as he taught her. 'What was the name of the school you went to when you were twelve? Did you think about college? Have you left many friends behind?'

It's Daniel who rescues Abi. 'Mum,' he says, flashing Abi a look as he speaks, somewhere between an eye roll and a smirk that makes her like him, 'enough with the interrogation.'

'Was I interrogating?' Sarah raises her eyebrows and glances at Daniel then Michael. Hurt glows in her eyes. 'I'm sorry, that wasn't my intention. There's just so much we don't know, I—'

'It's OK,' Abi cuts in, saving Sarah from another sorry-not-sorry apology. 'I don't mind. I have a lot of questions too, but I'm quite tired.' She pushes her chair back and stands. 'If it's really OK for me to stay here, then maybe we could talk more tomorrow?'

Sarah nods. 'Of course.'

Abi can see the questions still forming in her mind, but at least she stops voicing them.

Rebecca springs up from beside Abi. 'I'll show you where everything is.'

'Thank you, Rebecca,' Sarah replies, her eyes softening as she smiles at her youngest daughter. She moves her gaze to Abi and the warmth disappears, sending a chill racing down Abi's spine. 'Let us know if you need anything,' she adds as though Abi is an unexpected guest – someone to be courteous to and nothing else.

A force of emotion hits Abi. Tears blur her vision. This is not how it was supposed to be.

*I'm your child*, Abi wants to scream then but doesn't. 'Thank you for dinner. It was delicious.' She smiles at Michael. 'If that's the kind of food you cook, Michael, then I can't wait to taste your food some time, Sarah.'

Michael laughs, a loud bellow that lacks any hint of humour.

'Did I say something funny?' Abi glances at Rebecca.

'Sarah doesn't cook,' Michael replies, downing the last dregs of wine from his glass.

'Oh.' Abi frowns. 'It's just, I thought with the cookery show...'

Rebecca links her arm through Abi's and pulls her away. 'I'll explain it all tomorrow. Come on – your room's next to mine.'

Rebecca leads the way back to the hall, where Abi collects her backpack before following her up the sweeping staircase. Her trainers sink into the soft red carpet that runs up the centre of the stairs. She looks ahead to Rebecca's white socks with the black Nike tick and thinks of Ryan's bare feet in the kitchen. She wonders if she was supposed to have taken her trainers off.

No one asked her to. But then when would they have done that? The second she was through the front door, Sarah was throwing accusations at her, and then they were setting the table and eating, and now this. With everything else going on, it shouldn't matter, but it does.

The flames of heat burn Abi's face as they round the corner of the stairs and reach the first floor. There is no manual for how to act in people's homes, she thinks. It's assumed, learned in childhood, from parents, but Abi was always stuck in that awful room with Caroline. No playdates, no friends, no visits to the park. No time to learn all the little things about polite society that everyone seems to know except her.

The upstairs of the house is just as grand as the downstairs.

There's a wide hall with two doors either side and another corridor at the end leading off to the right.

Rebecca points left first, then right. 'My room, your room, bathroom, Daniel's room. Mum and Dad are around the corner and that's where...' Rebecca's voice trails off.

She pauses then starts again as though nothing happened. 'They have their own bathroom, which is so unfair. I hate sharing with Daniel. He's so hairy.'

A burst of unexpected laughter escapes Abi's mouth and Rebecca laughs too.

'Sorry,' she says, grinning. 'Too much information, right? Here, this is you.'

Rebecca opens the second door on the left into a large bedroom lit by the warm yellow glow of a beside lamp. There's a double bed in the centre of the room with a bedspread in pale blue, the same shade as the wallpaper with the delicate wild-flowers and green vines twisting around it that makes Abi think of the doubt she felt earlier.

'If you need something, like a hairdryer or anything, I'll be just next door. We've left you some towels there and some toiletries. Tomorrow, we'll get you tons more stuff. I really hope you like shopping.'

Rebecca gives a goofy wave, a final grin and disappears, closing the door behind her and leaving Abi to sink onto the soft mattress and kick off the trainers she hates that she's still wearing.

Her head spins with everything that's happened since walking into the police station. She feels somehow disconnected from it now, as though she was the onlooker, watching from the outside, like him.

Everything has gone to plan. The police believed her, didn't they? She's in her new home, isn't she? With her family. And yet it all feels so wrong. Abi unzips her backpack and pulls out her phone.

He said no contact. 'We have to make them believe it's just you. And the easiest way to do that is if it *is* just you.' But she longs for reassurance. Abi unlocks the screen, her fingers hovering over the message icon. Should she text him?

Before Abi can decide, her bedroom door opens. She jumps up, her heart lurching in her chest as she tries to disguise the phone gripped in the palm of her hand.

'Knock, knock,' Michael says from the doorway, his body swaying a fraction as he grips the door handle. 'I just wanted to check you have everything you need.'

'I do. Thank you, Michael.'

He stares at her for a moment, a glaze covering his eyes. Emotion? Alcohol? Both, Abi guesses.

'You can call me Dad, you know. If you want to.'

'I know. This is new for me.'

Abi stares at the man in the doorway. She's spent a long time imagining this night. Sometimes in her mind's eye it is emotional – she cries and they cry. Other times it's more joyous, with laughter and celebrations. And whilst there have been tears and laughter tonight, there has also been tension and confrontation. Neither of which she imagined on the lonely nights in that Buenaventura apartment after opening Jhon's letter.

Fresh tears spill from Michael's eyes and rest on the puffy skin beneath them. She drops her gaze. Unsure where to look or how to react to his emotion.

'I'll try... Dad,' she adds, more to fill the silence than anything else.

Michael smiles and steps forward, reaching his arms around her and resting his head on top of hers. Whiffs of wine and onions catch in her nose, and underneath it all is a familiar cologne she can't place.

He sniffs. 'I'm so sorry. What a mess you must think I am.

This is just so overwhelming. To have you home after all this time, Abigail.'

Abi tenses at the name. It's the first time anyone has used it since she's been in this house. Even Rebecca with all her friendliness has stuck to Abi. She wonders how much of what he's saying is the wine? A lot, she guesses.

'It's fine,' she says, her voice muffled against his chest. 'I understand.'

'Don't worry about Sarah – she'll come around.' His voice is low, the words quick, and then he steps back and stares down at her face. 'It's good to have you home,' he adds, his voice normal again.

'Michael.' Sarah's voice carries from the hallway. 'Let her rest and come to bed.'

'Yes, right, of course. Well, good night, Abigail.'

'Good night,' she says, following him to the door and closing it before Sarah decides to begin another round of questions – or worse, sees the phone in her hand and wants to know who she's messaging.

Abi stands by the doorway for a minute and listens for movement. The chink of light shining beneath her door disappears and she hears a door close from further down the hallway. Minutes pass and there's the distant sound of running water and a toilet flushing, and then the house falls silent.

She changes into a spare T-shirt and lifts the silky bed covers, releasing the smell of flowery washing powder into the air. The duvet is heavy, like a giant feather pillow on her body. Abi switches off the bedside lamp, throwing the room into darkness.

She grips the phone in her hand and unlocks the screen once more. What would he say if she called him now? Would he answer?

Before she can decide, her phone hums in her hand. It's him

of course. He is the only one with her number. Three messages appear in quick succession.

*Stick to the plan.*

*Don't worry about anything else.*

*Delete these! Don't reply!!!!!*

A weight settles in Abi's chest. It's hardly the reassurance she craved, but she does as she's told and deletes the messages, before switching off her phone and sliding it as far under the mattress as her hand can reach.

She lays on the pillow and closes her eyes, exhausted yet alert. She needs to rest. Today might have sapped every ounce of her energy, but it's nothing compared to what he promised tomorrow will bring.

# SIXTEEN

## ABI

### Then

'Please, please, please, Jhon, don't go again.'

'Abelia, I have to go.' He smiled, creasing the skin around his dark eyes.

'Why do you have to? You only come twice a month. Where do you go when you are not here?'

'I love you very much,' he said, ignoring her question. 'But I have other people who rely on me too.'

Tears dripped down her face. She stepped closer and snaked her arms around Jhon's leg. Her fists bunched the coarse material of his trousers. 'Momma doesn't love me,' she sobbed, rubbing her nose against his leg.

Jhon crouched to the floor in the bedroom and collected her into his arms. He rested her face against his so that the thick fur of his beard scratched against her cheek. 'She's sick, Abelia. She can't control it.'

'She can, Papa. It's always worse when you're gone. Really, really worse. She doesn't care about me.'

'I'll speak to her. I'll tell her to try harder. But look at the clock over there. Tell me, what time is it?'

Abelia wiped the water from her eyes and stared at the little round clock that sat on her nightstand. 'The big hand is at six and the little hand is at nine. It's half past nine.'

'And what time is your bedtime?'

'Half past seven.'

'Well then.' Jhon stood up, carrying her with ease and dropping her gently onto the bed in the corner of the bedroom she shared with her mom. 'Go to sleep now. I've left plenty of schoolwork for you. Two weeks' worth.'

Abelia glanced at the stack of papers on the floor. It would take her less than three days to finish.

'Remember your Spanish storybooks too,' he said, sweeping her hair away from her face.

'I will.'

'Escúchalos todas las noches.'

She nodded again, sleep pulling at the edges of her mind no matter how hard she fought against it.

'What did I say?' he asked with a wink.

'I must listen to them every night.'

'Good girl. Now sleep.'

He bent over and kissed her forehead. 'Be good for your mother.'

Fresh tears ran from her eyes, but she nodded again, before turning to the wall.

'Abelia?' he said from the doorway. 'The world is a dangerous place for a little girl. That is why you must stay in this apartment. Why you can never go out.'

Abelia sucked on a piece of hair and closed her eyes. She imagined waking in the morning to the smells of breakfast cooking and her mom singing. It was a fantasy. In the morning, Jhon would be gone, and her mom would sink back into her sadness, and Abelia would be all alone. But the fantasy helped her sleep and kept the nightmares at bay.

# SEVENTEEN

## SARAH

Friday, 10 p.m.

Anger settles over me, thick like the unfamiliar duvet I'm lying under. It doesn't help that Michael is next to me again.

Five years we've slept apart. Five years since I swore I'd never share a bed with him again.

My heard pounds in my chest, my anger for the girl heightening the memory of the fury I felt then too. Five years have passed but I still remember the pot of face cream in my hand and the desire to throw it. I didn't though. It cost far too much money to waste on my anger at Michael.

'How can you still be clinging to your charity after the mud you've dragged us all through?' I hissed.

It was one week into the scandal and the papers were becoming more inventive with their headlines. Today's had read 'MICHAEL DICK' and had thrown fuel on the flames of the scandal over Michael's affair and how his charity money had been used to pay for hotel rooms. I'd stopped looking at the papers days ago, but this one I saw. One of the children in

Rebecca's class had given it to her. A cruel joke by a ten-year-old kid and, I suspect, their parent.

'It's important,' Michael snapped, pulling his fingers through his hair, once, twice, three times, until tufts of it were standing on end. 'It helps families, and it helps me to help them. I won't let it go because of a stupid mistake.'

'Stupid mistake?' I made a noise in my throat, midway between a scoff and a laugh. It wasn't funny. None of it was. 'Is that what we're going to call embezzlement now? You've dragged Abigail's—' My voice choked. 'You've dragged her name through the mud too. Do you see that? You have to let the charity go, Michael. For Rebecca and Daniel's sake. The press and the Charities Commission will not stop targeting you until you relinquish your control. Let one of the bigger charities take it on. If you really care about Abigail's charity and what it stands for, then you'll do it.'

'I was cleared of embezzlement, Sarah. You know that. It was an accounting error, that's all. A mistake.'

'You were charging your lunches with all those desperate women to the charity. People did not walk, run, swim or whatever other fundraising stuff they did thinking of you having a sodding lunch at The Ivy.'

'I was developing contacts for bigger charitable investors. All the charities do it. No charity survives on bake sales alone.'

He dropped onto the edge of the bed, rubbing at his forehead. 'This may be hard for you to understand, but not all people handle things like you, Sarah. Not all of us wake up one morning and decide to just move on. The women you're talking about needed support, and I gave it to them. It's a big part of the charity's remit to help the families of the missing. I was helping them.'

I gritted my teeth and ignored the barb and his attempt to make what he'd done about me. About Abigail. About anything that wasn't him being a selfish, stupid bastard. 'They are not like us.'

'Yes, they are.'

'I read all about it in the papers, Michael. These are British women who married men from other countries, and were then surprised when the marriage fell apart and their husbands took their children back to their country of origin. Yes, it's tragic and must be very, very hard for them, but it's not the same as what we've been through.'

'They've still lost their children.'

'And the bill for the hotel room?' The words were out before I could stop them. I hated that I cared so much, hurt so much.

'Argh,' he cried out, throwing his arms in the air in a wild fashion. 'How many times do I need to say this? I told the hotel to charge it to my personal account but they didn't, and stupidly, I didn't check.'

'A billing error. The reason you've almost sunk my career and dragged your children into the centre of a media storm is because you didn't check the hotel bill after you'd finished screwing some woman.'

'You're the one making them go to school. Let them stay home for a while,' he hissed back.

'And what would that solve? Hiding out in the house wouldn't shield them from it either, not after that man knocked on our door today.'

'That was unfortunate,' Michael said.

'Unfortunate? I thought he was going to kill both of us.' He wouldn't shut up about his wife leaving him and how it was our fault he had nothing left. 'God knows how he saw your affair with his wife as my fault. Thank goodness the kids weren't home.'

'Come on, Sarah. I can take the blame for the affairs, but that man wasn't my fault. The police spoke to him and they don't think he'll come back. And please don't act all high and mighty in this. Let's not forget that in the weeks after Abigail was abducted you—'

'Don't you *dare* bring up that kiss with Ryan,' I cut in, fighting to keep my voice from rising to the scream I wanted it to be. 'That was a stupid, split-second moment that I told you about immediately and never repeated.'

'I'm sorry,' he whispered. 'I know what I did isn't the same. I was being unfair.'

My frustration petered out. What was the point of this argument? What did I expect to achieve? The answer was nothing. There was nothing Michael could say that I didn't already know – that I hadn't read about in every tabloid in Britain. Just as there were no words that I could fling at him in anger that would make any difference to the outcome.

I'd turned a blind eye to it – the dinners that hadn't ended until midnight. Overnight stays in London because of an early meeting. His affair – or affairs, as it turned out – had been in the periphery of my mind for some time, but I'd been happy with that. Michael needed to be wanted, appreciated, loved. I hadn't given him any of those things for a long time. For a while, he'd been too obsessed with finding Abigail to care about his physical needs, but even he had to stop when the wild goose chases dried up.

'What do we do now?' Michael's voice was muffled by the hands covering his face.

'I'm leaving you,' I said. 'Actually, *you* are the one leaving.' I stepped to the wardrobe and yanked open the doors before snatching at Michael's shirts and throwing them to the floor. 'Pack your stuff and get out.'

'Sarah.' Michael's voice was thick with emotion. 'Please. What about the kids? They've been through so much already.'

'And whose fault is that?'

'I know, all right. I know what I've done. But Daniel's GCSEs are coming up. He's going to find them hard enough as it is. We can't end out marriage now. You don't want him to have his whole life messed up by this, do you?'

I faltered then, hating Michael for making this about the children. I sat on the corner of the bed and clenched my jaw, pushing back the emotions. 'Fine. Stay. But as soon as his exams are over, this is over.'

Michael nodded. 'Thank you.'

'And don't think for one second that this is a marriage anymore. It's... it's nothing. It's an agreement. We live in this house and we do what's best for the kids. That's it. I'm never sleeping beside you again.'

'I'll move into the spare room,' he said.

'No. I will. It's closer to the children.'

Daniel worked hard and did well in his exams. The dyslexia made it harder, but he didn't give up. The years passed and I thought about telling Michael to go many times, but then Rebecca started senior school, and Daniel started at college and even I could see how important stability was to our family. And to be fair to Michael, he threw himself into the life of a stay-at-home dad. Cleaning, cooking, driving. All the mundane work I hated.

I still plan to tell him to leave at some point. I picture a time when Daniel has his own place and Rebecca is at university, and I find a little house somewhere. A two-up, two-down for me and Barley. I'm not sure how much Daniel and Rebecca are aware of our faux marriage. I'm sure Daniel is old enough to see the truth. If he does, he says nothing – another elephant in the room we all ignore. Rebecca is endlessly optimistic and too sweet to see the truth of what we are, I think. Or maybe I'm the one who's optimistic when it comes to how much Rebecca sees.

From beside me now, Michael draws in a breath as if he's going to say something, then exhales without a word. One, two, three, four, five times he does this – then he speaks. 'Are you OK?'

It's a stupid question to ask. 'Not really.'

'It could be her—'

'Don't,' I say.

'Can you just try and give her a chance, Sarah? That's all I'm asking.'

'I *am* giving her a chance. She's still here, isn't she?'

'I just mean... I know you have your reservations, but if you can just let your guard down for a minute—'

'Oh, what, and you're so sure that girl is our daughter now?' I interrupt again. 'What happened to waiting for the DNA test?'

Another exhale. 'I'm starting to think it could be. There is an undeniable familiarity to her. It's not so much something I see but something I feel.'

'You're drunk,' I reply.

'That's unfair.'

'I'm not trying to be nasty,' I say into the darkness. 'I know that's what you all think. That I'm heartless because I've not welcomed this girl like you have, but I'm trying to be realistic. How are you going to feel – how are Daniel and Rebecca going to feel – when the DNA results come back and tell us it's not Abigail? What happens then? We'll never be able to pick up the pieces again.'

Michael is silent beside me. I can't see his face, but I can sense the cogs in his head turning. 'So why get a DNA test then? Why don't we just accept that it *is* Abigail?'

'Michael,' I groan, failing to keep the frustration from my voice. 'You can't be serious. A complete stranger wants to live in our house and be part of our family and you just want to take her word for it?'

'Fine, you're right.' He matches my tone. 'Get the DNA test if it means that much to you, but remember she has the scar, Sarah.'

The scar. It keeps coming back to the chicken-pox scar.

Ryan said the same thing on the walk. Abigail had chicken pox when she was two years old and it left a circular white indent on her chest – this I know is true. The police in London have confirmed that the person sleeping in my spare room has a scar on her chest. To Michael, Ryan, the police and the girl too perhaps, this makes her Abigail. Why am I the only person who sees the fallacy in their reasoning?

My chest starts to tear apart and my head pounds in giant rhythmic throbs as I consider the possibility that I'm wrong.

Abigail is dead. I say the words in my head over and over and then I start to count again. One... two... three... four... I'm not sure what I'm counting anymore, but it helps me block out the questions I don't want to ask, let alone answer. One part of my mind counts, freeing the other part to think. Not just think but analyse.

'Michael,' I say, 'did any of the private investigators you hired ever suggest to you that Abigail might be in South America?'

'No.' He's silent for a moment. 'But that doesn't mean it isn't plausible. One of the PIs – this was early on, maybe the year after it happened – thought the man who'd taken Abigail had boarded a cargo ship at the docks in Felixstowe. The police worked on that assumption for a while too. Those big ships go all over the world, Colombia included. Why are you suddenly so interested in the search?'

'I'm trying to understand—' Trying to make you understand. 'Doesn't it seem strange to you that this girl has arrived here now, almost fourteen years to the day since Abigail was taken?'

'It's like DS Howard said,' Michael says, 'the people raising her died. She found a letter. What difference does it make if it's near the anniversary or not?'

'I just think it's odd, that's all.'

'I thought you didn't want to know any of this,' he says.

I shake my head on the pillow. 'I didn't. But you've kept all the reports though, haven't you?' I ask, picturing the row of red ring binders locked in the filing cabinet in Michael's study. All of Michael's leads, every search by every private investigator he's hired. Each binder has the year written down the side in black marker pen with Michael's looping handwriting; 2009, the year Abigail was taken, is larger than the other binders and stuffed full of paper and news reports that stick out the top in haphazard fashion. The rest are slim, like the kind Rebecca keeps her science homework in, with no sign of what or how much is inside them. I have never opened the files to look.

'Yes, of course, but I doubt they can help. There were never any strong leads.'

'Are you sure there's nothing in them that can tell us about the girl in our house?'

'For Christ's sake, Sarah. Stop calling her *the girl*. Her name's Abelia, or maybe even Abigail – either way she introduced herself as Abi. You could give her the benefit of the doubt, you know. Innocent until proven guilty and all that.'

He twists away from me and slams his head into the pillow.

Frustration shakes me like a rag doll.

'You're doing it again – making out like I'm wrong,' I say, dropping my voice to a whisper. 'We don't know that's what's going on. We don't know anything. Tomorrow, I'm going to sit down with her, without Rebecca and Daniel. I'm going to ask her to tell me what she told the police. If she has questions she wants to ask us, then I'll answer them too. There's nothing wrong with wanting some answers, and I'd appreciate it if you stopped making me out to be the villain here.'

'Fine,' he says. The muffle of covers does nothing to mask the razor sharpness of his tone. 'But I want to be there too.'

'Fine – we'll do it together.'

'Fine.' Michael pulls the duvet up so it covers half his head. End of conversation.

The frustration continues to build and swarm, a storm inside me. There is so much more to say, to talk about, but Michael and I, we are no longer the team we once were, but maybe he's right too. Calling her 'the girl' isn't helping anyone. *Abelia*. I say her name in my thoughts.

Michael's voice echoes in my head. 'I thought you didn't want to know any of this.' He's wrong. Of course I want to know. There's nothing I want more than to know what happened to Abigail and to have her back with us.

I remember the polite *tap-tap-tap* of knuckles on the white cottage door. I remember the desperation for any news ravaging and raging inside of me. I remember digging my fingernails into my palms until it hurt, just to stop my hands from reaching out and clawing at the detectives so they would stop with the polite *how are you*s and *as you know...* and tell me, just tell me, what they'd found. It was always nothing. The police found nothing.

Michael is wrong. I wanted to know.

Another memory fills my head. It's so strong that I can practically smell the chemical carpet-shop smell and I'm transported back in time to the empty room beside this one, with its new, ruby-red carpet, into which no one goes anymore.

# EIGHTEEN

## SARAH

Then

Light bleeds through the thin red curtains and hurts my eyes. I blink and realise with a nauseating guilt that I've been asleep. There is no moment of forgetting, no sense in those first waking seconds that all is as it should be. The knowledge is there, standing over me like a beast. My little girl is gone. I check the time. The calculation is instant. Seventy-three days and twenty-two hours since Abigail was taken.

What kind of mother am I if I can sleep whilst my little girl is out there, crying for her mummy?

The questions come thick and fast, adding to my nausea.

Where are you, baby girl?

Who has you?

Are you having nightmares?

Are you hungry? Thirsty?

There are no answers.

Abigail disappeared without a trace. Not a single sign, or clue, or hint of where my little girl is – not since the woman who called 999 because something in her gut told her to. An alarm in her head telling her that there was something wrong about the man with dark hair, wearing a baseball cap pulled low and pushing a little girl in a buggy with the sunshade pushed out towards the foot ferry near Felixstowe docks.

Not a single trace since the grainy CCTV footage from the fish-and-chip restaurant of a boat gliding over the waves, and the two skinny legs visible from the pushchair. Skinny legs too long for a pushchair. Where was he taking her? What did he do with her? Nausea burns my throat.

I turn my face away from the daylight and feel the carpet as soft as teddy fur on my cheek. It's brand new, laid the day before we left for the holiday. Boxes of furniture are stacked to one side. A bed, a wardrobe, a little dressing table Abigail wanted so she could be just like Mummy in her own grown-up room, no longer wanting to sleep in the bottom bunk of Daniel's.

From somewhere below me, I hear Rebecca's babbling calls. The noise tugs at the shattered pieces of my heart. The hurt of missing Rebecca and Daniel adds to the pain, but I'm in no state to see them. I'll wait until the sky is black and the house is still, and I'll creep into their bedrooms and kiss their foreheads, just as I've done every night of their lives.

There's a tap at the door before it opens.

'Sarah, are you awake?' Michael asks.

I nod and glance at him. His face is pale beneath his stubbly beard. His lips are chapped and sore, his hair messy and unbrushed. It's a reminder that we're both living this nightmare. I want to reach out to him, but I don't.

For the first time, I notice the tray in his hands. He drops down to a squat and slides it closer. There's a tall glass of water on the tray and a sandwich too. The meaty smell of the ham catches in my nose and flips my stomach. I don't remember the last time I ate, but I'm not hungry. How can I eat when my little girl might be starving?

'Do you want anything else?' he asks, just as he's done every day.

I shake my head.

'Mrs Dillinger is here from next door. She's offered to take the kids to the park. They've gone a bit stir-crazy. Even Rebecca is irritable. I thought doing something normal, away from the house, might help. I thought it might get Daniel talking too. Is that OK with you?'

I nod, trying not to think about Daniel and Rebecca leaving the house and all the dangers. The cars, the road, strangers snatching. Tears prick my eyes and I push the thoughts back. Mrs Dillinger is a retired schoolteacher and a grandmother. She's always been so kind to the children; I know she'll take care of them.

*Like you didn't.* The voice in my head is a hissed accusation that punches the breath out of my lungs.

'The vicar stopped by this morning,' Michael continues. 'I told her you didn't want to be disturbed, but she left her card in case you wanted to talk. Abigail has been put on their prayer list.' He stands up and steps back to the door. 'I'll come see you later.'

The door begins to close, taking most of the light with it. The question springs from my mouth before I'm even aware I'm thinking it. 'Daniel still isn't speaking?' I ask, pulling myself up to sitting. The room spins and a hammer pounds down on the top of my skull.

Michael shakes her head. 'No. He's not said a single word to me. I tried getting him to write something instead, but that didn't work either. He'll be OK. He just needs more time.'

The door closes, plunging me back into the gloom. I push the tray further away and lay my head back against the carpet.

I didn't notice it at first – none of us did. There was so much going on in those early days, and Daniel has always been a quiet child. Then it was shock, we guessed. I remember a whispered conversation with Michael and Ryan in the kitchen, Michael pacing back and forth as if I was holding him against his will, stopping him from calling God knows who else.

'Daniel isn't talking,' I said. 'I don't think he's said a word since...' I couldn't finish the sentence.

'He's scared,' Michael replied. 'He's in shock. He's old enough to know what's happening, isn't he? Give it time. He'll speak when he wants something badly enough,' he added.

But it's been seventy-three days and we're home now and Daniel is back at school, and still he hasn't uttered a single word.

The sound of the front door slamming echoes through the house. Then Michael's mobile rings from somewhere downstairs. I no longer hold my breath, waiting to see if he'll rush up to tell me something.

I glance at the tray and reach for the water. It's cool in my mouth, but I only manage a sip.

A single tear rolls out of my eye.

Daniel isn't speaking. His sister, his best friend, is gone, and he can't talk about it. He can't cry in my arms, because I am up here, in this room that should be Abigail's; my prison, my purgatory. Daniel isn't speaking. Rebecca is irritable. They need their mother, just as Abigail did. I've failed her, and now I'm failing Rebecca and Daniel. The guilt; the hurt is a noose around my neck, pulling tighter and tighter until I can no longer breathe.

I draw the tray towards me.

Abigail is gone.

I force down the nausea and chew every mouthful of sandwich, only swallowing when it has become tasteless mush and can slide down my throat without making me gag.

Lying in this room, wishing I'd been there, praying she comes home... it isn't helping her. It isn't helping Rebecca and Daniel. It's only me that this room serves.

But how do I carry on with my life while my daughter is out there somewhere? Scared and alone and crying for me?

Tears spring from my eyes. She isn't out there. She isn't coming back. The thought swimming through my head isn't new. It's been there all along, but I refused to acknowledge it until now.

One, two, three, four, five, six, seven bites until the sandwich is gone. My hand reaches for the water. Three gulps and the glass is empty.

I failed Abigail. I will not fail Rebecca and Daniel too.

All of a sudden, the silence in the house consumes me. It is absolute, and makes me want to flick on the radio just to drown it out. My mother's voice tinkles in my ears as I stand up and force myself out of the room. 'A noisy home is a happy home.'

I don't have a single memory of being in the three-bed terrace of my childhood home that doesn't have the radio murmuring in the background, filling the house with the noise my mother craved.

For the first time in my life, I'm glad I'm an only child. And I'm glad my parents are dead. They died within a year of each other and missed my graduation. My father from his heart, my mother from her lungs. They would've loved being grandparents. They'd have doted on the children. In a parallel world, I'd always imagined my father taking the children crabbing, and building forts, and my mother teaching them to bake and sew. But now I'm glad they're dead. I'm glad they've been spared this.

I pull up and out of Abigail's bedroom and force myself to shower and dress, to brush my teeth and my hair. When I'm done, I find Michael in the living room. The door is ajar and it creaks as I push it open. The sound is too loud in the silence. He's sitting bolt upright in the armchair that's usually beside the fireplace but has been dragged in front of the TV. He's so close that if he reaches out his hand, he could touch the screen.

It's the first time I've seen him motionless since it happened. The skin on his face is sallow and sinks in around his cheeks. He's been crying. Not just crying but sobbing. His shoulders are hunched forward. His face is wet and swollen.

Has something happened? My heart freezes. I fall towards the arm of the chair and stare at the screen.

Sky News is on but the sound is muted. My gaze darts across the screen and I watch a scene from the House of Commons – MPs bickering over a European currency. I catch Abigail's name on the yellow banner moving across the bottom of the screen. *Police scale back manpower for Abigail Wick abduction*, it reads. It's not news. Not to us anyway. They came and told us in person. Was it yesterday? Or the day before?

They're out of leads. They're very sorry, but there are no more avenues of investigation. They have to redirect their efforts to other cases, other missing children.

'We won't give up, Sarah,' Michael croaks. 'I've hired a private investigator. The best money can buy. I'm going to sell the business and set up a charity for missing children. No one else should suffer what we have. We can help others at the same time. We won't give up...'

'I can't.' The words tremble as they leave my mouth.

'What choice do we have? We must keep looking for her.'

'I can't,' I say again. 'I can't wait for news anymore. It's been months. She's gone. I can feel it.' I clutch my stomach, concave from starvation. 'The police have found nothing, because there's nothing to find. She's dead.'

Michael's mouth gapes and a noise catches in his throat. A strangled cry. 'How do you know?'

I shake my head. The concept is still so fragile in my mind that it could disintegrate at any moment. I have to believe it though. I have to survive. 'I can't fail Rebecca and Daniel the same way I failed Abigail.'

'You didn't fail her.' Michael stands up and pulls me into his arms. It's familiar, but I find no comfort from his touch and step away.

'I don't want to know about the traces and the potential sightings,' I say. 'I don't want to know about a girl that looks like Abigail, or dead ends and wild goose chases. Don't tell me any of it.'

'But, Sarah—'

'It's OK. Carry on searching if it's what you have to do, but I have to stop or I'll die. I know I will. And I can't die, because then Daniel and Rebecca won't have a mother and I can't do that to them. So unless a girl turns up calling herself Abigail, don't involve me.'

Confusion and hurt are drawn in the lines on his face, but he nods. This is how we will carry on – Michael choosing hope, and me choosing survival.

The front door opens and I hear Mrs Dillinger's high-pitched, 'Coo-eee.'

We stare at each other for another second before I follow the noise. Rebecca squeals in Mrs Dillinger's arms as I step into the entrance hall.

In a single second I feel my heart rip to shreds for what I've lost, and what I still possess. Daniel steps back as I run towards them, scooping Rebecca out of my elderly neighbour's arms and into my own.

I can't be the mother my children need and continue hoping Abigail is alive. I can't be the mother they need while dwelling on what happened. I have to look forward, and the only way I can do that is to believe Abigail is dead. Convince myself some-how, grieve and... move on. It feels impossible – unimaginable – but what choice do I have? I will do anything to protect Daniel and Rebecca. Even this.

\*

SATURDAY

# NINETEEN

## SARAH

Saturday, 6 a.m.

I wake to the sound of air catching in the back of Michael's throat with every inhale and the throb of a headache already pushing down behind my eyes.

I lie still for a moment as thoughts move in and out of my mind, knocking against each other. I was dreaming of the day Abigail was taken again. Not the beach this time but later. Janie and I running through the streets of the seaside village, screaming Abigail's name. I swallow and for a moment I can still feel the soreness in my throat from the shouting.

I think of Janie and the call I tried to make last night. For the first time in years, I wonder what she's doing now, what her life has become.

She left so quickly after Abigail was taken. As soon as the police would let her go. Phil had been in a car accident, she said. 'I hate to leave you like this. I'll check he's OK and I'll come back.'

I nodded, barely listening.

She never came back. She never called. The police spoke to

her again of course, but I never did. After the shock and the devastation, after we went home, after I picked myself up and forced myself to go on for Daniel and Rebecca, I tried to call her. I thought maybe I'd missed her calls, or maybe she was giving me space, waiting for me to make the first move. Maybe Phil was in a bad way and she had her own problems.

It stung that she hadn't tried to contact me. Janie was my best friend and I needed her more than ever. It stung even more when she didn't answer any of my calls or reply to a single message. I started to worry after a while that something had happened to her, but eventually I got a text from Phil.

*Janie doesn't want to talk to you. Please stop trying.*

I couldn't understand it. We'd argued earlier that day, before Abigail was taken from us. It was a stupid fight. Bickering really. Was that why she didn't want to talk to me anymore? It seemed petty, and Janie wasn't the type to hold a grudge. Or was it that I'd left it too long when I'd known Phil had been in an accident? Surely she would've understood. I was living through the worst thing imaginable.

I tied myself in knots over Janie's silence for a while, but, in the end, I gave up. *Look forward not back.*

Nearly fourteen years have passed, but the urge to talk to her returns. Her mobile might not be working anymore, but I'm sure I've got her home number in an old address book somewhere. I'll dig it out later.

My thoughts move on. I think about what awaits us today. Our DNA will be collected – mine and Michael's and Abi's – and the seventy-two-hour wait will begin. Three days, and then what? How will we cope on Tuesday when the results show she's not Abigail?

A sound pierces my thoughts. The clink of the cutlery drawer in the kitchen opening then closing.

Is it her? Is she snooping through our house?

Last night, I promised Michael that we would talk to Abelia together, but the chance to do it alone is too appealing, and quickly I'm out of bed and throwing an old fleece on over my pyjamas.

I count the stairs even though I know exactly how many there are: eighteen. The number floats in my head along with all the others, and I wish I could tip them out as easily as a glass of water can be emptied into the sink.

The scents of last night's stew linger in the air, stale and unwelcome, as Barley and I enter the kitchen. Nausea threatens from the smell and the thought of food. I will make myself eat at some point, but not right now.

I hear metal tap against china in the extension then the distinctive chime of Rebecca's mobile. Not Abelia then.

Rebecca lifts her head and beams at me as I step into view. Barley shoots to her side to receive an ear scratch and eye a stray cornflake that's fallen onto the table.

'Good morning, sweetheart,' I say, trying to sound normal. To be normal.

'Mum, you look dreadful,' she says, slurping a spoonful of milk.

I run my fingers through my hair and shrug. It's the least of my worries. 'You're up early,' I say by way of reply, dropping a kiss on top of her head. Her hair smells of the oatmeal-and-honey shampoo I gave her for her birthday.

'Couldn't sleep,' Becca replies before stuffing another mound of cornflakes into her mouth.

I stare at my daughter for a long moment. Even her wide grin can't detract from the dark smudges under her eyes. I wish I could say something. Tell her it will all be OK, while warning her that it won't. She's expecting a happily-ever-after, but there isn't one for us. Maybe Daniel can give her some reassurance if she won't listen to me. He won't be awake for ages yet, but I'll talk to him later, check he's OK too.

I must tread carefully. Rebecca has always hated conflict. I asked her once, when she was six or seven, 'How was your day?'

'Terrible,' she replied. 'Two of the older boys started fighting over who scored a goal and got sent to the head teacher.' It didn't matter to Rebecca that the fight had been nothing to do with her; it still affected her, just like the tension of last night will have done.

Barley trots to the French doors, tail wagging as he presses his nose to the glass. I open it a fraction, just enough for him to slip through and bound into the garden, enough for a blast of cold, dewy air to blow through the room. I can still see the damp indents of footprints on the frosty grass – mine and Ryan's. Above it, the sky is bright but grey.

'Come for a dog walk with me?' I say to Rebecca as the familiar urge to escape fills my body. Maybe if I can coax her to come with me, I'll find the words to prepare her. I wonder briefly about waking Daniel and asking him to come too. The urge to scoop my children up as though they're still babies and take them away from here is overwhelming. I drop the thought. Daniel will only grumble and fall back to sleep. He might be twenty, but he's not yet shaken the teenage urge to sleep.

'Sure,' she says with a shrug. 'What about Abi? Shall I see if she wants to come too?'

*Absolutely not.* I shake my head. 'Let's—'

'Come where?' Abelia says from the kitchen. Her accent still sounds unfamiliar. Her command of the English language is perfect, not a word out of place, but it's mumbled and soft – a Spanish-like drawl. I can hear American in it too, in the upward inflections at the end of each sentence, something Rebecca does when she's been watching too many American shows.

*You're not my daughter. You're not Abigail.*

She appears in the archway from the kitchen in the same

jeans and dark jumper she was wearing last night. Frays of navy cotton dangle from the hem and the sleeves. Her jeans are in better shape, but the denim is faded and sags around the knees.

'To take Barley for a walk,' Rebecca chirps from beside me. 'We can show you the village too.'

The girl nods. 'That would be nice.' She looks like she might say something more and then stops.

'Is there anything you need?' I ask. 'You're very welcome to stay here if you prefer.'

The girl frowns a little as if trying to decide how to answer. 'Eh... no, I'd like to come, but I wondered... can I use your washing machine please, Sarah?'

Her cheeks colour as her brown eyes stare into mine, and for the first time since she walked into our home yesterday, I feel something loosen inside of me. Yesterday's anger bubbles beneath the surface, but there's something else there now. Yesterday, I was certain she was tricking us, but maybe there's another reason. According to Ryan, Abi learned of her true identity after her father died. She has no other family. Could the death of her last remaining parent have triggered a mental breakdown? Could she have convinced herself she's Abigail?

I shake the thought away. It's easier to be angry.

'Is Abelia a common name in South America?' I find myself asking.

She smiles and shakes her head. 'I was named after someone in my moth— in Caroline's family. It's an American name. It never really took off. Most people call me Abi.'

'You speak Spanish, I'm guessing?'

'Si.' The girl grins and reels off a sentence with rolling Rs and a barrage of Os.

Rebecca sighs from beside me. 'Now I wish I'd kept Spanish for my GCSEs instead of French. I'd defo have got an A star with your tuition.' She laughs. 'Oh, Mum, that reminds me, I forgot to ask you last night – can we go shopping today? Abi needs some more clothes, don't you, Abi? She only brought one tiny backpack with her.'

'It's fine.' Abi shakes her head, dropping the T so it comes out *iss fine*. 'A washing machine is all I need.'

I look again at the girl – Abi – and suddenly she seems so much younger than she did last night. Not much older than Rebecca really.

'Mum?' Rebecca says again.

'Sure.' I nod, my eyes still fixed on Abi. She stares back and I think I see her own silent battle with her thoughts rage behind her eyes. 'I can take you two into Ipswich this afternoon.' My voice sounds far away, as if I'm listening to myself in the next room.

'Yessss.' Rebecca grins and jumps to her feet. 'Come on, Abs, I'll show you where the washing basket is. You can dump your dirty clothes in there, and I've got some leggings and a hoody you can borrow today.'

'Thanks, but I do my own washing.'

'Why? Dad does it. Come on.' Rebecca takes Abi's arm and pulls her away. A moment later, a burst of Rebecca's giggles carries from the stairs. The sound that usually lifts my spirits today causes dread to crawl over my skin. So much for preparing Rebecca.

There's a clatter from behind me. Paws on glass. I turn to see Barley at the door, two brown paw-shaped smudges on the glass and a smear from his nose.

'Hang on, Barley,' I say more to myself than to the dog. I pick off a soggy cornflake from the edge of Rebecca's discarded bowl and nibble it between my teeth. 'Looks like it'll be a while.'

I step into the kitchen to make coffee, listening to Rebecca and Abi's chatter carry from upstairs. The vice-like tension returns to my chest. Every second Abi is here is increasing the inevitable hurt that will come down on Rebecca – and Daniel.

My thoughts turn to Daniel. He might be an adult now, but

he's still my boy. My child. He might act cool, but this will be affecting him too. I must find time to talk to him as well.

I flick on the coffee machine and wonder about this girl's motives again. Is she mentally ill? Confused? Or is this something else? Does she want something from us?

———

*I keep the gun close to hand now. Taking it out of its hiding place anytime I get the chance, feeling the weight of the cold metal in my hands.*

*It's been a while since I fired it, but I still remember how.*

*Soon, very soon, I'll take from them what they took from me all those years ago.*

*Love. Family.*

*They mean nothing now.*

# TWENTY

## SARAH

'All set, Mum?' Rebecca calls from the kitchen.

My gaze darts to her before dropping to the mug in my hands. The black liquid is no longer puffing hot steam, and the curved china wrapped inside my cupped hands feels cool against my skin. I haven't taken a single sip.

'Are you ready to go?' Rebecca asks again.

I nod, gulping back two tepid, bitter mouthfuls.

Only as I walk through the archway into the kitchen do I see Abi, standing beside Rebecca. Her hair is tied back into a high ponytail and she's wearing a pair of black leggings and one of Rebecca's Abercrombie & Fitch hoodies. The arms of the pink jumper are stretched tight from where she's pulled them over her hands. She looks young and pretty. She looks normal, I realise. A normal teenage girl.

'Have you eaten?' I ask her out of habit. In recent years, Rebecca's friends have become more body conscious, cutting down their snacks and skipping meals, and I like to make sure they eat something when they're here.

Abi smiles. 'I'll be fine.' And then a second later: 'Thank you.'

We pile into the small mudroom beyond the kitchen. There really isn't space for three people and my arm brushes against her; the coffee rises up and stings my throat, and I'm glad I've not eaten.

The same questions pummel my thoughts again.

Why are you here? What do you want?

My ankle knocks the chrome shoe rack that sits against the wall. The jolt displaces the delicately balanced piles of shoes and boots, causing an old ballet slipper of Rebecca's to fall on top of a pair of newish walking boots I assume are Michael's.

The row of coat hooks on the opposite wall is in no better shape. I reach up and unhook my walking jacket from one of the overloaded pegs, knocking Michael's fleece and a navy-blue jacket of Daniel's to the floor.

'Here.' I ignore the fleece and the assortment of rain macs that have fallen, and hold out a coat to Abi.

She hesitates, glancing first at the item in my outstretched hand, then to my face. Up close, I can see the flecks of amber in her eyes, and it makes my heart race – pound in fact. I can hear the beating of it in my ears and feel the rush of blood to my head, as if my body knows something I don't.

I pull in a ragged breath and tear my eyes away. 'It's a spare,' I say, stepping back and grabbing Barley's lead. 'I got it for Daniel in the sales, but it wasn't black enough for him.'

'Thank you,' Abi says, sliding the jacket on and zipping it up to her neck. The hem reaches to her knees and her hands have been swallowed in the sleeves, but it will protect her from the wind on the open fields. I find her some wellies too, before hurrying to escape the close proximity and the desire to grab her face and stare into her eyes again.

Out in the garden, Barley dashes around my legs and unleashes a whimper more like a yipping fox than a spaniel. The fur on his legs and stomach is already soaked from the dewy grass.

He jumps up, leaving two paw-shaped mud prints on my jeans.

'Down, Barley,' I call, running a hand over his back.

Barley drops to the ground and skitters around Rebecca and Abi's legs, causing Abi to lurch back towards the door. Her arms are in the air and her eyes are wide with uncertainty. Barley whimpers again and nudges the girl's legs with his nose before wagging his tail with renewed ferocity.

Rebecca laughs, pulling Barley towards her and running her hands over his body. 'He won't hurt you. He's a cuddly teddy bear,' she coos as if speaking to a child. 'Aren't you, Barley Boo?'

I should step in and put Barley on the lead, but I don't. I'm still recovering from whatever happened in the mud room when I stared into Abi's eyes. Those amber flecks that jolt like an electric current. So familiar... And yet I can't... I won't...

'We almost called him Teddy, didn't we, Mum?' Rebecca says as Barley flops to the grass and rolls onto his back, desperate for Abi to rub his tummy. 'He looked just like a little teddy bear when we got him.'

I smile, allowing myself to be taken back to the afternoon I brought Barley home, six months after the news of Michael's affairs broke. Barley was a distraction from our marriage and another way to pretend we were a normal family.

The memory feels safe and wraps me in warmth. Barley – a small, quivering ball of fur, timid and curious, all in the same panting breath. The four of us – Rebecca, Daniel, Michael and I – sitting on cushions on the hard wooden floor of the living room as Barley, no bigger than a guinea pig, hopped and jumped between us, rolling onto his back the moment he was in touching distance to receive a belly rub whilst simultaneously trying to nip our hands with his sharp puppy teeth.

We all love Barley. He connects us, bridging the cracks in our family that seem to grow wider every year.

'He's cute,' Abi says. Her voice throws ice water on my

memory. 'I... I just haven't been around dogs. Where I lived there were two types of dogs – guard dogs and strays – both likely to bite you for one reason or another.' She shrugs and drops her hands into the deep pockets of the jacket.

Questions leapfrog in my head, pushing against my skull, desperate to be set free. Why were there guard dogs? Did they belong to your father? Do you remember Mrs Dillinger who used to live in the cottage next door? And Mrs Dillinger's shaggy golden retriever – Willow – who you spent hours playing with the year Daniel started school? I swallow hard and shake my head, a slight movement but enough to force the questions away. Of course Abi doesn't remember Mrs Dillinger – how could she?

I whistle two short blows, sending Barley scurrying to the gate.

'Hey,' a voice calls from behind me. 'Wait up.'

I spin around and see Daniel lolloping towards us – as though he's walking on the springy gymnastics floor that Rebecca learned to do somersaults on when she was nine.

In the seconds it takes Daniel to reach me, memories zip through my thoughts, like watching a hundred home movies on fast forward. I see Daniel at four and Abigail, two, thick as thieves, collecting up every cushion in the house, piling them up in the living room, and screeching at me to jump out of the crocodile-infested water that was our carpet when I tried to bring them a drink and a biscuit.

'Please.' Daniel's favourite word, always mimicked a second later by Abigail's garbled 'Pleash'.

'Please, please, please can I have a bunk bed? Please can Abigail stay in my room?'

'Pleash, pleash.'

I see the Daniel who'd launched himself into my arms at any and every opportunity; played make-believe for hours with Abigail and an imaginary boy called Seth. I feel the warmth of

Daniel's five-year-old body tucked up next to mine as I read him Enid Blyton.

I see the tantrums too. The sullen 'It's not fair', pronounced with a 'th' so it sounded like 'It's not there'. I see the time in Sainsbury's when I'd been pregnant with Rebecca, and Daniel had wanted a Spiderman comic and had thrown the loose rolls in the bakery section; screaming at the top of his voice when I'd tried to stop him. The snippet that followed in one of the tabloids floats in my mind: **Out-of-control children for** *This Morning* **host.**

The anger came with the start of school. At first, we put it down to the new routine and how unfair he found it that Abigail was spending time at home with me in the afternoons. But then it got worse. Screaming fits. Angry fists. Abigail asked for her own room.

The dyslexia diagnosis came a few months after Rebecca was born. His teacher suggested we take him for tests after he struggled with the first reading books.

And then everything got better. Daniel got the help he needed. More support at school and at home, and he was no longer frustrated or angry. We had the old Daniel back. He and Abigail became friends again. Except, a few months later, she was taken, and Daniel spiralled once more. Silence that time, not anger.

My throat tightens a little as I watch the twenty-year-old version of that boy. Sometimes it feels like I didn't just lose one child on that warm day in May; I lost two. Everything that had made Daniel who he was disappeared – the playfulness, the make-believe stories, the dinosaur obsession. All of it gone, vanishing without a trace. Just like Abigail.

It was a year of visits with Dr Hall before he uttered a single word to anyone. Even when he started to speak again, he came back to us slowly – quieter than the boy he was once but not unhappy.

'Wait up,' Daniel calls again as he reaches me, his voice carrying past me to Rebecca and Abi.

'Daniel,' I say. 'I didn't think you'd be awake yet.'

He turns to look at me. 'I don't suppose any of us got much sleep,' he replies. 'You look awful, by the way.'

'Thanks,' I sigh. My children are nothing if not honest.

'A walk is a good idea,' he continues. 'A chance to show Abigail the village and get some fresh air.' He falters and our eyes meet. Both of us heard the slip. 'Abi,' he corrects. 'I didn't mean... I know it might not...'

'It's OK. I get it.'

'Where's Dad?' Daniel scoops his hair behind his ears and glances back at the house.

'I don't think he'll be surfacing anytime soon.'

'Why does he always have to drink so much? You know he's got a drink problem, don't you?'

'I...' Yes, is the answer, but I can't bring myself to say it. 'Let's not discuss this now, Daniel.' I glance ahead to Rebecca and Abi, out of earshot and already strolling through the back gate. 'How much your father drinks is hardly top of my list of priorities right now.'

'Or any other time,' he mutters before jogging to catch up with Rebecca and Abi and falling into step beside them.

Daniel has a point. Michael's drinking has grown steadily heavier in the five years since the scandal over the affair and his charity. When he allowed Abigail's charity to be absorbed by one of the bigger missing-persons organisations, it was as though he lost his purpose in life. He talks of the book he's writing about Abigail, but I've never seen him at a computer, and I wonder sometimes if he's written a single word.

But Michael never drinks if he needs to drive Rebecca somewhere and he never loses control. Except last night. All that wine. All that emotion. The tears I'm sure made Abi uncomfortable, then suggesting we don't bother with a DNA test. Ridiculous.

I reach the gate so that the picture before me is framed in wood. Three teenagers strolling beside the river, Barley at their side. My breath catches and I realise the world is spinning around me, the emotions rocketing through me – déjà vu but in reverse. The image in front of me isn't one I've seen before, but one in my future, a future where Abigail is home.

I bite down on the side of my mouth and count the steps. One, two, five, ten, until all I see is the present. I can be kind, I can treat this girl like she's one of Rebecca's friends, but I will not pretend.

I pull out my phone and text Ryan, asking him if he has a time for when the DNA tests will arrive. We must get through the next three days and get this girl out of my house before the rest of the world finds out.

# TWENTY-ONE

## ABI

Saturday, 9.03 a.m.

Abi's face is numb. Her ears ache with the biting wind buffeting against them. Her toes are like ice in the wellies Sarah gave her. They're a size too big, and each step causes her heel to rub uncomfortably against the boot. She thought London was cold, but the open green countryside rolling either side of a winding river is something else. Her face is numb and the only part of her that's warm is the space inside her chest that comes from the safety of being nestled between Rebecca and Daniel, and the easy conversation that's batted back and forth between them.

She feels Sarah's eyes on her from two paces behind them. A narrow, assessing gaze. All the questions she wants to ask build in the space between them.

'Dedham is basically the most boring place on earth,' Daniel says from beside her, waving an arm in the direction of a row of trees with branches that curve and droop into the black water of the river.

Rebecca laughs. 'It's not that bad,' she says, squeezing Abi's arm. 'Besides, it's hardly the middle of nowhere. There are two big towns, like, fifteen minutes away.'

Daniel shakes his head at Rebecca. 'The people around here only take their heads out of their own arses long enough to make sure they know everyone's business – especially our business.'

Rebecca rolls her eyes. 'They care about the village and the people in it, that's all.'

Abi knows nothing of nosy neighbours. In her world it's always been a curt nod and eyes averted to the ground quick, so quick. Seeing too much on the streets has consequences, something she doubts Rebecca's innocent mind can comprehend.

So Abi allows Rebecca and Daniel's chatter to wash over her as she takes in the landscape. It's just as Jhon had described. 'Green for as far as the eye could see.' She wishes she could enjoy it, but Abi is acutely aware that every time her feet sink into the squelchy mud, she's one step closer to the next phase of his plan. That thought alone is enough to cause a jittery heart-racing panic to pump through her.

The conversation moves on to the shopping trip Rebecca has planned for the afternoon and the dozen shops she wants to visit. 'You need everything,' she says with the gleeful look of someone who's never worried about money.

Abi grits her teeth at the sudden flash of annoyance. It's not Rebecca's fault. Her whole life has been cushioned in a world of money and comfort. But it's more than Rebecca's innocence grating on Abi. It's that this is the life Abi should have had but didn't. And yet how can she pierce Rebecca's innocence – how can she make this lovely, kind girl see that Abi can't go shopping with her? That she doesn't have, nor has she ever had, disposable money to spend on clothes. Just the idea of shopping for clothes makes her feel slightly sick.

Rebecca moves on to school and her friends, and Daniel seems content now to let her talk. Abi likes listening to Rebecca.

She talks fast, one word merging into the next, like Jhon, like the few people she knew in Buenaventura. It's as though Rebecca is sharing every thought and every memory in her head as a way to bridge the distance between them, the time they've spent apart, and the vast difference in their upbringings. It's an impossible gap, but Abi loves Rebecca for trying.

Eventually the mud under Abi's feet hardens and they walk along a path with a canopy of spindly branches over their heads. The red-brick buildings of the village come into view, causing Abi's pulse to ramp up another notch. She's lightheaded, nervous.

It's nearly time.

Dedham is exactly how Abi imagined a quaint English village to be. Old houses painted in pastel pinks and yellows, lining both sides of the high street. At one end, a red-brick church-like building advertises rugs and homewares. At the other end of the street sits the real church – a vast stone structure, watching over the handful of gift shops and cafés.

A steady stream of cars moves slowly around them, parking in haphazard fashion outside a small supermarket with dark-green awnings and buckets of flowers outside.

Rebecca steers Abi down a road with an old-style pub on one side and a café on the other. Abi spots a couple sitting at one of the outside café tables, wrapped up in hats and coats, hands cupped around steaming mugs. The woman glances at Abi and then behind her at Sarah, before looking quickly away and whispering something to her partner. He turns to stare before pulling out his phone and holding it up as though he's recording them.

The air disappears from Abi's lungs as she drops her gaze to the pavement and pretends not to see.

'You've been hiding in the shadows too long,' he'd told her. 'It's time for the Wicks to see their daughter again. It's time for the world to meet you.'

'We've basically done a large loop,' Rebecca says from beside her, oblivious to the couple with their phones out and the sense of anticipation and fear now zipping through Abi's body. 'The front of the house is just up here.'

The pavement narrows into a single-lane path. Rebecca goes first, then Abi, then Daniel, then Sarah and the dog. There are cars everywhere. Some are parked, tyres bumped up on the verge, others are moving slowly, steering their way through the bedlam, searching for a space or a way through, Abi isn't sure.

'Hang on,' Sarah calls out to them as they squeeze along the space between a parked car and a hedge. 'Something isn't right.'

'It's just the usual Saturday morning tourists,' Rebecca calls back.

They keep moving, rounding a bend in the road. Abi's feet are concrete blocks inside the boots, each step harder than the last. It's happening, she thinks. Just like he said.

'Oh, my phone's ringing.' Rebecca reaches into the pocket of her coat and pulls out an iPhone in a sky-blue case. 'Wow, 180 WhatsApp messages, and Dad's calling,' she says, pressing the phone to her ear. 'He's probably wondering where we all are.'

The red roof and yellow walls of the house come into view. It looks even grander in the daylight, but Abi barely notices. She repeats the words in her head over and over.

I'm Abigail Wick.

I'm Abigail.

'I can't hear you, Dad,' Rebecca says, a step ahead of Abi, covering her free ear with her hand. 'There's something going on ahead of us.'

Another step around the corner and Abi sees the black gate and thick green bushes that surround the Wick property. But it's the large group of men and women outside the gates that draws Abi's gaze.

There are so many. A dozen or more. Cameras are being

held in the air, pointing over the gate towards the house. To one side is a row of larger cameras resting on tripods with people standing in front of them, better dressed than the others and holding microphones.

'No,' Sarah cries, pushing past Abi and reaching her arm around Rebecca.

The gesture is so protective, a mother caring for her child, that it stings Abi's heart for reasons she can't dare think about.

'Turn around now – we'll have to go back.'

There's a moment where they're all on top of each other – Sarah moving Rebecca back, Abi trying to step out of the way, Daniel right behind her. And between them all is Barley, pulling against the lead in Sarah's hand as he skitters around their feet.

He barks. A flurry of loud woofs that carry to the group and suddenly everyone is turning. Staring.

'We have to go back,' Sarah says again, lifting her hand to cover her face. But Daniel is stepping forward, taking Barley's lead in one hand while holding Abi's arm with the other.

'Isn't it too late for that?' he asks as he watches the group of reporters. 'They're already filming, Mum. It'll look weird if we turn back.

Sarah pauses, eyes darting back and forth as the yells of the photographers and journalists now reach them. 'No one say a word,' she says, voice low. 'They've got no way of knowing who she is.'

*She.* She?

They start to move again, faster now. Daniel and Barley, then Abi, then Sarah and Rebecca.

'Keep your heads down,' Sarah hisses as they draw nearer.

'Sarah,' a woman shouts from the group, 'is Abigail home?'

More questions follow, flying at them like bullets.

'Who's the girl?' a man calls over the heckling as he steps forward and points his camera at Abi.

It's now or never. She has to do it, but the words don't leave her mouth. She didn't think it would be like this. Loud and abrasive. Scary.

'Why are you keeping Abigail's homecoming a secret?'

'When will you be making a statement?'

'Abigail, where have you been?'

'Who's been holding you prisoner, Abigail?'

'How long have you been home?'

It all stops at once. They're upon the group now, outside the gate. Every eye fixes on her and she lifts her head. There's movement beside her, the sound of wood banging, and suddenly it's not the group staring at her that she feels now, it's him – his eyes, his gaze, willing her into action.

'I...' she starts, voice trembling but clear. 'I'm...'

But out of nowhere she's moving, being pulled back, feet stumbling in the stupid boots. The rest of the words are lost.

Abigail Wick.

I'm Abigail Wick.

It's too late. She's pulled and then pushed as Rebecca and Sarah follow through a small black gate to the side of where the police car drove through yesterday. Sarah slams it shut, blocking out the faces but not the noise – a roar of questions and annoyance.

Abi spins around. Daniel and Ryan are standing side by side. She has no idea who pulled her back or why Ryan is on the driveway at all. She steps away from them, a chill of fear trickling through her. She's failed. All she had to do was tell the reporters her name and now it's too late.

What the hell is she supposed to do now?

# TWENTY-TWO

## ABI

Then

Footsteps pounded on cement somewhere behind her. They were getting faster, louder, nearer – she was sure of it. The night was closing in too quickly. To the shop and back, that's all she meant to do. Some bread and a few extras, if the change she'd taken from her mom's purse allowed it. But the air felt so fresh on her skin. It was the first time she'd been outside in weeks. She hadn't stopped at the first shop, or the second. She'd kept walking. And now the sky was all kinds of purple and black and she'd stayed out too long.

The footsteps behind her continued.

Abelia broke into a jog, the bag in her hand knocking against her leg with every step.

Jhon's voice replayed in her head. 'The world is a dangerous place for a little girl. Never go outside. No matter what.'

'But I had to, Papa,' she imagined her reply. 'There was no food and Mumma wouldn't move. I had to go out. I had to eat.' Abelia couldn't stand the hunger anymore. And she wasn't sure she believed him anymore either.

There was an episode of *Columbo* her mom had made her watch last week. A man had been living a double life. He'd had two families. She'd gone to bed that night remembering Jhon's words. 'Other people rely on me too.'

She'd always thought it was his work keeping him away, but he used to come more often. Weekly. Now it was every two weeks. And sometimes three weeks between visits. He doesn't stay the night anymore either. Abelia wanted to believe it was work that kept him from them, but she didn't.

She reached the front door and stood on her tiptoes to reach the lock. The footsteps seemed to echo from all around her. She was no longer sure which direction to look in, or which way to run.

A sob tore from her throat. She couldn't reach the lock on the front door. It was too high. She was too short. No, no, no, no, no. The key scratched at the bottom of the lock, but she couldn't push it in at the right angle. She was stuck outside.

Abelia knocked her fist on the door. 'Momma,' she whispered as loudly as she dared. 'Let me in, Momma.'

Abelia held her breath and listened to the noise of the TV from inside the apartment, but there was no sound of movement.

She yelped as more footsteps pounded around her. Her gaze darted into the dusky night, but she saw only shadows. She bit down on the inside of her cheek and stretched her arm up as far as she could. Her muscles screamed in pain, but she didn't stop.

'Hey, you,' a woman's voice called, echoing in the cement corridor.

The key moved in Abelia's hand, slipping into the lock. She'd done it.

'You dropped your cheese,' the voice said, closer this time.

Abelia turned then, her eyes lifting to a woman in a pale-grey raincoat. She was old. Older than Abelia's mom, even older than Jhon. Her hair was white, the colour of snow, and her mouth was surrounded by a hundred tiny wrinkles. The woman narrowed her small eyes, but her voice, when she spoke, was kind.

'I didn't think I'd catch you,' she puffed. 'You dropped this,' she added, handing over a small wedge of cheese wrapped in wax paper.

'Thank you,' Abelia mumbled.

'Where's your mother?'

'Inside.'

'How old are you, little girl?'

'Seven. How old are you?'

The woman laughed; a gravelly choke that ended with a coughing fit. 'Old enough to be out on my own.'

'Momma's sleeping. She's ill. I had to get food,' Abelia said as if it was Jhon she was speaking to.

The woman eyed the bag in Abelia's hands and nodded. 'Sleeps a lot, does she?'

Abelia shrugged. The skin under her clothes felt itchy and hot. She desperately wanted to go inside, away from the woman and her prying, but her feet wouldn't move. Her mom hadn't spoken to her for days.

'What's your name?' the woman asked.

'Abelia.'

'Ain't that a type of flower? That's a funny name for a little girl with a funny accent. Where are you from?'

'Here.'

'You look familiar. Do I know you?'

Abelia shook her head.

'I'll call you Abi, and you can call me Flo. Who takes you to school?'

Abelia's eyes dropped to the bare concrete floor. She focused on the woman's shoes – black and square, with thick laces. Abelia's toes pushed against the end of her trainers. Next time she would wear some of her mom's.

'Do you do things at home? Maths and English?'

Abelia gave a furtive nod and shuffled towards the door. She had the sudden feeling of being in trouble for something, although she wasn't quite sure what she'd done.

'Four-two-three. Can you remember that number? Say it back to me.'

'Four-two-three.'

'My neighbour's daughter is a bit older than you. I bet she has some clothes you can have. Four-two-three. Remember? I'm on the floor above. Come tomorrow afternoon. But don't go expecting me to feed you or anything like that, OK? I've got my own problems.'

Abelia nodded and reached for the key. Her fingers hurt with the effort of reaching and twisting but it gave, and the door swung inwards, unleashing a flurry of gunfire and shouts from the TV.

Her mom's eyes were closed. Greasy clumps of blonde hair lay across the sofa. An arm flopped to the floor. Abelia grabbed the remote; it was slick from her mom's grip. Abelia had meant to turn the TV off, but at the last minute she flicked to the local news.

She sat cross-legged on the floor with a plate of bread and cheese, and listened to the voice of the news anchor.

'A funny name for a little girl with a funny accent,' the woman had said, making Abelia's cheeks feel hot.

She concentrated on the voices of the TV and repeated their sentences until her voice began to sound like theirs.

# TWENTY-THREE

## ABI

Mud smears and footprints cover the entrance-hall floor. It looks to Abi like the group of reporters outside have been traipsing around the house, not just Rebecca, Sarah and the dog rushing in before her.

Brown spatters mark the walls around the doorway to the kitchen too. Abi slips off the boots and stands for a moment. Unsure. Forgotten. Is she supposed to follow Sarah, Rebecca and Daniel into the kitchen or stay out of the way? Should she turn around, fling open the front door that Ryan has just closed and scream the words at the top of her lungs like she was supposed to. 'YES. IT'S ME. I'M ABIGAIL WICK.'

She asked him once why it mattered that the world knew and he told her, 'We can't let them hide you away. It has to be out there. We have to be the ones in control.'

Abi nodded, pretending she understood. He always spoke like that. So certain and matter-of-fact, like she was an idiot if she didn't understand. Now she wishes she'd asked more questions.

'Are you OK?' Ryan asks from beside her, voice low in her ear.

She shrugs. 'This is my fault.'

'It'll be OK,' he says. 'Come on. Let's get you a hot drink.'

Ryan walks into the kitchen with the confidence of someone who belongs. He's already turning on the coffee machine as Abi reaches the doorway and takes in the scene. Rebecca is sitting on a stool at the island in the middle of the kitchen, lost in her phone. Daniel is leaning on the counter, pushing his hand through his hair. Sarah is pacing back and forth by the sink and throwing questions and statements out with the same force as the journalists a few minutes ago: 'Who did this?' and then, 'Someone must have told them.

'This is completely out of control. I knew this would happen. I knew this was a mistake.'

'Well done, you,' Michael says, sarcasm dripping from every word. 'Who cares how we're all feeling right now? The important thing is that Sarah was right.'

'That's not what I meant, and you know it,' Sarah throws back.

'Isn't it?'

Sarah draws back, hurt sparking in her eyes. There's a beat where no one speaks. Tension crackles in the air.

It's Michael who breaks first.

'I'm sorry. That was uncalled for.' He sighs. 'We need to come up with a plan and quickly.' He looks first to Sarah before turning to see Abi in the doorway. He looks at her, a different man from the one she met last night. His face is an off-grey and the skin beneath his eyes is puffy, sagging onto his cheeks.

'Come in, Abi,' he says, nodding to the stool beside Rebecca.

Abi doesn't know if it's an offer or a command, but she does as she's told.

'It was scary out there,' Abi says, leaning close to Rebecca so their arms are touching.

'Yeah.'

Guilt swarms, angry bees inside Abi. She did this.

'Rebecca?' Sarah says from across the room. 'Are you all right?'

'Yeah,' she says again before holding up her phone. 'Ellie's calling me.' She stands, slipping out of her boots, already answering the call as she hurries out of the room.

'So crazy,' Abi hears Rebecca say, wishing she could leave too.

'How do you think they found out?' Sarah asks, her gaze flicking from Michael to Abi, but it's Ryan who answers.

'We're not sure,' he says, placing three blue-and-white striped mugs of coffee on the counter before sliding one to Abi. It's black and smells strong, exactly how she likes it. A jug of milk comes next, but Abi cups her hands around the mug and takes a sip.

Daniel takes Rebecca's vacated seat, beside Abi, and pulls up a news site on his phone. Sarah and Michael move to watch over his shoulder as a male reporter with a microphone stands in front of a camera; the black gates of the house visible behind him.

'Can you tell us what the mood is like there, James?' a female voice asks.

'It's exciting, Sian, that's for sure. Just a few minutes ago we saw the Wick family enter the house through this gate' – he strides a few paces to the right, the camera lens following – 'and there was a teenage girl with them.'

'We're playing that footage back for the viewers now, James.'

He nods, shrinking to a thumbnail in the corner of the screen as the footage of their hurried walk to the gate replays.

Abi holds her breath, transfixed by the image of herself. She is wide-eyed with shock and innocence. He'll be happy about that at least.

'As yet,' the reporter continues, returning to full screen, 'we've had no confirmation from the Wick family that their daughter – Abigail Wick – who was abducted from a holiday cottage on the Suffolk Coast nearly fourteen years ago – has returned. But the girl we just saw does bear a striking resemblance to Daniel and Rebecca Wick, Abigail's brother and sister, who we can also see in the replay.

Abi stops breathing for a moment. They think she looks like Daniel and Rebecca. They believe her. She sees it then; why telling the press mattered. They all see the connection, and now maybe her family will too.

'The news of Abigail's possible return was broken online by both *The Sun* and the *Daily Mail* in the early hours of this morning, and Suffolk Police have confirmed that the Abigail Wick investigation has received new information. This of course is the first piece of new evidence since the CCTV footage captured Abigail's abductor in 2009.'

'We're playing that footage now too.'

Abi's breath catches in her throat at the grainy black-and-white video on the screen. It's a fight not to grab Daniel's phone, snatch it up and zoom in. The enormity of what happened then, and is now happening fourteen years later, hits Abi with a tidal wave of horror and clarity.

She's home. She's where she's supposed to be, but there's so much these people – her family – don't know, so much that's wrong, and seeing the video playing on the screen before her, she isn't sure it will ever be right. For the first time, Abi sees just how broken these people are. Her life has been desperate and empty and tragic, but so has theirs.

'Is there any word from the family regarding a statement?' the female in the studio asks, pulling Abi back to the room.

'Not as yet, Sian.' The reporter touches his ear as he speaks. 'What will be interesting is whether we see Michael Wick, Abigail's father, out here at some point this morning. As I'm sure you'll remember, he tirelessly led the campaign to find Abigail up until five years ago but disappeared from the spotlight after the charity he set up, Abigail's Angels, became the centre of a financial scandal—'

'Turn it off.' Michael's tone is sharp, and immediately Daniel closes down the website and tucks his phone into his pocket.

Abi drains the last of her coffee. It's the first half-decent coffee she's had since landing in England, and the caffeine pumping through her blood gives her the confidence to ask, 'What happens now?'

'Don't worry about it,' Daniel says with a shrug. 'They'll sort something out. Come on. Let me show you the living room since no one else has bothered.'

She looks at Daniel then, this man-boy, her brother, and an idea starts to form in her head. Abi wonders if there's another way she can still tell the world she's Abigail Wick. A better way.

---

*Poor Sarah. Did you really think no one would find out? Did you think I'd let you hide this from the world?*

*You think you're in control. You think you're so clever.*

*All those secrets you're hiding beneath that steely glare.*

*You think no one knows the truth.*

*But I know.*

*I know what you did!*

*It's almost funny that you still think there's a way out.*

*There isn't. Not one that you'll like at least.*

*There's only one way this will end. With death and truth. And I really don't care what order they come in.*

# TWENTY-FOUR

## SARAH

One, two, three, I count as I pace up and down the kitchen. Four, five, six. All the way to eight. The number rolls around my head like one of those white lottery balls, except no one is winning today.

Eight.

Eight possible ways the press on my doorstep found out about the girl. Abi, I correct myself, hating again how close her name is to Abigail.

I've been so stupid. Of course the news leaked. Eight ways. Eight!

What was I thinking? The truth is, I wasn't. I haven't been thinking clearly since the shock of DS Howard's words, the appearance of Abi and the clash of hope and reality in my mind. Judgement couldn't compete with that.

Rebecca, Daniel, Michael, Ryan, Essex and Suffolk Police, the police in London, and me.

Eight.

'Here, drink this,' Ryan says, pressing a mug of coffee into my hands and stopping my pacing as Michael storms off to take a shower and 'clear his head'. My stomach lurches at the prospect of eating or drinking anything right now.

'It'll help,' he adds as though reading my mind.

'Thank you. And thank you for coming back today. I wasn't sure if you would.'

He shrugs. 'I didn't know whether to either. There's not exactly any written guidance for this situation, but then I thought there was no harm in dropping by.'

'I'm glad you did. I just wish I knew how it got out,' I sigh, the frustration still clenching every muscle in my body.

Eight ways.

Was it Rebecca or Daniel? Should I have taken their phones away last night? Did one of them confide in a friend who told a friend who told someone else? I know it's plausible, more than plausible, but the volume of men and women outside the gates isn't the result of one teenager phoning a tip into a tabloid hotline.

My boots tap the floor, my legs urging me to keep pacing, but Ryan is still in my path. I glance up at his face, and the words leave my mouth before I can pull them back. 'Was it you?'

'Sarah.' There is no anger in his face, just concern glowing in his eyes.

'I know, I'm sorry,' I say. 'I'm going out of my mind here. This is the last thing we need to be dealing with today.' I shake my head, hating the lump that's taken hold of my throat. 'If you mentioned something to your wife or girlfriend, I won't mind. I understand. I just have to know—'

'I'm divorced,' Ryan cuts in. 'And I don't have a girlfriend. I do have a son – Jack. He's nine, but he's with his mum this weekend. I left here at gone ten last night. I drove to my house. I slept. I woke up. I drove back again.'

'Oh. Have you eaten?' is all I can think to ask.

Somewhere in my mind I register his comment and realise I know nothing about the man in my kitchen. In my head, he's still the lanky family liaison officer I met in the cottage during the worst days of my existence. Somehow, it didn't occur to me that his life would continue after he left to help another family. That he'd marry and have a child of his own.

'Yes, now talk to me, Sarah. What are you thinking?'

I glance around the now empty kitchen. 'I'm thinking someone did this on purpose to rattle me.'

There, I said it.

Ryan frowns and I know what he's thinking – paranoid. I'm being paranoid.

'I'm aware how crazy that sounds,' I add, 'but I feel so... so...'

'Out of control,' he finishes. 'That's OK, Sarah. We can't control everything that happens in our lives.'

I bite down on the sides my mouth. *I can.* Tears are building in my eyes, and I know if I look up at him again or try to talk, I won't be able to stop them.

'Keep going,' he urges. 'What else are you thinking?'

Eight. I focus on the number and wait for the calm it brings.

Rebecca, Daniel, Michael, Ryan, Essex and Suffolk Police, the Met, and me.

I can strike Michael off the list of culprits. Once upon a time I might have believed he'd be capable of such a stunt, but after what happened to his charity, his hatred of the media is raw and absolute. He's as upset as I am.

'Who would do this? How did the press find out so quickly?' My voice trails off.

Nine. Not eight but nine, I realise. Abi makes nine. Was she behind it? Exasperation fills my body. I can't shake the feeling that I'm being moved places against my will.

She left her home and everything she knows. She's seventeen. She has no one. I try to hold these thoughts in my head, to be reasonable, but I still wonder if she called the papers. I think of Daniel's slip when he called her Abigail, and Michael's drunken suggestion that we don't bother with the DNA test. Rebecca, too, is already treating Abi as a sister. And now it's not just my family who are starting to believe. The entire world will too. I am alone in this.

A sob catches my voice and I'm powerless to stop the torrent that follows. The tears fall fast and hot down my cheeks as exhaustion and emotion engulf me.

Ryan moves closer, his arms out as if he's planning to catch me again, but he stops and steps back. The scene is eerily familiar to me too: tears in the kitchen, and Ryan, a shoulder to cry on. His body pulling me close, his lips touching mine. Kissing him with the desperate need to forget the nightmare I was living in. One moment of insanity.

I wipe my eyes and lean against the counter, widening the distance between us and pulling myself upright.

'I hate to admit it, but the leak probably came from inside one of the police forces. I'm sure it wasn't vindictive or even information sold to a newspaper for money. Just drinks in the pub and the buzz of knowing something no one else knows.'

I nod.

'What do you want to do?' he asks.

'I'm not sure,' I say, but the question grounds me. Dwelling on the who or even the why isn't going to achieve anything. I have to control it. *Look forward not back.*

'Can you get a police car here?' I ask. 'Get them to move the reporters away from the gates? They're blocking the road for one thing, and if they haven't got such a prime view of the house, then they might not linger for so long.' I wipe my fingers across my damp cheeks, feeling more like myself.

Movement in the doorway catches my eye. I expect Michael, but it's Daniel.

'Er, Mum, you do know there's mud everywhere.'

He's right, I realise, seeing for the first time the scuffs of brown and the dark boot prints across the tiles. The worst is by the sink where I've been pacing. I scan the floor for Barley and find him lying under the table in the extension, tail flicking droplets of liquid mud across the floor.

I grit my teeth at the mess before me. It's insignificant and yet I feel immediately out of control again. 'I'll sort it out,' I mumble, crouching down to unlace my walking boots.

'You've got enough going on. I'll do it,' Daniel says, stepping over the worst of the dirt to reach the cleaning products under the sink. He grabs a spray bottle and cloth before whistling for Barley and leading him into the garden.

'Where's Becca?' I ask.

'In her bedroom,' he says without turning around. 'Abi's up there too, in case you were wondering. Becca's showing her some photo albums.'

In case you were wondering.

There's a barb to his comment, I think. Another sign that he's seeing this girl as his sister. That it's them and me. I don't blame him. He and Abigail were so close. And yet it's another reminder of the battle ahead of me and the destruction this girl will cause.

'Daniel, I...'

Michael appears in the doorway before I can formulate a reply. He's wearing jeans and the red polo shirt I bought him for Christmas. His hair is wet from the shower and he's lost part of the greenish tinge to his face.

'I think Ryan should do it.' Michael nods as he speaks, as if he's agreeing with himself. 'Let's not give them any more ammunition. You don't mind, do you, Ryan?'

'Since when have the press needed ammunition?' I ask. 'And what do you expect Ryan to say exactly? Yes, there's a girl staying with us, who may be our daughter, but we're waiting on a DNA test to be sure?'

Michael shoots me the look again, the one between hurt and hate. I don't blame him. I have to get a hold of myself and the situation, and alienating him further isn't going to help.

I swallow and soften my voice before I speak again. 'It'll look like we're hiding if we send Ryan out there. Not to mention the fact that it isn't his job.'

'I guess... maybe' – Michael swallows – 'with some more Dutch courage, I could go out there.'

'That might not be a bad idea,' Ryan says from behind me.

'No.' I shake my head and ignore the word 'more' in Michael's sentence.

'I'll speak to Don,' I say before turning to Ryan. 'He's my agent. We'll come up with something – I don't know what, but something. He can release a statement to all the necessary channels, and that might buy us some time and some peace.'

'Why don't you go out there, Mum?' Daniel asks, and we all turn towards him. 'That's what they want. You and Abi stood side by side.'

'Don't be so naive.' I regret the words the moment they're out. 'If we go out together, then we're confirming the girl is Abigail. I won't do that without the DNA test.'

Without a word, Daniel places the cloth and bottle he's been using on the island in the middle of the kitchen, and with a shake of his head and a 'Whatever', he walks out.

'Daniel!' I call after him. He doesn't turn around.

'Sarah, maybe Daniel's right,' Michael says suddenly. 'Maybe we're looking at this all wrong. Would it be so bad if we all went out there? Power in numbers and all that.'

'No, I'm calling Don.' I grab my phone from the sideboard and stride from the room.

A plan formulates in my head. It's simple, but it helps. We'll stay inside this house for the next seventy-two hours. We can send Ryan out for supplies and we'll wait for the DNA results and then we'll pick up the pieces of our lives. It's a circus outside the gates, but they'll move on soon enough if we ignore them. If.

# TWENTY-FIVE

## SARAH

The living room is cool and smells faintly of the cherry-wood log Michael set on the fire yesterday. The charred log is still in the grate, surrounded by a layer of dusty ash. I shut the door and realise how enclosed the room feels compared to the expanse of the kitchen and the extension. A thin layer of dust covers the TV stand in the corner, as well as the marble fireplace. There's a stack of Rebecca's gossip magazines scattered on the coffee table. Two cream sofas sit in an L shape facing the television. The turquoise cushions on both sofas are squished down and out of shape.

I drop to the footstool and sit for a spell, allowing the silence to wrap itself around me. My head spins. My vision blurs. I have to be strong for Daniel and Rebecca. I have to be the one in control. But it's quiet in this room and so I allow myself a moment to crumble, covering my face with my hands and crying again.

Only when an emptiness takes hold do I unlock my phone and call Don.

One, two, three, the phone connects. There's a stutter of a ring – a split second of noise, before Don picks up.

'Don, it's Sarah,' I say, although I'm sure he knows this already; I'm sure he saw my name flash on the screen of his mobile, just as I'm sure he'll be dressed in his usual crisp white shirt, planning a full day's work despite it being the weekend.

'Sarah, what the bloody hell is going on there? Is it true?'

Relief and uncertainty battle for space in my head. Don is as close to a friend as I have now. Other than Michael and the children, Don is the one person who knew me before Abigail's abduction, and who I allowed to stick with me afterwards. Hearing his voice reminds me of the twenty-something years we've shared, the long lunches when I was just starting out, and the alcohol-fuelled promises of my blossoming career as a TV presenter.

But despite the years together, Don is not my friend; he's my agent. And when all is said and done, I'm a client like any other. I was stupid to think Abi's appearance would remain under the radar of the British press. I won't make the same mistake now. Don is not someone I can trust with my darkest thoughts.

'I... it's complicated,' I say. 'A girl turned up last night. She says she's Abigail.' My words sound dull, emotionless.

'That's insane. You guys must be over the moon.'

Don hasn't heard me. Like Michael, Daniel and Rebecca, like the reporters outside my house, and every person in the country scrolling through the headlines on their phones. He's making a leap.

'What can I do?' he asks.

'We're waiting for a DNA test to be sure. I want you to release a statement. Something vague asking for privacy. And whilst you're on with the editors, stress the privacy part. We need some space to deal with this. I'll sit down with any reporter they like on Friday, but until then, they've got to give us some space.'

'Sarah, sweetheart, I'd do anything for you, you know that.

But not even I can get them to agree to leave you alone. This is too big.'

Exhaustion kneads into my brain. 'Offer the same deal but tell them to keep away from Rebecca and Daniel. No photos of them, no side stories. Nothing. Understood? The more they leave us alone, the more forthcoming I'll be on Friday.'

I rub the palm of my hand against my forehead and try not to think about the hours of interviews I'm promising, or what I'll say. Friday seems a lifetime away, but before these next six days are up, I'll know more – I'll know the truth. The thought knots my stomach and I grind my teeth against another wave of frustration rocketing through me. Why is this happening? Who is this girl? What does she want?

'Got it. They'll want to start lining up the interviews ASAP. Do you want them to come to Essex?'

'No. I don't want them in the house. Do it in London. Back-to-back. I don't want to be hanging around any longer than I have to.'

'I'll set them up over coffee at the Landmark or maybe the Savoy,' he replies.

I hear Don's fingers punch the keyboard and I picture him hunched over his desk in the two-roomed office he rents by Marble Arch. I've always thought that Don's bulldog physique and bald head would lend him to a career as a bouncer, but his razor-sharp mind took him another way. Don is the only person I've met who sees the world as a series of complicated games. Like chess, but with ever-changing rules, and where a win one day is a loss the next. Don is the grand master of the game, always seeing five moves ahead when the rest of us can't see one. Whether at his desk, or at a client dinner, he has one eye on the news and social media, and one eye on the room and the people in it.

'Right. The statement. Something vague. Fire away,' he says.

'I... I'm not sure how to word it.' A girl is claiming to be my daughter, but I'm waiting for a DNA test because I don't believe her. I want to douse the flames of the media's interest, not add to it.

Don's keyboard is tapping again. 'Yesterday at approximately – we'll fill in the specifics in a minute – we met with a seventeen-year-old that we have every reason to believe is our daughter, Abigail Wick. This is an overwhelming time for all of us, da de da de da – I'll polish that bit later. We kindly ask all members of the public and press to allow us privacy during this happy time. Thank you. Is that the gist?'

Happy time?

'I guess so. No mention of a DNA test?'

'We don't want them waiting with bated breath for another announcement. You wanted vague – this is as vague as it gets.'

'You're right. Thanks. Can you get it finished and send it out this morning?'

'Of course. Sweetheart, you sound odd. Are you OK?'

I swallow back the emotion threatening to consume me again. I can't keep breaking down, but Don knows me too well. He's been by my side through it all – Abigail's abduction, my return to work, Michael's scandal.

'Sarah?' Don's voice echoes in my ear.

'Huh?'

'Have you been listening to me? Someone's making a statement right now. Live on TV.'

'What? That can't be. We agreed a written statement would come from you.'

I'm up and by the window in a shot, but all I can see is the gravel drive, the black gates and the flash of cameras on the other side.

'Well, Sky News is going live outside your house as we speak.'

'What?' I grab the remote and switch on the TV. One, two,

three, four excruciating seconds for the box to whir into life and for Sky News to appear on the screen. Don is right. The image on the screen shows the dark gates and the green of the laurel bushes on either side.

'I'll call you back.' My voice is barely a whisper, but I hang up anyway.

The pack of journalists falls quiet; the heckles die out. The only sound from the TV is the pop of the camera flashes pointing at my family – Michael and Rebecca either side of Daniel and the girl.

I'm torn; hypnotised by the screen and frozen to the spot while my mind is screaming at me to do something, to leap in front of the wheels that are already in motion. But it's too late. I can't stop it.

I expect Michael to say something, but it's Daniel who lifts his head up and looks straight down the lens and, it seems, straight at me. His shoulders are pulled back in a way I've never seen him do before. He looks so much like Michael that I'm slammed with a memory of another time, another press statement. Not black gates behind us but the narrow front door of the holiday cottage, and Michael thanking the group.

I feel myself pulled back to that time after Abigail was gone – Rebecca and Daniel inside the cottage with Ryan, me and Michael on the front steps, the closed front door behind us, Michael's hand in mine doing nothing to detract from the loneliness I felt. I remember wishing Janie was with us too and feeling hurt that she wasn't.

'Four weeks ago,' Michael began, 'we arrived on our holiday a happy family; today we leave a broken one. Our decision to go home is not an admission of defeat; we are not giving up the search for our daughter, Abigail. We're going home because we believe that it's the best thing for our children.

'We would like to thank Suffolk Police for their continued efforts in the hunt for Abigail. And we'd like to thank everyone who's distributing our posters of Abigail and helping to find her in any way they can.'

He pulls in a shuddering breath before he speaks again. 'I have a message for the stranger on the boat. Wherever you hide, we will find you. I will never stop searching for my daughter. We will find her.'

I remember the pause, the silence filled only with a rustle of movement as cameras continued to flash, and the pain in my chest – deafening, all-consuming.

# TWENTY-SIX

## ABI

Saturday, 10.40 a.m.

Abi's heart hammers inside her chest. A pounding, rhythmic, 'Do it. Do it. Do it.' She pulls her hands into the hoody she borrowed from Rebecca and wishes, just like yesterday on the steps of the police station, that she had a coat. A thick and expensive-looking green parka like Rebecca's wearing. Something cosy and warm against the cold grey of the day.

She scans the crowd of men and women stood before her. They look cold too, and dishevelled, but their eyes are bright with anticipation. Plan B, she thinks, fighting to hide the smile pulling at her lips. Better than his plan. A blurted, 'Yes, I'm Abigail.'

This way it's not her, it's them. Her family. And there's nothing Sarah can do about it now.

Daniel clears his throat and a hush falls around them. 'For those who don't know me, I'm Daniel Wick, the eldest child of Sarah and Michael Wick, and I'd like to read a statement.' His voice is clear and confident, as if he's been speaking in public his entire life. 'Yesterday afternoon, my parents, my sister,

Rebecca, and I received the news we've waited nearly fourteen years to hear. My sister, Abigail, is alive.

'I was six years old and Abigail was four when a man abducted her during a holiday in Suffolk. These past fourteen years have been a nightmare for all of us, and one we're now thankful to wake up from. There are no words to describe how elated we feel to have Abigail back home where she belongs.

'We'd like to thank the public for the support they've shown us over the years, and we ask now for a little privacy so that we can give Abigail the welcome home she deserves. Thank you.'

The silence continues for several seconds and then the noise explodes around them, questions firing from every direction. All of them directed at her. She lifts her head and gives a nervous smile. She won't let him down.

'Where have you been, Abigail?'

She takes a breath. A second to collect herself, to line up the words just right. 'I've been living with a couple in Colombia. I found—' She stops then, swallows, as if the emotion is too much. Daniel's arm wraps around her shoulder.

'Sorry,' she says. 'This is all so new for me. I only found out my real identity very recently.'

'Were you held prisoner, Abigail? Who is the stranger on the boat? Who is the man who took you?'

'No, I wasn't held prisoner. I was raised by two people I thought were my parents.'

A sudden tension grips her body. Parents. What does that word really mean? It can't be what she had. Abi sees herself then as a little girl, trapped in that room, alone and ignored by the one person who wasn't supposed to ignore her.

More questions come, but it's Daniel who takes them now. Abi is barely listening. She thinks instead of those first messages early on, before the secrets and lies, the smoke and mirrors, that spinning roulette wheel, when all they shared was the truth.

*I swear to you I'll make this right.*

*You deserve so much better.*

She wishes it could be like that now. He told her this was the only way. Sometimes she believes it and other times a fire-ball burns inside her with the injustice of it all. Whatever happens next, she's trapped in the lies now.

Daniel's arm moves from her shoulder, dragging Abi back to the moment.

'Abigail, what were the names of the people you lived with?'

'I'm afraid,' Daniel answers for her, 'that we're unable to give you any details about Abigail's life in Colombia at this time. My sister's abduction is part of an open investigation and we don't want to do anything that would hamper the police efforts. The people who took my sister from us must be held accountable.'

'Abigail,' a voice calls from the group, 'how does it feel to be back?'

'It feels... unbelievable. I finally feel home.' Tears roll in lines down her cheeks. She wishes it was true and wonders if it ever will be. It has to be, she decides. Or what is this all for?

'What do you plan to do, now that you're home?'

'Right now,' Abi says, 'all I want to do is spend time with my family and get to know them again.'

'Michael, how does it feel to have your daughter home?'

Michael coughs before saying in a voice choked with emotion, 'A dream come true.'

'Where's Sarah? Why isn't she with you?'

'As I'm sure you can imagine,' Daniel says, 'Abigail's home-coming has been a huge shock for all of us. My mother is extremely emotional and has been told to rest by her doctor. She's kept our family together all this time, and I can't begin to explain how hard she's worked to keep us all strong. She sends her deepest gratitude for all your support. We're planning a TV interview next week as a family. Thank you again, but if you don't mind, I would very much like to introduce my sister to the delights of a proper British fry-up.'

A spattering of laughter breaks through the group.

Daniel smiles, raises his hand in a wave and turns towards the gate. 'There will be no more statements. Please respect my family's privacy.'

'Welcome back, Abigail,' someone shouts as they file onto the driveway.

Michael closes the gate with a firm thud, blocking out the cameras, and Abi sighs. If his plan was to tell the world of her existence and to cement her position in the Wick family, then she smashed it. And yet, she can't shake the feeling of discomfort that's coiling around her body.

If this is where she's supposed to be, then why does she still feel so alone?

'You were brilliant, Abigail,' Daniel says.

'You were the brilliant one,' Abi replies. 'I couldn't have done that without you. You'll have to teach me how to speak like that to them. It was amazing.' Her words come out in a rush. It's an effort to slow down her breathing, to think clearly.

'I don't need to teach you.' He smiles. 'It's in our blood.'

'I think you were both brilliant.' Rebecca grins, pushing a cold hand into Abi's and squeezing tight. 'You OK?' she adds.

Abi nods, her gaze moving to the house. In the window of the living room, Abi sees Sarah, arms folded across her chest. Even through the glass and across the driveway, Abi is sure she can sense Sarah's fury. 'I'm not sure Sarah's going to be happy about what we just did.'

Michael huffs. 'Don't worry about Sarah. I'll tell her it was my idea. It was the right thing to do. She'll see that once she's calmed down.'

Abi isn't so sure, but she's happy for Michael to take the fall.

She hangs back a little as they walk towards the front door then falls into step beside Rebecca, hoping Sarah's obvious love for the teenager will protect her from the firing line she's sure she's walking into.

They step into the house, and Abi catches the lemony smell of cleaning products. There's no sign of the mud they traipsed in an hour ago. Abi spots Ryan in the doorway to the kitchen, a cloth still in his hands.

'Ryan,' Michael says, 'how did we do?' His voice is bouncing, ringing with false cheer.

Ryan opens his mouth to reply but stops at the sight of Sarah striding out of the living room.

'What the hell was—'

Sarah's words are loud, but her fury is cut short by the phone ringing in her hand.

'Nobody move,' she hisses, placing the phone to her ear.

'I'm here,' she says. A silence follows.

Michael points to the kitchen, and he and Rebecca and Daniel disappear. A moment later, plates clatter and the boiling kettle purrs. Abi stays where she is.

'I know, Don, I know,' Sarah sighs. 'We'll have to do it. Put it on Friday before the other ones... No. It should be on *This Morning*. They stood by me when...'

Her gaze lands on Abi. Heat rises in her cheeks under Sarah's penetrating glare. And in that moment it seems as though Sarah can see through every lie, every half-truth, right down to Abi's core.

Guilt twists and knots inside Abi for everything they're doing, and yet even as she wishes in the seconds that pass that she could undo it all, disappear back to her pathetic nothing life, another thought finds its way into Abi's mind. A question really – something that's only just occurred to her.

Here is a mother broken by the abduction of her daughter and the weight of heartbreak she's carried for fourteen years.

And here Abi stands with the round chicken-pox scar on her lower right breast, with the same hair and the same coloured eyes, telling them she's Abigail. She belongs in this family.

So why is Sarah so certain she isn't Abigail? What is it she knows that no one else does?

# TWENTY-SEVEN

## SARAH

I hang up the phone as a dizzying anger spins in my head; the result of my pounding heart and the blood now rushing to my brain. My hand drags along the smooth plaster of the wall in the hallway, anchoring it in my sights, whilst the rest of the room spins with fairground-like fury in front of my eyes.

And alongside the anger are the memories I don't want to remember, seeping through cracks in my armour, clouding my thoughts.

I have to eat. I know this now. I've forgotten my art of survival – eat, sleep, work, look forward never back. And if I'm not surviving, then I'm drowning. In grief. In despair. In all that I've lost.

I make it to the kitchen, aware of the eyes watching me – Rebecca and Michael and the girl, all stood frozen, waiting for my next outburst.

Ryan touches my arm as I pass, concern creasing his brow, but it's Daniel I focus on. He's standing by the open fridge, studying its contents and crunching on half a slice of buttered toast. Without asking, I grab the other half of the jagged rectangle from his plate and force myself to eat.

Chewing is a marathon. The toast tastes like cardboard, but I swallow it down.

'I'd have made you some if you'd asked,' Daniel says.

His voice, his entire manner, is relaxed, and suddenly I'm not sure if I want to hug him or shout at him.

Don's words echo in my head. 'Your boy is a natural, you know? That was superb. Not as vague as you wanted but he skipped over your absence like a pro.'

'Shall I make bacon sandwiches?' Michael chirps as he follows me into the room, buoyant now.

'What was that out there?' I ask him, forcing a calm into my voice that I don't feel, but I want answers more than I want to yell.

'Well, I...' Michael gaze darts around the room before landing sheepishly back on me. 'The statement was good, I thought. Well done, Daniel.'

'Thanks,' Daniel says, raising his eyebrows and pulling a face so the one word lands somewhere between a statement and a question in that way only teenagers seem to manage.

'I told you I was going to ask Don to release a statement. Until we know more—'

'A statement was never going to be enough,' Michael cuts in. 'Come on, Sarah, you know this business better than anyone. This is too big. Daniel did a great job out there.'

'I'm not saying he didn't; what I'm saying is that we need to think about what we're doing as a family. We need to agree. When did you decide you were going to do this? Whose idea was it even? And why did no one tell me?'

Michael clears his throat. 'You heard what Ryan said. He thought it was a good idea and I agreed.'

I turn my gaze on Ryan. Did he suggest something to Michael while I was out of the room? He starts to say something, but Daniel cuts him off.

'What's the big deal anyway?' He closes the fridge and

turns towards me. 'The news is everywhere anyway. They've got an image of Abigail walking into Bethnal Green Police Station, they've got the police on record saying that they've had new information—'

'You don't understand a thing about the media, Daniel. You should have spoken to me—'

'How would you know?' His voice has taken on an edge, and even though he's leaning oh-so-casually against the counter, I notice the muscles in his neck are taut. 'How would you have the first clue what I know and don't know about? Did you know I changed from computer science to media studies? No, you didn't.'

His comment lands with a slice of guilt.

'You're right,' I say, nodding. Now I'm the one who's calm – the eye of the storm has reached me. 'I don't know much about you, Daniel. But whose fault is that? You tell us nothing. You come and go, day and night, treating this place like a hotel.' The emotion is rising in my throat. I can see by the colour draining from Daniel's face that I, too, have hit a nerve.

He pushes himself off the counter and stands up straight, shooting me a final look. There's the faintest of smiles on his lips, as though he's saying 'Touché' and that he's sorry but also that he's right. Maybe I'm reading too much into it. But when he walks out of the kitchen, I let him go.

'Sarah,' Ryan starts, 'I'm sorry—'

'It's fine,' I say, turning to leave as well. I need a moment.

In the silence of the living room, a loneliness descends like the rolling fog that pushes across the fields on spring mornings. I'm no more alone now than I have been for the past five years, the past thirteen years, ten months and ten days, and yet it feels different. I'm outcast from this family, and even though it feels petty to admit it, I'm hurt that they made the statement without me. But then what choice did I give them?

I consider calling Don back, but he'll be busy arranging

interviews now. My gaze falls to the bookshelf – a long, thick frame in knotted wood that takes up half of one wall and is filled with a mix of books and photo frames and chunky silver ornaments. A heart on one shelf. A bird on another. And there at the bottom, forgotten and hardly used, stuck in with the cookbooks from Rebecca's baking phase, is my old address book.

I pull it from the shelf. The cover is polka dot and scuffed at the edges. I open it up and find Janie and Phil's address. They lived near Ascot, West London, fourteen years ago. Phil had a job with racehorses back then, but they could be anywhere now.

I wonder again why Janie stopped contact. Why the day of Abigail's abduction was the last time we spoke. Just an hour before the abduction, we were laughing together, running along the seafront in a last-ditch attempt to make up for the mountain of fish and chips I'd eaten that week.

And then our conversation turned serious. I was worried about her marriage and how unhappy she was. It led to a stupid fight that was meaningless given everything that followed so soon afterwards.

'Just leave him, Janie,' I said, my breath coming fast as we ran side by side, completely unaware that my life was about to be crushed. That less than an hour after these words left my mouth, my daughter would be gone and I would never see her again. 'He's making you miserable. I wish you could see that.'

'We're going through a tough time, that's all. The IVF hormones have made me crazy. I've been a total cow.'

'Which he should understand,' I said as we weaved around a dad with a young son wobbling on a bike.

'He does. He just doesn't want to keep trying for kids and I do.'

'He's not being fair.'

She huffed then, shooting me a look so fierce that I slowed my pace and reared back.

'It's easy for you, isn't it, Sarah?' she said, the blustering sea breeze carrying the anger in her voice. The dad with the boy on the bike looked up at us. 'Telling me to leave my husband and give up on my dreams while you sit there having it all. Little Miss Perfect, with her perfect husband and three perfect children.'

A sob shuddered through her, and I stopped running and tried to take her arm.

'Don't,' she said, pulling away. 'Just let me be angry. Carry on your run. I'm going to head back.'

'Janie, I'm sorry. I didn't mean to upset you,' I called out as she turned and ran back towards Thorpeness and the cottage. I stood watching her for a moment before carrying on the run. It was useless chasing after her when she needed to calm down.

I felt bad for being pushy, but I also knew Janie. She'd cool off and we'd have a glass of wine and laugh about it later.

Except we didn't.

The next time I saw her, I was running the streets, screaming Abigail's name.

'Sarah, what's happened?' Janie asked, grabbing my shoulders and holding me still.

'Abigail's gone. She was playing in the garden. Michael left her for a second and—'

'She'll be somewhere,' Janie said, and we searched together until there was nowhere else to look and we sprinted back to the cottage, praying for news.

My eyes fall to the home-line number below the address. I tap it into my phone and wait for it to ring.

A woman answers with a brisk, 'Hello,' and I know instantly that it's not Janie.

'Oh, hello,' I say. 'I'm sorry to bother you. I'm trying to track down an old friend. She lived at 247 Winchester Road, and this was her number.'

'Yes, that's where you've reached. Who are you looking for?'

'Janie Franklin.'

'The Franklins, yes – they lived here before my parents.'

'You don't happen to have an address for them now, do you?'

There's a pause on the line. 'I don't think so, sorry. I'm actually just visiting. My mum is unwell. It was so long ago. They must've moved in 2010, I think. I was away at university that year. I think Mum said they moved abroad for work. Look, I can ask my mum when she wakes up, but she's got dementia, so I'm not sure she'll be a lot of help.'

'Thank you. If it's not too much trouble to ask, I'd appreciate it.'

'You could try Facebook. If your friend isn't on there, then her daughter might be.'

'Daughter,' I stumble over the word.

Another pause. 'Yes. I'm sure Mum said she had a child. My bedroom was painted bright pink when I moved in and they left a swing set in the garden. Sorry, I'd better go. I can hear my mum getting up.'

She hangs up and I stare at nothing, trying to make sense of what the woman said. Janie and Phil moved abroad a year after Abigail was abducted with a daughter they didn't have in 2009. Not a baby. A child. A little girl old enough to use a swing set. Adoption is the obvious answer, or a mistake by the woman I spoke to, and yet a shiver still races down my spine that I can't quite understand.

# TWENTY-EIGHT

## SARAH

Saturday, Noon

The morning passes with stilted words. Polite requests and questions. 'Who wants another coffee? Anyone hungry? Pass the milk.'

My family look at me like I'm a grenade with the pin yanked out. I can't settle. My mind keeps turning over Janie and Phil and their daughter, and the girl in my house. I drift between the kitchen and the living room, watching the news repeat Daniel's statement over and over. There is nothing new said, no more presenters reporting from outside the house.

Daniel disappears upstairs at some point. Rebecca and Abi chat in the kitchen while taking it in turns to play *Among Us* on Rebecca's phone. I hover in the background, hoping to get Abi on her own and talk at last. But if I ask her for that conversation, I know my family will close in around her again and I'll get nowhere. I have to wait until she's alone.

Ryan washes up and makes sandwiches, a tea towel slung over one shoulder. He continues to throw me worried looks, which I ignore. My anger is not at him, and yet I'm still annoyed he gave Michael the final nudge into making a statement. I want to ask him what happened to being unobtrusive, but it's another question I keep in.

When I can stand it no more, I throw on my coat and take Barley into the garden, playing an endless game of fetch he will never tire of. I try Janie's mobile number again, but no one answers this time.

At some point, the back door opens and Ryan appears.

'Not now.' I shake my head. 'I'm fine.' I don't want his sympathy, his pity or his calm. I don't want to be told I'm overly emotional, a wreck. And I don't want to hear that Daniel did the right thing.

'The DNA technician is here,' Ryan continues.

I jump up, anger forgotten, and stride to the house with Barley at my heels.

Seven, eight, nine steps until I'm in the mudroom. I catch sight of Abi's trainers as I lift my feet out of my boots. They are unbranded and old; the lip by the toe is peeling away. I look away, suddenly uneasy. Unsure. A flash of her eyes – those amber flecks. The same questions return. Is she innocent? Or is this something more? I can't shake the feeling that it's the latter.

I look away, remembering instead the red trainers Abigail loved so much.

Everyone is gathered in the kitchen and I fight the feeling that I'm being excluded. Talked about. There's a man standing beside Ryan. He has a beaked nose and small eyes below a shock of curly black hair. He is half a foot shorter than Ryan and eye to eye with Michael. He's wearing a dark polo shirt with the name Bio Data Clinic written in aqua blue.

'Does your van have that logo on it?' I ask, pointing at his shirt. My voice is still sharper than I intend, but I don't have the energy for niceties or greetings.

He looks down at his T-shirt as he shakes his head. 'They're plain white. Look like any old delivery van,' he replies. 'Two police uniforms were moving the photographers back as I came in, if that's what you were worrying about, Mrs Wick. Most of them looked to be packing up and going home.'

My anger falls away. The sheer enormity of what's happened in less than twenty-four hours is pounding down on me. There are so many questions I need to ask the girl, the police, Michael and myself. There are so many things I don't know.

'Sorry.' The word spills from my mouth. 'I didn't mean to sound so abrupt.' I'm staring at the technician standing in my kitchen, but I'm thinking of Daniel. 'It's just...' There are no words to explain.

'Nothing to apologise for, Mrs Wick.'

I smile my appreciation as Michael steps over and shakes the man's hand. 'Thanks for coming back, Bob. Sorry about my state of undress this morning.'

'I see it all in this line of work,' Bob replies with a smile that seems to curl up around his nose.

'You were here earlier?' I ask, looking from Bob to Michael.

Michael nods. 'While you were out on your walk.'

'It was no problem,' Bob chips in. 'I had other deliveries to make so I said I'd come back later to collect them.'

'How soon before they get to the lab?'

'It's my next stop.' Bob examines his watch. 'All being well, the results will take seventy-two hours.'

'Thank you.' Seventy-two hours. Tuesday afternoon. I can survive until then.

Then what? The question is in my thoughts before I can stop it. Last night I was clinging to the belief that the DNA results would put everything back to normal. My family would realise I was right, the girl would disappear, and we would carry on with our lives. But even in the chaos I can see it's far too late for that. If we, if I, had kept the girl away from the house, put her in a hotel for three days, then maybe things would have been different. I think of Daniel and Rebecca. In their heads, they have their sister back. An image of the three of them walking and laughing beside the river floats across my mind.

'Shall we do it then? Where are the tests?' I ask, looking from Michael to Ryan and finally to Bob.

'I left them with you, Mr Wick,' Bob says.

'Did you?' Michael's eyes drift across the kitchen. 'I thought you took them with you.' He pats the pockets of his jeans as though they're a lost set of keys. 'I'm sure they're here somewhere. I wasn't really with it this morning. Not enough sleep last night.'

Too much wine. I keep the comment to myself.

'Ryan, did you move them?' Michael asks.

Ryan shakes his head. 'I don't think so.'

'Sorry about this, Bob,' Michael says. 'They're here somewhere.'

'Have you got any more kits?' I ask.

Bob shakes his head. 'Sorry. I'm all out. I would normally have more but it's Saturday and this is my final stop of the day.'

'Well, they can't have gone far,' I say, fighting to keep the frustration from my voice.

'I know that, Sarah,' Michael mutters as he surveys the kitchen. 'I swear I left them...' He spins, a full circle. 'Ryan, are you sure—'

'Oh, for goodness' sake,' I hiss, pulling open the nearest cupboard.

'I think I left them on the sideboard.' He makes a face, staring at the long wooden cupboard at the end of the kitchen. It's littered with letters from Rebecca's school, and there's a pile of jumpers and books that I made two days ago still waiting to be taken upstairs and put away. Michael and I arrive at the spot together. Our hands dance over each other to sort through the mess.

I yank open the top drawer, but something snags against the

runner and jolts the drawer back to closed, almost taking my fingers with it.

With more care, I wriggle my hand inside the drawer and push the blockage out of the way. The drawer slides open and there on top of the takeaway menus and a tangle of phone chargers are three small white boxes with the same aqua-blue logo on the front.

'Why did you hide them?' I ask.

'I didn't *hide* them, Sarah,' Michael snaps. 'Someone else must have put them there, or I don't know, maybe I dropped them in there whilst I was trying to call you all and warn you about the press on our doorstep.'

After last night's suggestion that we don't bother with the DNA test at all, I'm not sure I believe him.

I scoop up the boxes and hand one to Michael. The results of the test will bring pain and destruction on my family, but it will also bring the truth, and there has to be some comfort in that. I cling to the thought and turn in search of the girl.

Abi is standing beside Rebecca. The sleeves of her jumper are pulled over her hands and I'm struck again by how young she is.

'Here,' I say. 'I'm sorry I'm asking you to do this,' is all I can think to say.

'It's OK,' she says. 'I want to know the truth too.'

We stand on opposite sides of the island with its clear glass wine fridge and drawers full of tea towels and never-used utensils. A sudden burst of sunlight floods the room, showing up the smudges on the black granite worktop Michael insisted we get.

Michael joins us at one side, and a second later the technician places a small silver jiffy bag in the centre of the worktop.

'You'll find a clear tube in your box,' he says. 'Write your name in the space provided on the tube and seal your sample inside. Then place all three samples in this silver bag.' He points to the silver jiffy bag. 'Voila.'

I rip open the box and find an information leaflet folded over the top of the contents, reminding me, with a stab of sadness, of a pregnancy test. The result will be absolute. This girl is not my daughter.

Doubt, hope's ugly brother, creeps over me. My eyes are scanning the instructions and the simple line drawings that depict the steps. One, rub the swab against the inside of my cheek. Two, place it in the tube. Three, put the tube in the bag. Four, seal the bag.

My hands start to shake. I look around the kitchen at my family. Would it be so bad if we skipped the test? Would it be so bad to pretend? Isn't that what we've been doing for nearly fourteen years anyway? Pretending to be a normal family? Would it be so bad to let the questions I have slip away and look forward to a life where our three children are home?

The box and the instructions fall from my hand and drop to the counter. The words are forming in my head, and for a second I can see myself speaking them. I can see the future I think Michael sees. But Abi gets there first.

'It's OK,' she says, her voice barely audible over the rustle of paper and the clatter of the contents of Michael's box as he tips it onto the granite. But I hear her. There's something in her voice that sticks in my head. My eyes are on her in an instant. Her face is blank, unreadable. Did I imagine it or did the girl's accent just shift? There was no Spanish in those words, no American. The words had been clipped; the accent English.

My gaze darts from the girl to Michael. He's already rubbing the swab inside his mouth. *Did you hear that?* I want to shout to them all – to Rebecca, to Daniel, to Michael. Even Bob. *Did you hear her accent change?* I want to scream at them, and at her. But I don't. Nobody else is listening. Nobody else heard. Two words, that's all it was, but it was enough. Enough for me to remember that this girl is a stranger. There's no way I can pretend otherwise. I have to find out who she is and why she's here. But first of all, I need my family with me, and the only way to do that is to take this test.

'Shall I do it right here?' she asks in a louder voice, rolling the R in her mouth and lifting her tone at the end in an exotic blend of Spanish and American, and glancing between Michael and the technician, and then her gaze falls to me and I don't see innocence or youth in that stare. I see determination. I see trouble.

I pick up my box and count the steps as I do them. DNA doesn't lie, and in seventy-two hours, she will be gone.

# TWENTY-NINE

## ABI

Abi waits for Sarah's focus to return to the testing kit before she dares to breathe. Dropping the accent was a risk, but it wasn't a mistake. She could see Sarah faltering, questioning if they needed the test.

It was a moment of weakness Abi knew Sarah would regret. There's no way a woman so adamant that Abi isn't her daughter one day wouldn't start asking questions the next.

No. Better to get this over with. And besides, Abi needs this DNA test. She needs to prove to Sarah and to all of them that she's part of this family. Maybe then she'll start to feel like she belongs, like he promised her she would.

Abi opens the box and pretends to read the flimsy paper instructions. It's just for show. This isn't her first DNA test. He made her practise. They had to be certain the plan would work. There was too much at stake. There still is.

A sudden fear ignites inside her. It takes her a moment to process the feeling, to attach it to one of the dozens of thoughts fighting for attention in her head. Is it fear of failure? Knowing that all that awaits her outside of this house is a life on the streets, £89.61 to her name. No bank account, no qualifications.

The café work was always cash in hand, and even though Abi knows she's smart, that she could work out the change to give a customer before tapping it into the till, being smart isn't enough.

It's a scary thought but it's not what's causing the bolts of fear shooting through her body as she takes out the swab and rubs it against her cheek. It's him. It's how much could still go wrong. She has so much to lose, but so does he. There's no going back for either of them. He's put everything on the line for her, and Abi still isn't sure why and what he wants out of this, just that she can't fail him.

Was it only last week that she sat in that hotel room and asked him what they'd do about the DNA test? She remembers sitting on the bed and the feel of the covers beneath her hands, slightly damp in that way fabric feels when the room is so cold. She wished she could leave him sitting in the armchair and escape to wander London, to explore the city she'd heard so much about but never seen.

She craved the fresh air, the noise, the people.

'You're not listening to me,' he said, rubbing a hand across the back of his neck and digging in his pocket for a second before pulling out a half-eaten pack of mints. They'd been at it for hours. Going over every detail of her fictional life, every question the police might ask, and what answer she would give.

Exhaustion nagged at her thoughts.

'You have to concentrate,' he said. 'We don't have much time. I told you, Sarah will insist on a DNA test.'

'I thought you said they'd welcome me with open arms?'

'They will,' he replied with a crooked smile. 'But Sarah is practical. She'll want the DNA too.'

'And?' She glanced at the radiator below a single window that rattled with every passing bus. It was an old chunky thing painted cream, and it had orange-and-brown rust flaking around the sides. She'd tried in vain to turn the twisty knob a couple of times, but it was immobile. She hadn't thought she'd ever miss the stuffy, unmoving heat of Buenaventura, but she longed for it then.

It wasn't even six o'clock and already it was dusky outside, the room shrouded in gloom. She missed the daylight too. The endless sun.

He sighed again and shook his head. 'We've been over this. The DNA test, the police questioning you, it's all good. We want it.'

'But the results, I mean—'

'Trust me,' he cut her off and stood up. 'I've planned for this. I've been planning every detail for months.'

You've *been planning this. What about me?* She wanted to ask. What had she been doing all these months?

She sighed and chose a different question. 'Why are we doing it this way? Why am I not just knocking on their front door and telling them everything? The real truth, not just part of it. This feels so twisted. I can't make sense of it all. Why are you helping me? I wish you'd tell me everything.'

Out of nowhere, he moved, leaping onto the bed and landing beside her, his face so close she could smell the tangy mint on his breath. Abi's heart froze for a beat before thudding hard in her chest.

'It's the only way.' His voice was low and fast, and made the hairs on her arms stand on end. 'I promised you a future. I promised you a real family with nice parents and a brother and sister. They've even got a dog. You need to get it into your head that the truth won't help here. The truth will blow that precious family into smithereens. Then you'll have nothing.'

*And so will you,* she thought.

'They're damaged.' His voice softened as he spoke. 'The atrocity they suffered in the past has all but destroyed them.'

Abi lifted her gaze and looked at his face, hovering inches from her own. It was etched with sorrow and guilt, and she couldn't help wondering what he'd done.

'Sarah will never accept you. She's too protective of her children. But you can give them their daughter back,' he said, 'and you can have the life you're owed. Just think what that means to them and to you. You can go to college. You can become whoever you want – a doctor or a TV star. You can sit around all day and do nothing, if that's what you want, and they'll love you just the same.'

Tears throbbed at the back of Abi's eyes. A weight pressed down on her chest. Love. It was an abstract emotion. To be seen and read about but never experienced. Caroline hadn't loved her, not as a mother should love her daughter. Caroline had tried, but the depression, like a tornado, had consumed everything in its path. As for Jhon, Abi had thought she'd loved him, and he her, but after the lies he'd told her, and then the truth he'd shared only after his death, it didn't feel like love now. Jhon had been a coward.

What would it feel like to love and be loved by a family? Not just any family but *her* family. What would it feel like to live in a nice house and have nice clothes? What would it feel like not to worry about money every second of every day, and whether she could afford to eat that day?

'You can have the life you're owed,' he said, pushing the point.

Could she? she wonders as she rubs the swab against her cheek.

# THIRTY

## ABI

### Then

Jhon's hand pressed against her back as she wriggled the key in the lock and stepped into the empty apartment. Empty, finally.

Abi breathed through her mouth, a habit she wasn't ready to break. Her mom might be gone, but the smell of her still lingered in the air. If she'd expected the apartment to feel bigger without her mom's swollen body, it didn't. It was quieter though. There were no rasping gasps for air or hacking coughs; no gunfire or explosions from the TV. Just silence.

She stepped to the window and fiddled with the open curtains, pushing them a little further and allowing another inch of light into the room.

'I'm sorry about your mother,' Jhon said. 'What shall I do with these?' he asked after a pause, holding up the small wooden box the man at the crematorium had given them.

Abi shrugged.

'I could throw them in the sea?'

'OK.'

Something stirred inside Abi, but it wasn't sadness. She

didn't care. She didn't care about the ashes. She didn't care her mom was dead. Why would she? Her mom had kept her locked up her entire life. Twelve years in this stinking apartment with only her mom, and the depression like a beast living with them, and the TV. It was like the stupid *Rapunzel* fairy tale in the book Jhon had given her years ago, except no prince had ever come to rescue Abi.

Only in the last year had she plucked up the courage to upset her mom and leave the apartment on her own for longer spells; walking all the way along the main road into town, and wandering around shops she couldn't afford to buy anything in. Then, just as Abi had found a sliver of the freedom she'd craved, her mom had got sick, forcing Abi back to the sofa, watching those goddamn films, with the smell of body odour and death affronting her nose.

Cancer, the doctor had told them after Abi and Jhon had finally convinced Caroline to see a doctor. Breast and lung and other places too. Chemotherapy might have given her a few extra months, but what would've been the point?

No, it wasn't sadness Abi felt. It was something else. Relief? Guilt? Maybe both.

Jhon moved to the sofa. The springs had given up years ago and gave an irking creak as he sat down. The noise tickled the hairs on the back of Abi's neck. For one heart-stopping moment, Abi could sense her mom still sat there in her trance, watching the flicking images of the TV.

Abi gripped the curtains in her fists and pushed the thought away. Her mom was dead.

A force pressed down on her shoulders. She didn't want to spend another minute in the apartment, in her prison. Finally, she was free.

'What do I do now?' she asks, when what she really meant was, *Can I come with you?* She already knew the answer to that one. No.

Abi wasn't sure when she'd figured it out, or when Jhon had stopped pretending that when he left this place it was only to work and travel, but it had been a long time. She'd pieced together enough fragments of arguments. Enough 'Go on then – go back to her' comments from her mom to get it. She didn't know where his other family were – his real family – or how many children he had, but she knew they existed in the same way she knew her mom was dying before anyone had told her.

'Come sit with me for a minute, Abelia.' Jhon patted the cushion beside him.

Abi's skin crawled at the thought of sitting on that putrid thing, but she did as she was told.

'I would take you with me if I could,' he said, his voice soft but firm, as if she was a stray dog trying to follow him home. 'But my family don't know about you and it's hard to explain. I'm sorry.'

'I thought I was your family. You said... if I looked after Mom, then you'd look after me. You promised.' Tears blurred her vision. She looked up and watched the specks of black mould in the corner move across her eyes like spiders crawling from their web.

'I'm sorry, Abelia. I'll still come visit. It'll be like it always has been.'

'But I'm only twelve... I can't live by myself.'

Jhon sighed and Abi sensed his patience wearing thin.

'You've been looking after yourself for years. You looked after your mom too. It'll be easier now. You can go to school if you want. I'll help you find one, and I'll still give you a little allowance for food and bills. Nothing will change.'

He stood up, ending the conversation.

'You've got my number. You can use your mom's mobile. Any problems, I'm fifteen minutes away. I'll see you next week. Thursday. OK?'

Abi nodded and waited for the front door to click shut before sliding to the floor and pulling her knees to her chest.

Fifteen minutes away. All these years she'd pictured him travelling the world and he was only down the road on another sofa, kissing another child goodnight.

Stupid. Stupid, stupid.

Jhon's words circled her head. 'Nothing will change.' Abi wasn't free from any of it – the shitty apartment, the loneliness. She'd never be free.

# THIRTY-ONE

## ABI

'Excuse me.'

Abi jumps, expecting to see the red peeling walls of the hotel room, but only the sleek white cupboards and shiny black worktops of the kitchen lie before her.

'You need to put the cap back on and seal the buccal swab inside the bag quickly.' The DNA technician nods to Abi's hand. 'To minimise degeneration of the sample.'

'Oh, sorry,' she says, feeling all eyes on her. She's the last to finish her swab.

'It'll be all right, kiddo,' Michael says, handing her the silver bag with his and Sarah's samples already in it. The smile that crosses his face is small, but his voice is kind.

'Anyone want a drink?' Daniel asks from the other side of the kitchen.

Michael pats her shoulder and steps towards the sink. A moment later, the kettle begins to bubble into life.

'What about lunch?' Ryan asks. 'Anyone for a—'

'Don't say sandwich,' Rebecca groans. 'So boring. We'll get something out when we go shopping.'

Abi falters, trying to follow the conversation; trying to wrap her head around talking about a trip to the shops while inside her jumper, sweat clings to her skin. He made her practise this. She knows what she has to do now.

Do it. Do it. Do it. Her pulse hammers in her ears.

'Just one other box to tick,' the DNA technician says, unfolding a piece of pink paper. 'I understand we're billing you for the test, but the call came from... DS Howard at Essex Police. Do you want us to send a copy of the DNA results to him as well?'

'Yes, thank you,' Sarah says. The heat of her gaze leaves Abi's face.

Abi picks up the silver bag and pushes her sample inside. Her movements are clunky, but at least her hands aren't shaking. She holds her breath, waiting, expecting someone to say something, to shout a 'Hey' and grab her hand. She rips off the sticky tape, sealing her sample inside.

A second later, Abi steps back and leans against the counter. She waits a beat before looking up, but thanks to Rebecca, no one is watching her.

'So, what?' Rebecca says. 'We're not allowed out the house now? Mum, seriously, stop stressing. I wanted to go out there. I didn't say anything. I just stood next to Dad. And I don't see why we can't go shopping. Abi's got, like, no clothes.'

Sarah touches Rebecca's arm. 'Sorry, Becca, honey, I don't think it's a good idea. I don't want you being followed around town by journalists. Let's let things die down for the next few days.'

'That's so unfair.' Rebecca folds her arms across her body and finishes her sentence with a short huff that's almost comical. Attitude doesn't suit her the way kindness does, Abi thinks.

'Can't you get some things online instead?' Sarah asks, voice pleading now.

There's a pause, then a mischievous smile pulls at one side of Rebecca's mouth. 'Can I have your credit card then please?'

Sarah's shoulders sag. Then she laughs. A short exhale of humour – the first Abi has seen from her.

'Why do I have the feeling I've just been played?' Sarah reaches into a drawer and pulls out a purple card.

Rebecca's grin widens. She leaps forward, taking the card from Sarah and enveloping her mum in a brief hug.

Sarah turns towards her. 'Is online shopping OK for you, Abi? If we say five hundred pounds to start off with. And, Becca, only a few things for you please – you've got more than enough clothes.'

'I know, I know, don't worry. This is all for Abi.'

Becca gives her mum another hug and all the while Abi feels her mouth drop open, Sarah's words echoing in her mind.

£500. For clothes? For her? Abi wants to laugh at the absurdity of it. She's quite sure that if she added up every item of clothing she's ever bought or been given, found or stolen, the total amount wouldn't come close to £500.

'Come on,' Rebecca says, turning to Abi. 'Let's go shop.'

She grabs Abi by the hand, causing the object inside her sleeve to rustle. She tenses, waiting for Rebecca to notice, but she's still talking about a pair of wide-legged jeans she's desperate to get. Abi's heart continues to race. She really needs a moment to herself.

'This is going to be fun,' Rebecca says. 'We'll have a whole new wardrobe for you by this time tomorrow. What shall we look at first?'

Abi drops her gaze to her bare feet, remembering the rub of the boots that were too big and her old trainers. 'Shoes,' she replies, sensing again the glimmer of how her life might be. 'I don't know if this is OK, but I've always wanted a pair of Converse.'

'Of course it's OK. I love them. There's this shoe shop that does these really cool Converse trainers with, like, loads of different patterns on. Rainbows, sweets. Glitter. Oh, and there's this summer wrap dress I saw last time I was in town.'

Abi feels that warmth in her chest again as Rebecca flops onto her bed and opens up a sleek red laptop, but this time it comes with a desperation that feels like it might suffocate her.

*I am Abigail Wick.* She repeats the words in her head just like he told her to. Over and over.

The packet inside her sleeve feels heavy, a rock pulling her down. She has to hide it. If anyone finds it, everything is over.

'I'm just going to use the bathroom,' she tells Rebecca, spinning around and bumping straight into Ryan with an 'oof' of bodies colliding. She catches the scent of coffee and mint on his breath.

'Sorry,' she mutters, pulling her hands behind her back.

'I'm sorry,' he says, tone friendly, but there's something in his expression that sends a trickling unease through her body. 'I just came to ask if you wanted lunch after all? I was going to make sandwiches.'

'I'll have something later thanks,' Rebecca calls, already scrolling through rows of brightly coloured shoes.

'Erm...' Hunger rattles in Abi's body. 'Yes. I mean, yes, please. Thank you.'

He watches her for a long moment before nodding and leaving Abi to dart into her bedroom. She steps to the mirror on the wall, cased in a thick silver frame. She almost doesn't recognise herself with her hair tied back. She's never worn it like this before, preferring it down. Something to hide behind. In the mirror, wide eyes stare back. Startled. Face pale. She looks scared. Terrified.

'I am Abigail Wick,' she says to her reflection. Then she shakes her head, ponytail swishing. No matter how many times she says the name, it always snags. No matter how many times she tries to convince herself, she'll never feel it. Never truly believe the lie.

And that's what it is. A lie.

For all his talk of family and justice and belonging, it's all a lie. She's many things, but she is not Abigail Wick. The roulette wheel stops spinning in her head. Abi pulls out the DNA test hidden up her sleeve and stuffs it under the mattress with her phone, before turning on her heels and heading back to join Rebecca.

---

*There is a difference between being guilty and feeling guilt.*

*They are guilty.*

*I am guilty.*

*I feel guilt.*

*They don't.*

*Fourteen years is a long time to live with guilt – the kind of toxic malignancy that eats away at someone's soul. Believe me, I know.*

*I wonder what they're feeling now.*

*Are you scared, Sarah? You should be.*

*And now we wait for the truth.*

*They say the truth shall set us free, but I don't think it can this time. I think it can only destroy. And that's my plan.*

*I will destroy them.*

*I will end this.*

# PART II

MONDAY

# THIRTY-TWO

## SARAH

Monday, 4 p.m.

The wait is agonising. My phone is never out of my hand. The screen remains infuriatingly blank.

I count the hours like I count my steps.

One more night, I tell myself.

This time tomorrow.

Mantras that mean nothing because the moment they pass through my thoughts, they're followed by the same unanswerable question. Then what?

A weak ray of afternoon sunlight stretches through the glass of the extension. The sun arrived yesterday, bringing with it the daffodil stalks and blue skies, and the tourists fighting for spaces taken by the media. Their numbers have dwindled but the hardiest of them are still outside the gates, hoping for that family photo of us all together.

Despite the sun, a dark cloud still hangs over us. It's the waiting. A half-drunk cup of coffee sits on the table in front of me. Cold now. The other half is swilling in my empty stomach, adding to my jitteriness. I can't remember if the coffee is one I made myself or the one Ryan handed me an hour ago when he tried to coax me out of my robotic state and get me talking again, but I can't talk, not properly.

What is there to say? How can I explain.

My mind is a pendulum, oscillating one way and then the other. In the dead of night when I stare into the darkness, Michael snoring beside me and Barley sleeping at my feet, questions race through my mind until I have to fight the desire to shake Abi awake and ask her: *Who are you really? Why are you here?* But when dawn breaks and I drag myself downstairs, and I'm faced with my family and her, the certainty and the questions are gone, dying like a gust of wind running its course.

I don't believe Abelia is my daughter, but I can't ignore the glow on Rebecca's cheeks or Michael and Daniel's laughter bouncing through the rooms. She's no longer a stranger either.

I'm grateful for Ryan's presence. The one person in the house who doesn't think I'm crazy. Or perhaps just the one person who hides it well. I told him on Saturday that he didn't need to come back, that we would be fine. He saw through the lie and I didn't protest when he insisted.

A movement startles me. I blink and she's there, standing in the archway to the kitchen wearing a pair of tight jeans and a red top that falls off one shoulder. Her long brown hair is loose and lies in waves over her shoulders.

'Sorry,' she says, glancing behind her. I wonder if she's searching for someone to rescue her. 'I heard voices and thought Becca was back.'

'Michael's just popped out to collect her. Ryan's left for the day too. And I'm not sure where Daniel is.' I tap the home screen and register the time – 4.16 p.m. 'Becca won't be long.'

'Oh, OK.' She starts to turn and I see that the chance to talk that I'd planned on Saturday is now before us.

'Abi?' I say. 'Can we chat for a minute?'

Her gaze darts to the kitchen doorway as though she's

hoping someone might rescue her, but then she nods and one, two, three steps later she slides into the chair opposite me. Her eyes are wide and fearful. She's scared of me, I realise, and really, who could blame her?

'I'm sorry for how we started. I know I've not been a good...' My voice trails off. I search for the right word. Host seems too formal, but mother is all wrong too.

'I understand,' she says. 'You've all been very kind. Thank you for my clothes.'

I shake my head. 'You don't have to keep saying thank you. This isn't an easy situation for any of us, but whatever happens, I want you to know that we'll do our best to help you.' I pause, unsure if I mean the words or not. The pendulum swings again in my thoughts. Is she here to hurt us or does she believe she really is Abigail? 'Perhaps we could talk about—'

The front door opens and Rebecca's voice calls a 'Hello'.

'In here,' the girl shouts, jumping up, and I think we're both relieved. What good are questions anyway? The only answer that matters is the one we're all waiting for.

I think back to Michael's disbelief this morning. 'You're not really sending Becca to school, are you?'

'It'll do her good to see her friends, and falling behind on her schoolwork isn't an option,' I said.

I'm not sure if it was the right decision. It wasn't just the schoolwork, or the need to give Rebecca a little of something normal, away from the house and the girl, that made me send her. I needed to break up the day and the waiting, and Rebecca leaving and returning from school was all I could think to do.

Besides, I couldn't stomach another day of Michael's faux celebrations. Yesterday, he took it upon himself to treat Sunday like Christmas. Champagne and wine flowed from lunchtime. He either didn't notice or didn't care that he was the only one drinking. He cajoled Daniel, Rebecca and Abi into playing board games he unearthed from the back of a cupboard – dusty relics from his own childhood. *Monopoly* first, then *Cluedo*. I hid in the kitchen or the garden with Barley, drinking too much coffee – an outsider looking in.

Rebecca appears before us, dropping her school bag to the floor with a thud.

'What did I miss?' she asks. Her smile is wide but her eyes travel between me and the girl, betraying her concern.

'Nothing at all.' I force a smile. 'How was your day?'

'Terrible. Everyone was staring at me. I couldn't concentrate on anything. Do I have to go tomorrow?'

'I'm not sure,' I say, already shaking my head.

'I want to be here for the results too,' she says. 'Please.'

Rebecca's eyes turn glassy and I find myself shrugging.

'All right.'

The threat of tears is replaced with a wide grin, and Rebecca and Abi set about making snacks in the kitchen before disappearing upstairs. Idly, I pick up my phone and call Janie's number again. I must have called a dozen times since that first call and the man who answered. Each time it rings and rings. Except today it connects again.

'Hello?' I say into the silence. 'Hello? Janie, is that you?'

I hear something. A rustle of clothing, a breath. Someone is there.

I stand up and step through the French doors and into the garden. The sun is still bright, but the spring warmth has gone from the day and a chill pushes through the wool of my jumper.

'Hello?' My voice carries my impatience, but still no one replies. I sense them on the other end of the phone. Listening. Waiting. But why?

'Janie, I know you're there.' It's a lie. I don't know if it's Janie or a stranger but something makes the words rush out of me. Why aren't they speaking?

I wait, refusing to hang up. And then there's a voice, a distant, 'Mum, I can't find my trainers.' It's a girl's voice shouting from somewhere nearby and then a clunk, a hissed swear word and then the call disconnects.

For a moment, I do nothing but stare at my phone, trying to make sense of what I've just heard. I've been calling for days and days without really knowing why. But now someone has answered, someone with a daughter who sounded like a teenager. And that whispered swear word right at the end, that was Janie. It might have been fourteen years since we last spoke, but I'd recognise her voice anywhere. And yet, I can't understand, if it was Janie, and I'm sure now that it was, why she didn't say something.

My mouth turns dry as my thoughts connect the dots to a place I don't want to go. Janie was there the day Abigail went missing. Janie who couldn't have her own children but who loved mine with all of her heart, especially Abigail.

Questions charge into my mind until my head is spinning. It feels like these questions have been hidden somewhere inside of me all along and now that I've set them free, they are fierce and loud. Could Janie have run back to the cottage after our fight, coaxed Abigail away, hidden her somewhere, then come back to help me look?

It's farcical. The police questioned Janie more than once. They would've found something if she'd been involved. And yet the sound of that girl on the phone – that distant shout – sends another wave of jittering uncertainty through me.

I take a breath. I push the questions back into the darkest corner of my mind. I've allowed myself to be distracted by Janie and the past, but I must think clearly now about Abi, the girl in my house.

I need to be the one to look beyond tomorrow to the next day and the rest beyond it, but I don't know how. I desperately want to protect Rebecca – and Daniel too – from the fallout the DNA results will bring, but I don't know how.

As I step through the French doors, Abi rushes back into the kitchen, grabbing another bowl from the cupboard. 'Forgot this,' she says, flashing me a nervous smile before turning away again.

I watch her leave, the urge to shout after her rising up inside me.

*You're not my daughter; you're not Abigail.*

*Are you?*

\*

TUESDAY

# THIRTY-THREE

## ABI

Tuesday, 1.28 p.m.

The waiting has become a physical being, a person lurking in the corner of the room. A bad smell. Something ugly. Impossible to ignore.

It's in the tightness of Michael's jaw; the permanent pinch between Sarah's eyes; the grey tinge of Rebecca's already pale skin; and the relentless tapping of Daniel's fingers on the table. Abi can't remember the last time anyone spoke. The silence feels spiky and tense.

Any attempt at conversation has been swept away with the breadcrumbs and lunch plates. The only thing on the table now is Sarah's phone. Blank. Silent. Michael is beside Sarah on one side, Rebecca on the other. Daniel is in the corner, and beneath the table is Barley. She reaches out her foot and strokes his belly. It's soft and warm and even though he's a dog and Abi thought she hated dogs, Barley is the only one now acting normal and she's grateful for that.

A clink of china sounds from the kitchen. Ryan. He's

waiting too. His presence, like the waiting, is impossible to ignore.

'Why don't you call them again?' Michael says, glancing at his watch again.

Abi eyes the shaking of his hand and the sweat shining on his forehead. It's the first time Abi has seen him without a drink in the afternoon, and he looks like a man who badly needs one.

'I tried less than an hour ago,' Sarah replies, running a bony finger across the home screen of her mobile, checking something – her signal, Abi guesses. 'They know we're waiting for it. The receptionist promised to call the moment he has the results.'

Abi's mouth is dry. Her eyes too. She's scared. Petrified. She keeps forgetting to breathe, only realising when her lungs scream for air. She watches two pigeons in the garden, pecking at the lawn before taking flight and disappearing into the sky. The DNA packet under the mattress pushes into her thoughts and she wonders, for what feels like the hundredth time today, if this will work.

'How about another game of something?' Ryan says, leaning against the archway into the kitchen, a mug and a dishcloth in his hands. 'Watched pots and all that.'

Sarah shakes her head.

'I spy,' Daniel says, throwing a wink at Abi, 'with my little eye something that begins with S.'

Rebecca lifts her head up and glances around the room. 'Sun?'

Daniel shakes his head. Rebecca shrugs and returns her focus to her phone.

'Salt,' Michael says, nodding to the glass salt and pepper pots in the centre of the table.

'Sky.' Sarah swipes a finger across the screen of her mobile again.

'No and no,' he says. 'Abi?'

All eyes turn towards her. For the first time since she walked into the police station, Abi feels like the imposter she is.

She runs her tongue over the dry ridges of her lips and swallows. 'Sister,' she whispers.

Daniel's smile widens. He opens his mouth to reply but stops. All eyes fly to the phone on the table, now ringing into the silence.

Sarah snatches it up, fingers fumbling to swipe and accept the call before pressing it to her ear. 'Hello... yes, I'm here... Of course. Twentieth of January 1979.'

Abi stops breathing, struggling to hear over the thumping drum of her pulse in her ears.

The colour drains from Sarah's face. She swallows. The room falls away. It's just Sarah and Abi. Wide eyes staring into her soul, and in that moment Abi knows. She knows it's worked. The DNA is a match.

She expects relief but feels only the same fear that's dogged her for days, months even. She's not Abigail. She doesn't belong in this family. She never did and she never will.

What has she done? What the hell has she done?

# THIRTY-FOUR

## SARAH

'What?' My voice is feeble and distant. 'What did you say?'

The secretary on the phone clears his throat. 'I said the DNA results are a match.'

I hear it, but I can't... The words won't sink in. It's not true. It can't be true.

Abigail is dead. She has to be dead. Otherwise, what have I been doing all these years? Living my life, moving forward. Always forward. The only way to survive was to convince myself that my beautiful little girl with the auburn eyes flecked with gold and the laugh that lit me up inside was dead. Otherwise, how could I stop searching for her? How could I be the mother Daniel and Rebecca needed me to be if I was consumed by the constant questions of where Abigail was, who had her, was she crying, was she being hurt? There was no end in that. Only madness.

I had to tell myself Abigail was dead. It was the most unimaginable cruelty, but I did it for Daniel and Rebecca, to protect them from the pain of losing their sister, to give them the normal life they needed.

A trembling takes hold of me. 'How... certain are you?' I ask.

Their eyes are on me. One, two, three, four, five. Watching me, my face, my reaction. Michael is leaning forward, willing me to look at him, but I don't. I can't. It's a mistake. It has to be a mistake.

'These tests are ninety-nine point nine per cent accurate, Mrs Wick. The two samples you've given us are a parental match. I've got the printouts in front of me. I'll pop them in an envelope and they'll go in the post to you this evening.'

Ninety-nine point nine. The number floats away, another number off to play with its friends in the back of my mind, but his words are stuck. And all I can think of is those first frantic hours in the holiday cottage, before Ryan and the police arrived. When it was just Janie and me and Michael, gripping each other's hands and waiting for the crackle of the PC's radio, waiting to be told that Abigail had been found wandering around by the boat lake or the playground; tearful and tired but otherwise fine. But the radio hadn't crackled. Not with that news anyway. Abigail hadn't been found, she'd been seen – captured on CCTV with a man running to catch a ferry. She'd been taken. The information hadn't fit then, just as this piece doesn't fit now.

'Mrs Wick?' the voice says in my ear.

'Um,' is all I can manage.

'Is there anything else I can help you with?'

I shake my head, freeing tears I didn't know had formed in my eyes and whisper, 'Thank you.'

The phone slips from my hand and lands on Barley's head before clattering to the floor. He sighs but doesn't move. My eyes find Abigail's.

'Mum?' It's only one word but it's enough to convey the excitement, the apprehension, in Rebecca's voice.

DNA doesn't lie.

Abigail is scared. Her eyes are wide, huge O-like things. I'm studying the contours of her face again, just as I've been doing for days now. My breath catches in my throat. I blink and look at her again. Her nose – how did I not notice it before? The way the tip points up a little at the end. Just like Michael's. Just like Daniel's.

Michael starts to stand, his hands gripping the table as if the effort is monumental. 'Let's all take a second—' he starts to say, but I'm already on my feet, moving around the table towards my daughter.

'I... I'm sorry.' The words choke me. 'I... was wrong.'

The tears gush out of me. The river bursting its banks. My shoulders are heaving and my vision shimmers with the water of my tears, but I don't close them; I don't stop staring at her. Abigail.

'I... I told myself you were dead.'

Abigail's expression is now pained with sadness. 'You don't have to—'

'I do.' I drop to my knees beside her. 'I told myself you were dead. I made myself believe it because I couldn't carry on living knowing you were out there somewhere. I couldn't stop imagining all the things that might've been happening to you. I had to think about Rebecca and Daniel. I had to tell myself you were dead. Or they'd have lost a sister and a mother.'

Chairs are scraping from around the table. Michael is standing; so is Daniel.

'I knew it,' Rebecca cries from beside Abigail.

Abigail is up on her feet too, standing over me. For a moment I think she's going to walk away. I know I'd deserve it if she did. The way I've treated my own daughter; the suspicion, the coldness I've shown. Fresh tears flood my eyes.

But Abigail doesn't step away; instead she drops to the floor beside me and hugs me.

My hands touch her back. Loose waves of her hair tickle against my fingers. Her body is warm and I can smell the coconut scent of her shower gel. A hand touches my shoulder, then another. Michael is closing his arms around us both. Then Rebecca is with us, and Daniel.

We stay like that, kneeling on the tiled floor, holding on to each other for what feels like a lifetime. A lifetime of grief and sorrow that flows out of me with every shed tear. It's Michael who unbalances us. Or rather Barley's eagerness to join in.

Michael makes a grunt from behind. An 'Oof' and all of a sudden we're all crying out, all falling backwards into a heap of bodies. My stomach muscles tense, stopping my head from hitting the tiles. Abigail is half on top of me and half on Michael, with Daniel and Rebecca landing either side.

Barley's tongue is warm and wet and unrelenting in its quest to lick all of our faces. I'm no longer crying, but my body is shaking; so is Abigail's. Laughter and yelps from Barley fill the room.

The joy of the moment floods my body and I drink it in; the happiness.

I know there will be challenges ahead of us. It won't all be tears of joy and laughter. I'll have to accept my mistakes. All of them. I'll have to find a way to deal with all the hundreds of ways I've been wrong. But right now, I don't want to think about that. I want to feel. I want to be happy. Because I can. Abigail is home.


'Are you sure you'll be all right?' Ryan asks as he pulls on his jacket. 'I can still pop in tomorrow?' The silver on the edges of his hair and in his beard catches in the light. He looks older than when I saw him on Friday, as if he's lived through a year each day in our home, but then, I imagine I do too.

'There's no need.' I smile and hug my arms to my body. The entrance hall is cool now that the sun has started to set and is no longer spilling warmth through our windows. 'Thank you for all you've done. I don't think I could've made it through these past few days without you here.'

Dark circles surround Ryan's eyes. For the first time, I realise how exhausting his job must be. The line between support and intrusion is thin and by no means is it straight.

'You all have a lot to process. I can help with that.'

'It's OK. Go back to living your life. Honestly, we'll be OK now.'

'Will you call me at least? Let me know how it's going?'

I nod.

'Tomorrow?'

I shrug. 'Sure.'

He pauses as though searching for the next words. 'I hope I haven't overstepped—'

'You've been the friend I needed,' I cut in.

Ryan doesn't want to leave. I can see it in his hesitance to move towards the front door. If he wants reassurances, then I'm happy to give them. He's been my anchor in the storm, but right now I want him to go. Right now, I want to be with my family.

'I can't thank you enough.'

'I don't see many happy endings,' he says after a pause. 'I'm happy for you, Sarah. I care a lot about you; I always have.'

His words hang in the air, causing my heart to beat faster, but I don't want to think about why. I shake my head and drop my gaze to the floor. 'Don't say anything else. Please – don't make this awkward.'

He laughs, short and quiet, forcing my eyes back to his. 'I was going to say' – he smiles – 'don't stop asking questions. There are still a lot of things you don't know. You've been driving yourself crazy with questions. Knowing Abi is your daughter is only one piece of the puzzle.'

Warmth tingles across my cheeks from my mistake. 'It's like a veil's been lifted. I needed to hear the DNA results to see it for myself.'

'Yes, but—'

'I know.' I nod, moving to the front door. 'You're right. There are still questions that need to be asked... and answered. And we'll get to that, but...'

'You want to be with your family.' He smiles, mirroring my thoughts.

'Thank you,' I say again. 'For everything.'

We hug and his body is warm and firm. I step away quickly, ignoring my body's reaction to his touch, and open the front door. Outside, the sun has almost gone and the sky over the house is a smouldering orange.

'Call me tomorrow,' Ryan says as he steps away, and I nod and close the door.

Immediately, the house feels strange without him. Ryan insisted on being here every day since Abigail returned. It was obvious just now that he didn't want to leave us, asking me to call him tomorrow, as though he's expecting me to have something to say other than the happily-ever-after ending rolling out before me.

His words push into my thoughts – 'Don't stop asking questions' – and I wonder if he's seen something. If I've missed something. The doubt and suspicion rise up inside me, but I push them back.

DNA doesn't lie, and there's no way I'll question my daughter again.

\*

THURSDAY

# THIRTY-FIVE

## SARAH

Thursday, 9.40 p.m.

My feet stop on the landing outside Rebecca's door and I listen to the sound of giggling teenage laughter carrying through from the other side. A smile pulls at my mouth at the sound of Abigail's laugh. It's the kind of laugh that starts right down in her belly and ends in her nose with a snort, sending both her and Rebecca into another giggling fit.

I lean on the door frame and close my eyes, allowing the noise to flood through me. I could almost believe that four-year-old Abigail is sitting behind the door.

The house has been filled with laughter since our fall to the floor on Tuesday, and I wonder, with a pang of guilt, if I'd heard Abigail's laugh when she first arrived almost a week ago, would I have behaved differently? Would my belief have been immediate? I like to think yes, but my judgement was fogged, like the windscreen of my car in winter. I couldn't see her.

I couldn't see the cow's lick of hair by her parting that sticks up first thing in the morning before she's brushed it.

'Mummy, when did a cow lick my head?' an almost four-year-old Abigail asked me at bedtime once, lying in the bottom bunk in Daniel's bedroom before she'd decided she wanted her own room. 'Did it lick me when we were on a farm or did it come into the house? How did it get up the stairs?'

I remember the way her forehead had creased with the battle in her little head – should she carry on asking questions or wait for the answers to the ones she'd already asked?

I couldn't see the way Abigail tilted her head to her right when she was listening to someone. It's just a fraction now, the shadow of the way her younger self had tipped her head almost horizontal when she concentrated.

I couldn't see the shape of her nose, just like Michael's. The thickness of her hair – that one's from me. I couldn't see the sweetness within her. I couldn't see my daughter.

A surge of sadness echoes through me. This isn't the constant deep wound of grief I've carried with me for fourteen years but something else that jumps out at unexpected moments. We've missed so much of Abigail's life. I can spend the rest of mine getting to know her again, and there'll still be things I don't know, things she doesn't remember about her childhood that have shaped who she is.

One day I hope she'll tell me more about her time away from us. Now that I can see her clearly, I can see she carries her own emotional scars. I want to help her, but she needs time first. Time to settle in her home and to feel part of it. Time to trust me again.

My hand is out and I'm knocking one, two, three light taps on the door before my thoughts lead me further into the murky sadness.

'Oh my God,' Rebecca is saying with short gasps for air as I stand in the doorway. 'You should be on TV. That is hilarious.' She looks up at me and waves her hands, scrambling up to sitting. For a moment she's laughing too much to say the words I can see her fighting to get out. 'Mum, oh my God, you *have* to hear this. Abi does *the* most wicked impressions.'

I smile and laugh at the pair of them. 'Do you have a moment to talk about tomorrow's interview?'

'Sure,' they chorus before looking at each other and laughing again.

'I just want to make sure you're both happy to do it. I don't want you to feel scared about the fact it's live TV. You won't have to say anything if you don't want to. And just wear normal clothes, jeans and jumpers. We're not dressing up. The questions will mostly be for me and your dad, but Abigail,' I say, staring at her beautiful brown eyes, 'they'll want to hear from you as well.'

'Oh.' The smile on her face remains but it's lost the light behind it.

'Is everything OK?' I search her face, desperate not to be the cause of any more pain. 'I can have a word with the producer and keep the questions light, focused on the future.'

She nods, the light in her eyes returning. 'I'd like that.'

'When will it be over?' Rebecca asks. 'I've got a mock biology test after lunch tomorrow.'

'We should be finished at the studio by ten, so you can head home with your dad and go into school at lunchtime. I need to stay in London for some other press stuff I've promised to do, but I'll get the train back in the afternoon and be home before dinner.'

Rebecca nods and makes a face. 'Guess I'd better do some last-minute cramming,' she sighs.

'You'll ace it,' Abigail says. 'I wish I was half as smart as you.'

Rebecca beams ear to ear, her cheeks blushing red with the compliment. My heart clenches, but not with pain. Even in the short time Abigail has been back, she's boosted something in Rebecca.

Rebecca has always been confident, a seeker of the limelight, but it's always seemed tinged with whispers of desperation – to me at least. She's always been so eager to please. Since Abigail has been here, Rebecca's confidence seems more natural, and the strain that lingered in her eyes has disappeared.

'Don't stay up too late.' I smile at them. 'We have to be out the door and leaving by six. Your dad's planning to do eggy bread before we go.'

'Ewww.' Rebecca pulls another face and sticks out her tongue. 'That's gross, Mum.'

I laugh. 'You both used to love it.'

'Well not anymore. Yuck.'

I step further into the room and kiss the top of Rebecca's head. 'I'll tell him not to bother.'

Abigail steps away from the bed and stands beside me. 'I'd better get some sleep,' she says.

There's a second of awkwardness. I don't know yet how much of it is remnants from my behaviour towards her, and how much is just a seventeen-year-old in a new place, a new home. The second passes and she reaches forward, wrapping her arms around me in a brief embrace.

'Night, Rebecca,' she says, releasing her hold and turning to the door.

'Night,' Rebecca calls back in a silly voice that makes Abigail smile.

In the hallway, Abigail's feet stop; she looks at me. 'Night, Mum.'

She turns quickly and walks into her bedroom. The word no longer grates against me. Instead, I'm filled with hope, and I like it.

'Good night, Abigail,' I whisper.

. . .

I find Michael stretched out on the bed looking at his phone as I enter the bedroom. He looks up and exhales a short laugh as he looks at me.

I smile. 'What?'

He does it again. 'Nothing. You just look... happy.'

'I am.'

We stare at each other for a long moment before Michael slides from the bed and stands. We're a metre away from each other in almost the exact places we stood five years ago when I told him to get out, that our marriage was over.

'Sarah,' he starts, 'I... I just want to say I'm sorry we did the statement without you on Saturday, and I'm sorry that I've been a terrible husband. I'm sorry I ruined us.'

Hurt balloons across my chest. There are tears swimming in my eyes, and I can tell that he means it.

'Is it too late for us?' he asks, voice thick with emotion.

I shake my head. 'I don't know.'

'I still love you. We've been through the worst thing anyone can live through. I know nothing will change overnight, but could we try again? Could we just try? Not for the kids, but for us?'

The hurt pushes through me. Years and layers of it. Hurt for Abigail and for Michael and what he did. But I know deep down that the state of our marriage before his affairs wasn't all his fault. I pushed him away, built up my armour. I couldn't be strong and rely on him, let him in. And Michael needs to be needed. I don't know what I want now, or if what he's asking is possible.

'Please, Sarah,' Michael says, taking a step towards me. 'Could you ever forgive me?'

'I don't know,' I reply at last. I can tell by the way his face falls that it's not the answer he was hoping for. 'But I'm willing to try.'

He smiles. Relieved.

I'm not sure which one of us moves first, but we meet in the middle, his arms wrapping around me and mine him.

'I'm sorry,' he says again.

'I'm sorry,' I whisper, wishing away the sadness threatening to take over. I don't want to be sad anymore. Abigail is home. We can finally be the family I've pretended we are for all these years. It's time to stop pushing everyone away and let people in.

*

FRIDAY

# THIRTY-SIX

## ABI

Friday, 9.26 a.m.

Electricity hums in the air and in the crew with their trendy ripped jeans and headsets, and in the audience hanging on every word. It hums in the two presenters sitting opposite Abi – a man and a woman Abi only recognises from watching the show the previous day. The first, Greg, is a fifty-something dad-like man with silver hair and a belly that looks bigger in real life. The woman, Tina, is younger. A younger version of Sarah. All blonde hair blow-dried to sleek perfection, tanned legs and layers of make-up that shimmer under the hot studio lights.

Michael is talking, his gaze swinging between the presenters and Abi, at the other end of the long red sofa, where she's cushioned between Rebecca and Sarah. Michael is in his element – charming and gracious, smiling in a way Abi's never seen before. But Abi is only half-listening. The electricity is zipping through her too, making it hard to concentrate on Michael's 'life can now move on for all of us' spiel. It's the same blah blah blah they've all been spouting for the last twenty minutes.

Abi likes the buzz inside her, humming and jiggling, dancing. The nerves, drowning out the serpent voice in her head whispering and hissing and stabbing at her with guilt for what's done, what she's doing to this family.

She thought they could be hers. He promised they would be. Funny, kind Rebecca. Daniel with his intuitive way of seeming to know just what to say to her and when. Michael, trying so hard. Even Sarah, now showering Abigail with all the love he promised her.

It's everything she wanted. It's the reason she's travelled halfway around the world and tangled herself in so many lies that she doesn't recognise herself anymore. She thought the DNA results would cement her place in this family. She thought it would put an end to the narrowed eyes, the suspicions, the fear gnawing away at her.

She is Abigail Wick.

Except she isn't. And it's not better at all. It's worse.

The more they accept her, the harder she's finding it to keep up with her lies. The fear has grown too. It's no longer just about him and what he'll do to her if she fails. It's about this family – especially Rebecca, who she's really started to care about – and what he'll do to them too.

What is his plan? It was always about fixing the DNA test, making them believe. They never spoke about afterwards, and that thought alone makes her pulse quicken, her chest tighten. She's exactly where she's supposed to be, but now what?

Greg, the presenter, is saying something to her. Abi homes in on his words as another burst of nerves adds to the rest.

'So what's next for you, Abigail?' Greg asks, leaning forward in his chair as if the answer she gives is the only thing in the world that matters to him.

'Exams, I imagine.' She returns his smile. Sweet and angelic. 'There wasn't much chance for education where I grew up.' She chooses her words carefully, weaving away from any follow-up questions that might involve Jhon and Caroline. She doesn't want to talk about them. 'I'd like to go to school, or college, if I can. After that' – she shrugs – 'I don't know yet. I think I'm pretty good at maths.'

'I think Abigail will be on the telly,' Rebecca chirps from beside her, slipping a hand into Abi's. It's clammy with the heat of the studio and the nerves of live TV.

Rebecca sits up straighter and flashes a wide grin at Abi before turning back to the presenters. Abi's pulse skips a beat. She takes a silent, sharp intake of breath as she sees with crystal-clear clarity what Rebecca is about to say next and there's nothing Abi can do to stop her.

'Really?' Tina and Greg say in unison.

Abi squeezes Rebecca's hand, willing her not to speak, but Rebecca flashes another smile and nods. The electricity humming through her morphs into a fiery panic.

Rebecca nods. 'She'll be on one of those comedy shows. Where they, like, pretend to be famous people. Impressionist stuff. Abi is amazing at it. She's such a good actress. Do your impression of Mum, Abi,' Rebecca says, already laughing.

Abi's face hurts from the pressure of holding her smile in place, of fighting against the urge for her eyes to widen and her head to shake back and forth. Why did she show Rebecca her accents? Abi knows why. She did it because Rebecca was stressed from studying, and tired, and something about a boy she liked ignoring her, and all Abi wanted was to cheer her up, make her smile.

There's only one way out of the hole Rebecca has dug for Abi. She swallows and raises her shoulders, mimicking Sarah's posture. Sarah is laughing now too as Abi clasps her hands together and mimics Sarah's opening to the cookery slot, capturing Sarah's public-school TV voice to perfection.

Laughter travels across the studio, but, under the make-up, fire burns on Abi's cheeks. It's harmless fun now. None of them have twigged what this means. But they will. And soon. Abi risks a glance at Sarah, but she's laughing along, oblivious. How long before she remembers that moment in the kitchen when Abi dropped the accent? How long before she starts to question which voice is real?

'I had no idea you'd seen any of my shows,' Sarah says, composing herself and nudging Abi's shoulder. 'Or how talented you are.'

'YouTube,' Abi mutters, and just for a second she thinks she catches a hesitation in Sarah, a moment when her smile freezes in place and a question plays behind her eyes.

'She can do anyone,' Rebecca says. 'Any actor, any voice, you name it, Abigail can do it.'

Abi tries to keep the smile in place, but it's hard now. Her body tenses. Freezes. He's watching her. She can feel his eyes on her. Sharp, hating eyes. His anger slices right through her skin and all the way to the pit of her stomach. Abi let her guard down, sharing too much with Rebecca. He'll want to know what other secrets might have slipped out. He'll want to remind her of everything she has to lose.

'What a talent.' Greg laughs. 'Well, it's been a pleasure to have you all on the show this morning. We've only got a few more minutes.' Greg fixes his gaze on Daniel, sat the other side of Rebecca. 'And I'm sure our viewers at home would like to hear from you, Daniel. The statement you read earlier this week was incredibly heartfelt. It must be amazing to have Abigail home again after so long apart?'

'It is,' Daniel says. 'It feels incredible to have my sister home. I wanted to read that statement because I wanted to do something for my parents, especially my mum. As I said in my statement on Saturday, Mum has been a rock for all of us over the years, and it's taken a long time for me to see that, and to appreciate it.'

Daniel leans forward, propping his elbows onto his knees,

his eyes fixing on Sarah. 'I love you, Mum.' Then he stands and so does Sarah.

'I love you too,' she says as they hug.

'All right, all right.' Daniel pats her back a moment later, his cheeks red. 'This is live TV, you know?'

Another spattering of laughter fills Abi's ears. The presenter is speaking again, the interview almost over, but she can't think beyond what just happened. He'll be so angry.

What will happen now? What will he do to her? The questions knot her insides.

# THIRTY-SEVEN

## ABI

The interview ends and straight away two producers are shepherding them away from the set and the cameras and the audience and into a corridor. A dizziness is spinning in Abi's head. She's shaking, uncertain how to move forward, to carry on with the fear gripping her so tight.

The lies feel suddenly so flimsy, like the silver layer on the scratch cards Jhon used to love. All it needs is a coin, a sharp finger, to expose who she really is.

They step into the green room – a long room with sofas and armchairs, and a dressing table with a mirror. There's a table to one side with a coffee machine and a plate of flaky pastries and chocolate muffins topped with fat chocolaty chunks someone has refilled since they left for the interview. On the wall a TV is playing. Abi glances up to see the two hosts have moved on, talking to a reality TV star she vaguely recognises.

'Abigail,' Sarah says, touching her arm, 'you did really well. How did you find it?'

Sarah is beaming at Abi. She looks younger now, Abi thinks. There's an energy to her, a glimpse of the person she was before.

'It was fine.' She forces herself to smile. 'I couldn't do it every day.'

'Not many can,' a voice says from behind Sarah.

'Don!' Sarah spins around, hugging the man beside her. 'I didn't know you'd be here.' She turns back to Abi. 'Abi, this is my agent, Don.'

Abi keeps her smile in place, shaking the hand of the bulldog-like man standing before her. There's something intimidating about him that rattles Abi, and she finds herself pulling her hand away, stepping back.

'You're a natural in front of the camera,' Don says to her, his gaze piercing.

'Are you trying to sign my daughter now?' Sarah shakes her head but she's smiling.

'Just paying her a compliment. Look,' he says, dropping an arm over Sarah's shoulder, 'this is all on the q.t. but a certain someone' – he flicks his eyes towards the set as he speaks – 'will be going on maternity leave in the autumn. They're looking for a stand-in to co-host the show for a few months. Libby just told me. She wants to know if you'll consider it. They had you-know-who lined up for it, but after the coke stuff came out, they want to go a different way.'

'And they want me?' Sarah's voice hits somewhere between joy and disbelief. She glances at Abi, her eyes shining. 'I guess. Give me a few days to think about it, and talk it over with Michael and the kids.'

Don nodded. 'Of course. But think about this too – you've spent over a decade doing what's right for your family. Now you can think about what's right for you. This can be your time. It's not too late.'

'OK. I'll think about it.'

'Just one other thing to ask.' He glances to Abi, winking at her with sharp blue eyes before refocusing his on Sarah. 'The

*Strictly* producers want to know if you'll consider coming in for a chat?'

'Don, no.' Sarah laughs again, shaking her head in a way that makes her hair swish back and forth. 'I cannot dance, and I will not be their token geriatric.'

'Hardly a geriatric, my dear.'

'Any female contestant over thirty-five is considered a geriatric. Sorry, Don. I know you'd love me to do it, but it's a no.'

'Fair enough. You know I've got to ask. Look, I've got another meeting around the corner. You all set for the interviews?'

Sarah groans but Abi can tell she doesn't mean it. 'Yes. I'll call you later.'

Don nods to Abi again before stepping away, leaving her unsettled, watched.

'All set?' Michael calls across the room, already shrugging on his jacket. 'I need to get this one back for her biology exam.' He throws an arm over Rebecca's shoulder and hugs her. 'You did brilliantly, kiddo. Everyone did.'

'Yes. Go. I've got twenty back-to-back interviews to get to,' Sarah says laughing.

Michael steps to Sarah. He pauses, then touches her arm. Abi waits for her to jerk away, but instead she leans into his touch. Rebecca catches Abi's eye and rolls her eyes, grinning too.

'Will you be OK?' he asks.

'Of course,' she replies.

Daniel steps into the room just as Abi is thinking that she did this. Through the guilt and the fear, she can see the wounds healing, the love returning to these people. Does that make up for all she's done? She hopes so.

'Mum,' Daniel says. 'Did you know Ryan was in the audience?'

'Is he? I had no idea.'

'He called me over to see how it's going.'

'That was nice of him to come.' Sarah's gaze moves to the door as though she expects him to appear.

'Dad,' Rebecca says in a pleading voice, 'can we go? I don't want to be late.'

Michael claps his hands. 'Yes, of course. Let's move. Ready, Abi?'

She nods, craving the fresh air and to be away from this building.

Sarah leans in, kissing Abi's cheek and filling her senses with the floral scent of her perfume. 'I'll call when I'm on the train. Michael, can you pick me up from the station? It'll be before dinner, hopefully.'

'I will,' Daniel says.

Sarah's smile widens as she looks to him. 'Thank you, Daniel. And for what you said in the interview. It means...' Her voice falters. 'It means a lot.'

'Mum, Dad.' Rebecca waves her phone in front of them. 'Can I go for a sleepover at Ellie's tonight?'

'Oh' – Sarah looks to Michael – 'it's quite short notice, Becca.'

'Please. I really want to. Some of the other girls in our class are going as well. We're ordering Domino's. And all the mock exams will be done.'

'She'll be fine,' Michael says, pulling Sarah to his side and tucking his arm around her tiny waist. 'It'll do her good.'

'OK.' She nods. 'Sorry, of course it's fine. I should be home in time to drop you round to Ellie's this evening.'

'No need.' Rebecca grins, already halfway to the door. 'I'll go straight from school. I can borrow pyjamas and stuff from Ellie.'

They all move, hurrying now to leave the studio – Daniel and Rebecca striding ahead, followed by Michael and then Abi and Sarah. They walk down one corridor and then another before reaching a flight of stairs. Five minutes later, they're standing in the brightness of a day that promises to be warm but hasn't quite got there yet.

Sarah hugs Abi again and this time the fear overwhelms her. Panicked tears sting at her eyes. They can't see the mistake she's made or the fragility of this new happy existence they're all living in. She might not know him very well, but she knows he won't let this go, just as she knows at some point today or tomorrow, when Sarah has a moment to herself to think, she'll replay the impression Abi did and the seeds of doubt will grow again.

'I could come with you to the interviews.' The words rush out sounding as desperate as Abi feels. 'We can spend some time together on the train that way too.'

'No.' Michael's reply is quick. 'You should come with us.'

Sarah shoots Michael a look, confused by his outburst, Abi thinks. Then Sarah smiles and sweeps Abi's hair from where it's dropped over her face. 'Of course it would be lovely to spend more time with you but your dad is right. I'm not quite ready to put you in front of the tabloid reporters. It won't be like it was this morning. I don't have any sway on what they'll ask. Better you go with your dad and I'll see you later on.'

Abi nods and allows Michael to guide her towards the car park.

One thought begins to circle her head. The same whispered thought she had stepping into the police station a week ago. The same thought she had when Sarah's phone rang with the DNA results. But this time it isn't a whisper, a hint, a suggestion. It's a loud ringing alarm, pulsing one word into her thoughts.

Run.

# THIRTY-EIGHT

## SARAH

Friday, 10.29 a.m.

The air is cool in the shade of the buildings as I make my way through the side streets of Waterloo. The buildings are packed together here – giant concrete lumps that stop the sun from reaching the pavements. It's a different world to the sleek glass and grand Victorian architecture of the City on the other side of the river.

There are people here and there. Office workers queuing out of a sandwich shop, a delivery man on a bike. I'm not alone and yet I feel weary, on edge, as though someone is watching me.

It's apprehension for the press interviews, I decide, ducking along a narrow side road with a red-brick wall on one side and grey concrete on the other. I'm in no rush. I have half an hour before I meet the first journalist, and the Savoy is only across the river, but my pace is still quick; London pace.

My thoughts turn over the live interview. It went well. No awkward moments, no slip-ups, no mention of Michael's scandal. And yet something is nagging in the back of my mind. I can still feel the tightness of Abigail's touch against my body, her plea to stay with me. She seemed... I'm not sure. Scared is the word that springs into my thoughts. But why?

I'm almost out of the shadows of the buildings. Ahead, I can see the pedestrianised South Bank and the river beyond, tourists, people. But the noise of a carousel and the shouts of a street entertainer aren't enough to mask the footsteps coming quick from behind me. I throw a glance over my shoulder and stop dead.

'Hello, Sarah.'

I gasp. The woman in front of me is tall and slender. Her black braids are streaked with grey, but otherwise she looks exactly the same as when I last saw her nearly fourteen years ago.

'Janie. What are you doing here?'

'You've been calling me.' Her head tilts up a little, chin jutting out in the way I remember so well. Janie's sign of defiance. 'I heard you were doing this interview and I came to tell you to stop calling me and to leave me alone.'

'You came all this way to tell me to leave you alone? Why didn't you just do that on the phone instead of ignoring me?'

'I...' Her chin drops. She shrinks back a little as though she isn't sure of the answer.

My body is still pumping with the adrenaline of the live interview, so I ignore the dozen questions hopping into my thoughts. I ignore the suspicion and the anger and the desire to scream at Janie, to grab her by the arms and shake her until she tells me why she left me that day when I needed her more than ever. Instead, I point to the river. 'Shall we find a bench?'

She nods and we walk in silence.

I find a quiet bench in the sunshine, tucked at the back of a slice of green lawn behind the vast white structure of the London Eye. We sit side by side, facing out, pretending to watch the slow rotation of the glass bubbles.

'Why were you calling me?' Janie asks the moment we're sat down.

'I honestly don't know,' I reply. 'You know about Abigail coming home, I assume?'

'Yes, I saw the news.'

'At first we weren't sure if it was her, but Michael and Daniel and Rebecca... well, it felt like I was the only one questioning her and I wanted to speak to someone else who knew Abigail. It was stupid. But then you didn't answer and I started to wonder why that was and why you cut yourself out of my life... when I needed you most.' Despite the years, the hurt clogs my throat.

I thought I'd moved on from Janie, but all the *look forward not back* mantras in the world can't undo a friendship as close as ours was.

There's a pause that stretches out for so long that I turn my head a fraction to look at the side profile of her face. Close up, I notice the fine lines around her eyes and the anxiety swimming in them.

'Why did you disappear on me?' I ask again.

'Because I'm weak,' she whispers. 'I'm a coward, Sarah. Abigail's abduction broke my heart, and seeing your devastation, I couldn't... I just couldn't be around you. It was too hard. I started getting these panic attacks anytime I went to call you. In the end, I had to think about myself and what was best for me. I'm so sorry.'

A single tear escapes from my eye and I blot it with my finger before it can ruin the careful layers of foundation painted on by a make-up artist at the ITV studio this morning.

'Was Phil in a car accident?' I ask.

'What?' She sounds surprised.

'You told us that evening, when we were in the cottage waiting for news on Abigail's abduction, that you had to leave because Phil had been in a car accident.'

She gasps as though remembering and then shakes her head. 'I'm sorry.'

I let the sun hit my face and her words sink in. I think of the questions I asked myself earlier in the week, wondering if Janie was involved in Abigail's abduction. I was just searching for an explanation that made sense to me. Something more than my best friend being weak and selfish. But listening to and looking at her now, I know it was nothing more than that.

It still hurts but not too badly – the ache of a fading bruise when touched. I survived without Janie's help. I picked myself up and did it on my own, and maybe if she'd been there, I would have relied on her too much; I wouldn't have been able to carry on the same way I did.

'You have a daughter?' I ask.

'Yes. How did you know?'

'I called your old house.'

'Oh. We moved shortly after adopting Raya. She... she came to us when she was four and... it was hard. I worried constantly about what could happen to her, so we gave up London and our jobs and we moved to Anglesey, off the coast of Wales. I own a pottery painting studio and Phil does a bit of farming. Raya's going to Cardiff University this September to study engineering.'

Everything about Janie is lighter when she talks of her daughter, and despite everything, I'm glad for her.

She pulls a phone from her pocket, unlocks her screen and turns it towards me. The photo is of Phil and Janie, laughing at the camera with a teenage girl between them wearing a red football kit and grinning at the camera.

'She just scored the winning goal in the cup,' Janie says, smiling now, before tucking her phone away.

Janie takes a breath and turns in the seat to face me. 'I didn't really come all this way to tell you to leave me alone. I came here to apologise for being the worst friend to you when you needed me. It might have been the only way I could cope back then, but I will never forgive myself for not being stronger for you.'

We sit for a beat, neither knowing where to go from here. It's not a reconciliation. However much Janie might be sorry, however much I might be able to forgive her for leaving me when I needed her most, our friendship cannot be rekindled.

'It's unbelievable that Abigail has come home after all this time. It's a miracle. I'm so pleased for you, Sarah. You deserve to be happy. Everything will be OK from now on. I just know it.'

'I'm not sure it will be.'

My words surprise me, and I'm drawn back to the roller-coaster of emotions I've felt over the last seven days. I was so sure the nervous teenage girl stepping through my front door wasn't my daughter. Daniel and Rebecca, and even Michael, were so much quicker to accept her, to believe, than I was. But the DNA test came back and everything changed, and I've been so happy.

And yet... there's a feeling deep in my core that something isn't right. I've been ignoring it for days, but something about the interview has sharpened the feeling. I'm just not sure what or why.

'What do you mean?' Janie asks, startling me from my thoughts.

I shake my head, remembering that this woman beside me might feel familiar and safe, but she's no longer my best friend. Besides, I don't even know what I would say, even if I could.

'Oh, nothing. Just all the press. I don't know if they'll ever leave us alone.' I stand quickly. 'I need to go. I've got interviews lined up with the papers.'

Janie stands too and we stare at each other for a moment. Hugging is wrong. So is a handshake. In the end, I lift my hand in a half-wave and step back. 'Thank you for coming to London to see me.'

'Goodbye, Sarah.'

Only when I reach the centre of the bridge do I stop for a moment and take a long breath in and out. Janie's appearance, and my own confession that something isn't right, has knocked me, and I need a moment to gather myself before the interviews.

Waterloo Bridge, like the buildings I've passed, is a functional concrete structure, but the views are beautiful. To my right, the sun is high over the dome of St Paul's Cathedral and the City surrounding it. Its bright-yellow rays glint on the glass of the Leadenhall Building in the distance. The sun is warm, dispelling the mist that covered the fields and the city on our journey early this morning.

Below the bridge, the river looks calm – black, and dark blue in places, with tiny triangle waves that lap against each other.

My phone buzzes in my bag and I rummage under my heels and my purse in the stupidly large shoulder bag I use when I'm in London.

It'll be Rebecca or Michael, wondering if I want anything from Waitrose on the way home. Or Don, wanting to invite me to a restaurant opening. I saw the spark in his eyes earlier. He wants to relaunch my career, ride the coat-tails of Abigail's homecoming. I am no longer the tragic mother who lost her daughter; I am the woman whose daughter came home. The public will want to revel in the magic of it, and Don is five steps ahead as usual.

As I free my phone from my bag it reminds me that I should buy Abigail a phone. She hasn't asked for one. She hasn't asked for anything, but I'm sure it would be nice for her. I've seen her watching Rebecca and Daniel tap away on theirs. She'll need a bank account too, and an allowance. A list begins to form in my mind as I stare at the text on my screen. It's from Ryan.

*Well done on the interview!! I was in London for a meeting
and thought I'd swing by to watch. You were all great!*

I think back to Abigail's impression of me. It was brilliant. I
didn't realise she'd watched any of my shows. I shouldn't be
surprised. And if I'm honest with myself, then deep down one
of the reasons I pushed to stay in front of the camera, a reason I
never told a living soul, was because I hoped that one day a little
girl eating her cereal or playing with her toys would turn on the
TV and see me, her mother, and she'd tell someone. It was a
stupid dream, but it was there along with all the other reasons.

I start to walk again, slower now. A feeling is creeping over
me. Something about Abigail. That hug, the pleading I now
think I saw in her eyes, and the way her voice changed so effort-
lessly to mimic my tone and accent.

I hear Rebecca's voice in my thoughts. 'She's such a good
actress.'

A question begins to form, pushing out from a hidden part
of my mind. It's on the tip of my tongue and I'm just about to
reach out, grasp it with both hands, when my phone rings with
an unknown number.

'Hello?'

'Mrs Wick?' a woman's voice asks me.

'Yes,' I reply.

'My name is Detective Constable Cara Swain. I'm part of
the Metropolitan police force and I work out of Bethnal Green
Police Station. I was the officer who first spoke with Abelia
Pérez last Friday.'

The officer pauses and I wonder what I'm supposed to say.

'OK,' I say, and then, 'Her name is Abigail.'

'I've been following up on some of the information' – she
pauses for a second and then continues – 'Abi gave us last week,
and I'd very much like to speak to her again in the presence of
you or your husband please.'

'That's not a problem. When were you thinking?' My mind is moving forward to next week. Perhaps Abigail would like to come up to watch one of the *Loose Women* shows. Michael too. We can have lunch first and swing by the police station on the way home. The thought sends a burst of love and hope through my body.

Abigail is home. Everything has changed. I have changed.

'Today,' the detective replies. 'As soon as possible.'

The first sense of worry worms through my body. 'Oh, right. Is it that urgent? Because I'm afraid you've just missed them. We've all been in London for a press thing, but Michael and the kids have gone back to Essex already.'

'Perhaps you could phone them and ask them to turn around? It's important that we speak with Abi, and with you and Michael. There are some' – she pauses again – 'inconsistencies in Abi's story that we'd like to clear up.'

'Inconsistencies? Like what?' My tone is curt, harsher than I intend, but my instinct is to protect my daughter. I don't know yet what I'm protecting her from, but I sense it in me – an innate force.

'These aren't details I can discuss over the phone,' she says. 'It would be better to speak face to face.'

Whatever it is this detective wants to know, I don't want Abigail to be ambushed with it. The relationship, the trust we've built over the last few days is delicate, the silk of a spider's web. I can't risk damaging it by dragging her to a police station to be questioned.

'Why don't I come in this afternoon?' I reply, reaching the end of the bridge and darting across the road. 'Maybe there are some details I can help you with. If it really is as urgent as you say, then I'll drive Abigail back to London myself.'

'It would be better if we could meet with Abi as soon as possible.'

I feel myself waver under the officious voice on the other

end of the phone, but then I picture the shell-shocked expression on Abigail's face after the interview this morning.

'I'm sorry,' I reply in a tone that says otherwise, 'but Abigail has had a rocky week, mostly because of me. She needs to rest. I'm not prepared to make her sit down in a police interview room and be grilled because of a few inconsistencies. So you can either meet with me this afternoon and all of us next week, or—'

'What time?' the detective cuts in before I can finish my threat.

'Three thirty.'

'I'll see you then, Mrs Wick. Bethnal Green Police Station. Ask for DC Swain at the front desk.'

There's a brief pause and she's gone.

I scroll through my contacts until I find Michael's name. My finger hovers over the call symbol, but I change my mind. Our relationship is also a delicate thread waiting to be broken.

If I call Michael, then he might agree with the detective and take Abigail straight to the police station, and I don't want that for her. I shield my phone from the sun and fire off a text to Daniel and Michael instead.

*Popping into Bethnal Green Police Station on the way home for quick chat with a detective about Abigail's visit last week. Nothing to worry about. Will grab a taxi home from the station x*

I'm late, I realise, dropping my phone back into my bag and picking up my pace. The first journalist will be waiting.

Inconsistencies. The word lodges in my thoughts. What kind of inconsistencies? The answer doesn't matter, I realise. Abigail is seventeen, a kid. Even if she wasn't hurt – and I say a silent prayer that that's not one of DC Swain's inconsistencies – even if her life was normal, she's still had to cope with the deaths of the people who raised her. Still had to come to terms with the lies they told her. So what if she made a mistake when she spoke to the police? I'm sure there's a good reason. I'm sure when we give Abigail the trust and the time to explain, we'll understand.

I think back to my accusation: 'You're not my daughter.' It stings my heart and burns my cheeks to remember. I push the memory away as I switch back into my heels. All that matters is the future we have together.

I rake my fingers through my hair and pull back my shoulders before stepping into the foyer of the hotel. There's nothing the detective can say that will change anything for me. My daughter is home. I will do anything to protect her.

---

*It's time.*

*Time to end this. Time to go back to where it all began.*

*To pull off the mask I've been hiding behind and show them all the monster beneath; what they made me.*

*It's time for all of us to pay for what we did that day.*

# PART III

# THIRTY-NINE

## SARAH

Friday, 3.55 p.m.

I'm late. It is almost four by the time I step out of the Tube at Bethnal Green. My head is pounding. A combination of too much coffee and the constant effort of being on my guard, of smiling and evading the questions I wouldn't answer. The afternoon was intense and there was no time to think about Abigail or DC Swain's inconsistencies.

The street is busy with parents and children, pushchairs and scooters. I watch them for a moment, seemingly oblivious to the thrum of traffic. The air smells of fried chicken from a takeaway place across the road. A group of teenagers Rebecca's age are gathered outside, eating from boxes while staring at their phones.

I open Google Maps and follow the blue line the three minutes to the police station, and now that I'm here, standing at the bottom of the steps, the worry is back. What did the detective mean by inconsistencies? What am I walking into?

Above the door is the CCTV camera Abigail looked into a week ago. It took so much courage for her to leave her home, to travel halfway around the world and walk through the doors ahead of me. The thought powers me forward. One, two, three, four steps and I'm standing in a small waiting area. There's a young woman, with a toddler on her hip, talking to the desk sergeant about a stolen pushchair.

I'm about to take a seat when a door to one side opens and Ryan is standing there in a blue shirt and grey trousers. He smiles and beckons me over.

'Hi,' I say. 'What are you—'

'DS Howard called me at lunchtime about new evidence. He said you were coming here, and as I was in London anyway, I thought I might be able to help.' He motions for me to step through the door.

I catch the spice of his aftershave as I pass through the doorway. It's only been three days since I last saw Ryan, but it feels like weeks. So much has changed. I've changed. I think of our final hug goodbye and the heat it unleashed in me, and then I think of Michael and the promise we made to try. It's early days but already I sense a thawing. It's in the way we look at each other when we talk now, and the touch of an arm or a hand as we pass each other. It's too early to know if we have any kind of future together, but it's a start.

'Come on,' Ryan says, 'it's this way.' He pushes the door closed behind me and I follow him along a grey corridor.

The niggling worry expands like a black parachute, collapsing over me. 'Ryan, what's going on? Do you know?'

Ryan frowns, the concern pulling at his features. 'It's about Abi. She's—'

Before he can finish, a door opens beside us and a woman appears. 'Mrs Wick,' she says in a voice I recognise, 'I'm Cara Swain; we spoke on the phone.'

I pull my gaze away from Ryan. What was he about to say?

DC Swain takes my hand in hers. Like her voice, her grip is

officious – cool and firm. She's wearing a navy trouser suit with a navy silk blouse.

'Would you like to take a seat?' She steps back to reveal a meeting room with a long, oval table and ten or so chairs spaced around it. My eyes are drawn to the two whiteboards at the other end of the room. Both are blank, but they sit on hinged frames that make me wonder what information is on the other side.

A bitter taste fills my mouth. Too much coffee, or maybe it's nerves. I have the sense of standing before a curtain that's about to be pulled back to reveal... What? I don't know.

'What's going on?' I ask, throwing a pleading look at Ryan. His presence is suddenly unnerving. For the first time it occurs to me that he was there the day Abigail was taken. He was there last week when she returned. And he is here now.

The detective motions towards a chair on the opposite side of the table. 'Please sit down. I'd like to ask you a few questions if I may – and show you something.'

I do as I'm told and wait for Ryan to sit beside me. Instead, he sits a seat away from me at the head of the table, in the centre point between DC Swain and myself. The seating seems deliberate and I wonder if they planned it in advance. Ryan isn't on my side. He isn't against me either, but he's not with me. Why?

'Would you like a drink? Some water?' she asks.

I shake my head. My insides are tangled in a heap of ropes, tight and knotted. 'Would someone please explain to me why I'm here?'

'Mrs Wick— May I call you Sarah?' She continues without waiting for a reply. 'First of all, I should explain that your daughter's case is being handled by Suffolk Police. I could have, or should have I suppose, passed Abelia's appearance here on Friday to a case officer in Suffolk to follow up with, but there was something about Abelia that didn't sit right with me. So I've been investigating parts of her story myself—'

'It's Abigail,' I cut in. 'Her name isn't Abelia; it's Abigail.'

DC Swain raises her eyebrows and continues as if I haven't spoken. 'The reason I wanted to meet with... Abi today is to go over some holes that have appeared in her story.'

'Like what?'

'Before I start, it's very important that we get hold of Abi. When was the last time you spoke to her?'

'This morning when we said goodbye after the interview. It must have been just after ten. Michael drove her home with Rebecca and Daniel.'

DC Swain nods, scribbling a note on a piece of paper in front of her. 'I've been calling your home phone and Michael's mobile all afternoon with no answer.'

'Maybe they stopped somewhere on the way back.' I shrug. 'Or they're busy. I'm sure there's a reason.'

'Would you mind trying to call from your mobile? Michael may answer if he knows it's you calling.'

I hesitate, the desire to protect battling against wanting to do as I'm told and help the investigation.

Ryan leans forward and touches my hand. His fingers are warm next to mine. 'This is important, Sarah.'

It's the final push I need and so I try Michael's mobile. It clicks straight to voicemail. Daniel's is the same. 'Their mobiles must be off, or out of signal. Why is this so urgent?'

DC Swain nods. 'I'll get to that in a moment if I may. First of all, I want to ask you about the DNA test.'

'What about it?'

'Perhaps you could start by telling me what you remember about the test? Ryan has already told me that you all did the mouth swabs yourselves, but he doesn't remember seeing Abigail do hers.'

'Of course she did it,' I reply. 'We were all standing in the kitchen together. You were there, Ryan.' I shoot him a look.

'I was talking to the technician. I wasn't watching,' he says.

It's a fight not to scream at this woman to tell me what she knows. It feels like we're doing a dance that I can't hear the music to. I'm out of step. Stumbling.

DC Swain flicks her cool gaze to Ryan then back to me. 'What was the order? Who did the test first?'

Frustration begins to wind through me, but I force my mind back to last week. 'Michael was first. Then me, then Abigail. Why?'

'You definitely put your sample in the bag?' she asks.

'Yes.'

'Who sealed the bag?' DC Swain asks.

'I don't know. Abigail, I guess. Why? What difference does it make?'

'Are you aware that the lab only examined two samples: Michael's and Abi's?'

'No.' I shake my head. 'That's not true. They must have mine too. They said on the phone, it's a match. They said...' I pause, wading through the emotions of the afternoon three days ago when I got my daughter back. My life back. 'The receptionist said the two samples were a match. My DNA and Michael's matched Abigail's.'

'I'm afraid that isn't the case.'

'Maybe there was an issue with my sample,' I say, looking between the detective and Ryan, feeling stupid but not knowing why. 'I remember the technician, I can't remember his name, he said to seal the bag quickly or the sample becomes degraded. Maybe I didn't seal it properly. Either way, I don't see what difference it makes. Whether Abigail's DNA was compared to mine and Michael's or just Michael's, the results are a match. She's our daughter.'

DC Swain reaches for a stack of papers on the table beside her. I watch her movement. Calm. Controlled. I have the sense of standing by the river on that cold wet night a week ago, the ground slippery and dangerous beneath my feet.

'As I said, Sarah, I've been liaising with Suffolk Police, who originally handled your daughter's case. They provided me with a copy of the original file, which includes a DNA sample that was take from Abigail's toothbrush during the investigation.'

Confusion spins in my mind. Half of me is still replaying the revelation about the DNA – why was my DNA not tested? Why does it matter who sealed the bag or what order we did it in? The other is following DC Swain's train of thought. Is she purposely trying to catch me off guard?

I don't have time to formulate an answer before the detective slides two pieces of paper across the table. The first is a graph with peaks and lines that make no sense to me.

'This is the DNA profile from the original investigation,' she says. 'Abigail's DNA taken in 2009.'

The second piece of paper is a photocopy of a photograph. It's grey apart from the blue *Thomas the Tank Engine* toothbrush in the centre. Abigail's toothbrush. The walls of the room close in. The insides of my cheeks tingle; my stomach turns. I swallow hard, fighting back the grief that hits me.

Somewhere in the very back of my mind, beneath all the layers of guarding I use to protect myself, I knew Abigail's toothbrush was blue. Her favourite colour along with red. She loved *Thomas the Tank Engine*, preferring to wear blue Thomas pants over the pink ones with Peppa Pig or Ben and Holly on. I reach out a hand and touch the piece of paper, fighting the desire to cry.

DC Swain's voice is gentle now. 'Abigail's toothbrush was taken for DNA.'

I nod.

'In case a comparison with clothing needed to be made or...'

'A body,' I whisper the word she's dancing around.

It's DC Swain's turn to nod. 'Yes.'

She's watching me, watching my expression. I don't know what the DC sees in it, but whatever it is, she continues. 'DS

Howard from Essex Police forwarded me the DNA test results you had done this week. He received a copy of them under your instruction, I believe.'

I nod again and take the white folded sheet DC Swain holds out to me. It's another graph. The same as the first, but the quality is better. The lines on the graph are sharper, the ink quality of the printer better.

'Please look closely at these two graphs.'

My eyes float back and forth between the pages. The lines blur under my scrutiny. 'I don't know what I'm supposed to be seeing.'

'This piece of paper is the DNA profile from the toothbrush – Abigail's DNA – taken fourteen years ago. This second piece of paper is the DNA profile from Abi, taken on Saturday.'

'So?' I ask, looking again between the spikes of the graph.

'They're not a match,' DC Swain says.

'What? I don't... but they are. The lab called us. They said it was ninety-nine point nine per cent accurate.'

'Abelia Pérez's DNA is a paternal match to Michael. He is her father. But Abelia's DNA is not a match to the DNA profile taken from your daughter's toothbrush fourteen years ago. I'm sorry, Sarah, but Abelia Pérez is not Abigail Wick; she's not your daughter.'

The noise of the wind across the fields roars loud in my ears. I think back to Tuesday, to the flood of emotion pushing through my body. How much joy I've felt this week. How alive. Snatched away from me in seconds. It's a mistake. It has to be a mistake.

# FORTY

## SARAH

A silence falls over us, disturbed only by the rustle of papers in the file DC Swain is opening.

'I don't understand.' I shake my head, freeing a tear that rolls slowly down the side of my face. 'What do you mean exactly? How can her DNA be a match to us but not to Abigail? That's what you're saying, isn't it?'

Ryan stands, reaching for a bottle of water and a glass and placing them in front of me. I think he might sit down beside me, take my hand, but he doesn't. He returns to his seat as I nod my thanks.

'Everyone's DNA is unique. A personal fingerprint of what makes them who they are. Our DNA is an equal blend of the DNA from our parents, and their DNA is made up of an equal blend from their parents. So,' she continues, tapping a pen against the notebook in front of her, 'if we compare the DNA profiles of a child and a parent, they'll have half the markers you see on this graph in common, and twenty-five per cent of the markers in common with that of their grandparents. Does that make sense?'

I nod. 'Abigail has half of my DNA and half of Michael's.' I take a sip of water. The cold liquid sliding down my throat almost gets stuck on the lump of emotion now lodged there.

'Exactly. Now, I'm not a DNA expert,' DC Swain says, 'but a colleague of mine is. I showed her the two profiles of Abigail in 2009 and Abelia Pérez just to be sure that they were from two different sources. She confirmed this to be the case, but when she studied the two profiles side by side, she said the results had' – DC Swain pauses for a moment and glances at a scribbled note in the margin of a page in front of her – 'some similar genetic markers.'

'So what are you saying?' All of a sudden my voice is loud, almost a shout. Exasperation curls inside me.

'I'm saying that the DNA profile of the girl who walked into this police station last week' – DC Swain pulls out the CCTV still of Abi taken from the steps of the police station – 'has twenty-five per cent of the same genetic markers in common with the DNA profile from Abigail's toothbrush that the police took from your holiday home fourteen years ago. This girl' – she taps the photograph again – 'is not Abigail, but she is related to her.'

'How is that possible?' I look between the woman and Ryan, waiting for the information to slot into place in my mind. It's there. Just out of reach. Abi's DNA is a paternal match to Michael. 'You're saying she's a half-sister to Abigail? That Michael has another child?'

'Yes. That's what we believe these results tell us. Does Michael have any other children that you know of?'

'No. I'd know if he had any other children, and he doesn't. There's been a mistake somewhere. Surely you must see that? Abigail is home. She's my daughter.' My voice is weak, pleading. A last-ditch attempt to go back to five minutes ago when my daughter was home at last. My gaze flicks between DC Swain and Ryan. Another tear escapes from the corner of my eye.

'Sarah.' Ryan reaches across the table. His voice is low and I know he's trying to calm me down. It doesn't work. 'Up until Tuesday, you were so adamant it wasn't Abigail. It was only the DNA test that made you think otherwise. If we take the DNA off the table – do you still believe she's your daughter?'

'Yes.' I blurt out the word but quickly shake my head. 'No. I don't know. So Abelia is Michael's daughter but not mine?'

'Your DNA wasn't compared, so I obviously can't say that, but my theory is that your sample was stolen on Saturday so that no comparison could be made, because one or both of them knew that a comparison with your DNA wouldn't be a match.'

'Stolen? By who?'

'I'm afraid we don't know that yet. All I can say is that it was someone who had access to the DNA samples before the bag was sealed.

The list of suspects is short, I realise. Michael and Abi were the only ones stood by the island while we did the tests. Ryan and Rebecca and Daniel were in the kitchen but I don't remember them coming near us.

Michael and Abi. Father and daughter.

'The two samples are a match,' I say, the words now taking on a new meaning. 'Michael's and... the girl's,' I finish, unable now to use her name.

'Yes. And there's more,' DC Swain says. 'We also believe Abelia is being helped by someone.'

I gasp. I thought it was paranoia on that first day, that first accusation. *You're not my daughter.* I felt certain she was after something from us, and I was right. But what? 'Who?' I ask.

'Sarah, can you think of anyone who might wish your family harm?'

'Um...' I shake my head. 'No, I don't think so.'

'Have you ever had a stalker? Anyone ever written into the show?'

I start to shake my head again but then stop. 'There was someone.'

'Who?' Ryan asks.

'It was five years ago though. Just after Michael's affairs became public,' I say, and despite everything, heat flushes on my face. 'A man knocked on the door while the children were at school. He started screaming at me and Michael, saying that we'd ruined his life. He was the husband of a woman Michael had slept with. She left him after that, and he blamed Michael and me. He said he'd had his whole life taken away from him. But Michael called the police and they spoke to him and he never came back. I don't even know his name.'

DC Swain makes a note before she flips open the cover of an iPad and positions it in front of me. 'We've been talking with authorities in Buenaventura in an attempt to verify the story Abi told us last week, but as I'm sure you can imagine, the flow of information is slow. So we've focused our efforts on Abi's time after she arrived in the UK, starting with tracking her journey from Heathrow on CCTV.

'One of the officers, who has an eagle eye for this sort of thing, found something rather interesting.' She slides the tablet towards me.

A video stream plays on the screen. One, two, three, four, five seconds and it's over. The girl walks onto a Tube platform and boards a train. Then another video starts. Another Tube stop. This one Hammersmith. I can see the red Tube symbol in the background. The platform is busy with commuters and other travellers, and by the dishevelled look of the passengers, I guess it's the evening commute. My gaze focuses on the girl as she steps from the Tube. The camera changes. Now she's in a walkway.

I thought she was Abigail. I thought we had our lives back. The pain of the realisation is the sharpest of blades slicing into me.

'I'm not sure what this proves?'

'Watch it again.' DC Swain taps the screen.

My head is spinning now. The pieces of information they're giving me blur – figures on a carousel turning too fast.

DC Swain points at something on the screen. I blink and try to focus.

'They're not looking at each other, and they could be complete strangers, but look, here... and again... here, at Liverpool Street.'

The man is wearing a long coat that skims his knees. The collar is large and turned up, shielding his face all the way to his eyes. He's wearing a baseball cap so I can't see his hair – not that I need to see it. My heart is beating so fast that one beat is indistinguishable from another.

Nausea burns in my throat and my breathing is sharp and loud in the quiet room. I feel DC Swain watching me. With a shaking hand, I tap the screen myself and watch another loop; this time it's the man I focus on.

'We've not found a good shot of his face yet, but we're still combing through the footage. As you can see, his hat is pulled down low and he keeps his face angled away from the camera, which in itself is impressive because we have a lot of cameras on the Underground now. Do you know who this man is, Sarah?'

'No.' I shake my head and grapple for control of my voice. I have to say something. 'I was so sure she wasn't my daughter, and then I was so sure she was, and now you're telling me that not only is she not my daughter, but that there's someone helping her to pretend that she is.'

DC Swain nods. 'I believe so, yes. We'll know more when we speak to Abelia. I'd also like to speak to Michael.'

The room falls silent. The detective's words hang in the air. A desire to watch the video again pulls at my mind, but I don't touch the screen.

Something occurs to me then, and I can't believe it's taken me so long to realise. 'The chicken-pox scar,' I say. 'You saw the chicken-pox scar. No one else knew—'

'She didn't show us the scar, Sarah. She told us about it, but we didn't see it.'

'Oh.' A chill takes hold.

'I can only apologise for the oversight. Um... I should have arranged for her to show a female officer the scar, but time felt of the essence and—'

'It still doesn't explain how she knew about it anyway,' I cut in, saving DC Swain from the rest of her apology. Regardless of the oversight, she's the only one now piecing together what's really going on. 'No one else knew about the scar.'

'Are you sure about that? Are you sure Michael didn't know?'

'He said he didn't.'

A memory catches at the corner of my mind. I stare at the photograph of Abigail's toothbrush. She loved that toothbrush. I can see her now, holding it in her hand in the living room of the holiday cottage, Rebecca in my arms and Michael two steps away in the kitchen. I'm lifting Rebecca in the air and making her giggle. Up and down. My arms aching with the effort.

Rebecca's babyish squeals ringing through the small cottage as I catch the sound of Michael laughing at us from the kitchen.

'Ready?' I grin, bouncing Rebecca back on my thighs. I feel her legs wobble and her weight press down on my legs as she tries to stand. 'One, two, three—'

'Mummy?' Abigail says. There's a concern in her voice that makes me stop bouncing Rebecca and turn to face her.

'Is everything all right?' I ask with a smile. Her brown hair is still wet from the bath, leaving damp patches on her red night-dress, and she's holding her toothbrush tightly in her hands. My eyes travel automatically to her feet and the red trainers I still need to convince her to take off before bed. A small smile plays on her lips as she catches me staring at her shoes.

'Mummy, I can't go back to nursery next week,' she announces, a small pout on her lips. 'I have chicken-pox again.'

'Have you been using the colouring pens?' I ask.

She shakes her head and lifts up her nightdress. 'Look.' She points at a white scar on her chest, the only blemish on her perfect skin.

Rebecca gabbles from my lap and reaches a chubby hand out towards her sister, desperate to be part of the conversation.

I smile again. 'It's not chicken pox, baby. It's just a scar. Sometimes chicken pox leaves a scar. It'll fade.'

'Oh.' Abigail frowns again, looking from the white mark up to my face and giggling. 'Can we have a story now?'

'Yes. Go get your brother and choose one each.'

She runs off, trainers thumping on the floors of the cottage.

'What was that about?' Michael asks, leaning down to kiss the top of my head and scoop Rebecca out of my arms.

'Nothing.' I smile and shake my head. 'Abigail has a chicken-pox scar on her chest. She thought it was chicken pox again.'

Michael laughs before blowing a raspberry on Rebecca's tummy. She releases another babyish giggle as Daniel and Abigail charge into the room with a book in each hand.

The memory fades and I shake my head now, gaze darting from Ryan to the detective. 'Oh God,' I say. 'I think he did know. I think Michael knew about the scar.'

DC Swain nods as though she's not surprised.

Oh, Michael. What have you done?

'What happens now?' I ask.

'Since we've had no luck reaching Michael, and therefore Abelia, it's probably best you go home.' DC Swain reaches into a pocket and pulls out a card. 'Please call me when you get there. I'd still like to speak to them tonight – or tomorrow morning.'

'I... I don't know what I'll say.'

I think of Rebecca and Daniel and how I'll break this news to them. They'll be devastated. This girl has repaired something in our family. We haven't been pretending everything is normal this week. It really is normal. Rebecca has stopped trying to fill every silence, and Daniel has been home more. I think of his 'I love you, Mum' comment from the interview and my heart breaks.

'I'll drive you back,' Ryan says, already standing up. 'I can come in with you too, and help explain this to Michael and the kids.'

'Thank you.'

The carousel appears in my head again as I count my steps, following Ryan to a car park at the rear of the station. 'I don't know who you are, or why you're here, but you're not my daughter.' The words spin with the rest. I was so sure then. Just as I was an hour ago.

It's all been a lie. A game. The girl is not my daughter. I say it again in my head, surprised how easy it fits now as though maybe a part of me, somewhere deep and dark and forgotten, knew this already. But she's not a stranger either. She's Michael's daughter. I think of the CCTV footage of Abelia travelling across London. I think of everything that's happened in a single week to repair and then destroy my family.

*Oh, Michael, what have you done?*

# FORTY-ONE

## ABI

Friday, 4 p.m.

For the whole journey back to Dedham and the house, Abi's mind raced with a hundred 'what ifs' and 'what next?'. She turned over everything she'd done, every lie she'd told, searching for a way out or maybe a way forward that would make it all better. But there was nothing.

So she carried on pretending. They dropped Rebecca to school, and she watched the blonde swish of her ponytail disappear through the tall iron gates. Then back home, Abi made coffee and lunch, all the while waiting for it all to come crashing down.

And now the waiting is over and Abi finds herself standing by the island in the kitchen, unable to move. She's frozen. A statue. Somewhere in the very back of her mind, a voice is screaming at her to breathe, but every inhale is a shallow gasp as she stares at the gun pointed at her face.

The rifle is big – a black metal barrel and a dark wood handle. Bigger in real life than in the hundreds of films and shows she watched as a kid. The fear is bigger too. Bigger than she ever imagined possible. The reality of the gun, and the bullets waiting to fire out, have cemented her legs to the floor. Stolen the screams before they can escape.

For a split second, Abi wants to laugh at herself and all the times she thought she was scared this week – scared of Sarah, scared of him, scared of what he'd do if she made a mistake. That fear is puny compared to what she's feeling now.

She can't move her eyes from the gun. The perfect O of the barrel staring back. The barrel, like the gun, like the hand holding it, is steady. It isn't shaking with the same fear that grips Abi's body.

Even without looking she can sense the furtive looks passing back and forth between Michael and Daniel. The same way she can sense the blades of fear slicing through them too.

No one speaks. They've tried reasoning, pleading, screaming at him to stop. Nothing worked. And now the gun says it all. But she has to keep trying. She's come too far for it to end like this, and it seems obvious that neither Michael nor Daniel will be the ones to save her.

'It's not too late,' she says to the gun and its owner. 'It doesn't have to be like this. Stick to the plan – isn't that what you've said all along?'

He laughs. A calm noise, not like a laugh at all. 'You stupid girl. This is the plan. This has always been the plan. True, I wanted it to happen on *her* anniversary. Maybe if you'd have played your part how you were supposed to then we could've got there, but this will work just the same.'

'What are you talking about?' Abi asks.

'All in good time.' He smiles and strokes the trigger with his finger, causing the fear to rise up to her throat. 'We need to wait for Sarah first.'

Reality dawns. His words sink in. This is the plan. This: the gun, the madness. This has always been the plan. Abi thinks of all the things she told him about her life, her pathetic stupid life. How easily he manipulated her.

Another thought hits, causing her heart to lurch inside her chest. Abi doesn't know what this is all about, not really, but one thing is clear: her part in it is over. He doesn't need her anymore. She's as good as dead.

The thought makes the walls of the kitchen shrink until the shiny cupboards aren't cupboards anymore but walls, the walls of her coffin, shrinking and shrinking until she can't think through the claustrophobia bearing down on her.

The phone rings again, echoing into the silence. It's the third call since the gun appeared in his hand.

Nobody moves to answer the phone. A message starts to record. It's Ryan this time instead of DC Swain. 'Michael, this is Ryan. Please call me as soon as you get this. It's urgent.'

The message clicks off and the room falls silent. Nobody speaks.

'Well,' he says, moving the gun so it points halfway between them, 'it seems we'd better hit the road. The police have been a tad more efficient than I expected. Abi, get a pen. I want you to leave a note for Sarah. Oh, and you can drop the accent now, don't you think? Bravo for that by the way. It was Oscar-worthy, truly it was.'

Abi dips her head, hiding her face as best she can from Michael and Daniel. She can feel their eyes on her; she can feel the hurt and betrayal hanging in the air between them.

'He tricked me,' she mumbles in her real voice, feeling suddenly exposed – as if she's stripped off her clothes. It's been months since she last spoke without the accent. All the time she was in Colombia, and for some time before that, she kept it up – practising and testing, trying it on for size.

She moves to the sideboard and picks up a pad of paper and

a pen. From beneath the table in the extension, Abi hears the uncertain thump of Barley's tail. He's scared too. She hopes he has the sense to stay still, keep himself hidden.

She forces herself to look at him. 'What do you want me to write?'

# FORTY-TWO

## SARAH

Friday, 6 p.m.

A pale moon follows our journey back to Essex. The sky is still light, the sun only just sinking towards the horizon. The mix of day and night in the sky is otherworldly, something out of a science-fiction movie, or a parallel universe where everything is twisted. Wrong.

Ryan's eyes are fixed on the road ahead and the stop-start traffic. I want to say something, but the words don't come. I'm still struggling to process everything DC Swain has told me.

'You all right?' Ryan asks.

I shake my head. 'No. Not really.' The hurt scratches my insides. It's dull, masked by the shock, but at some point soon I know I'll be broken again.

'In the meeting room, before, when you saw the CCTV of Abi in London, you looked... Well, to be honest, it looked like you'd seen a ghost.'

Ryan isn't wrong, but I can't tell him that. I'm not ready to believe it yet.

'If you recognised that man,' he continues, 'you should've said something.'

'I didn't.' The lie hangs between us. I'm sure Ryan knows, but I force myself to keep quiet.

Ahead of us, the traffic clears. Ryan increases speed. I count the lampposts we pass but there are too many to keep the number in my head.

'There was some other evidence DC Swain found. She didn't mention it. I guess she didn't want to overload you, and I think she's keen to talk about it with Michael and Abi too. But —'

'Tell me. Please,' I add as a text from Rebecca pings on my phone: *Can I go to the cinema tomorrow with Ellie? Be back for dinner!! xxxx*

I stare at her words until they blur into blobs in front of my eyes. I don't know how I'll tell Rebecca that the big sister she thought she had is a liar. The hurt it will cause lies on top of my own. At least Rebecca won't be home for the confrontation.

My reply is short: *Yes. Have fun. Love you xx*

'They ran the names Jhon Pérez and Caroline Pérez through the national police database. They got a hit. There was a Colombian-born man called Hector Jhon Pérez who lived in Birmingham. He died of bowel cancer just over a year ago.'

'Abigail—' I stop myself, hating my mistake. 'The girl said Jhon died of bowel cancer. Is it the same man? That's too much of a coincidence, isn't it?' I think for a moment. Turning this piece of information over in my mind, like a puzzle piece waiting to be put into place. 'But she flew into Heathrow from Colombia. She's spoken about her home lots of times. There's no way she could have made that all up, is there?'

'They have her flight records. She was on a flight that originated from Buenaventura. But it's not so easy to track how long she was there for. She could've flown in the day before, using a different passport.'

'A fake passport? This all feels so unreal. How easy are they to get hold of?'

'Not very. But the reason Hector Pérez – Jhon – is – was – in the police national database is because he was suspected by Birmingham Police of drug smuggling for a criminal organisation based in the Midlands and North of England. He may have got her one before he died. It's impossible to know what exactly she's lied about until we speak to her.'

I struggle to process Ryan's words. Drug smuggling. Fake passports. It's another world. 'What about the woman – Caroline?'

'There's nothing on her. All they have is a side note on Pérez's file. Under connections, an officer noted that Pérez visited a council tower block every month or so. The suggestion was that he was visiting a mistress or a family member. DC Swain is waiting for Birmingham Police to give her the address of the tower block and check the names of who lived there.'

The girl's words ring in Sarah's head. 'Where I lived there were two types of dogs – guard dogs and strays – both likely to bite you for one reason or another.' Could she have been talking about a tower block in Birmingham rather than the streets of a city in Colombia?

I think about her accent. The way she mimicked my English so perfectly this morning. Is the girl a con artist; an imposter, just as I first thought? Is this girl involved in organised crime? Have we been targeted?

This feels like it's about more than money, I think, as we turn onto the country lane leading to Dedham.

The questions turn over and over. I don't know what to think. But then I remember the CCTV of the man helping Abi, and I know one thing. This isn't about organised crime. This isn't even about the girl really. It's about the past. This is about what happened to Abigail fourteen years ago.

A shiver runs down my spine.

# FORTY-THREE

## SARAH

The moment Ryan pulls up to the house, I'm jumping out. I tap the code to open the gate for him before slipping through and running to the front door. I'm in the hall in seconds.

'Michael?' I shout but there's no reply. 'Daniel? Abi?'

Silence. The house is still, in that way houses are when they're empty. I don't need to go from room to room to know that they're not here. It's cold and dark, no lights on, no fire in the grate in the living room.

I step into the kitchen and turn on the lights, my gaze roaming the surfaces. There's a plate and a glass by the sink, left from breakfast. Everything is how it was when I left this morning and yet there's something in the air, an unfamiliar scent, or a feeling maybe, that things aren't right.

'Barley?' I call out suddenly, realising why the house feels strange. Where's Barley?

There's no reply. I don't expect one. If he was here, he'd have run out to greet me.

Then I hear a soft muffled bark. A yip.

'Barley?' I call again, whistling this time, following the noise of the barks to the extension and the French doors that lead into the garden. Barley is on the other side of the glass, tail wagging, tongue lolling. Mud and slobber cover the bottom of the doors and I wonder, as I let him in, how long he's been out there.

Barley's claws clatter on the floor. He dances around my legs and it's as I'm bending down to stroke him that I notice the note on the table. I snatch it up and scan the words.

*Sarah,*

*Taken Abigail and Daniel on a trip down memory lane. I thought it would be nice to go back to where it all began on the coast that day.*

*You must come.*

*Michael x*

'Sarah?' Ryan calls through the house.

'In here,' I shout back, stepping to meet him in the kitchen. 'I found this note.' I hold out the paper and, as Ryan reads, I scan the words again, searching for a hidden meaning, but all I see is the scratch of handwriting that isn't Michael's – and the threat: *You must come.*

'The holiday cottage,' I mutter. 'They've gone back to the holiday cottage, but Michael didn't write this note.'

'Who did?'

I shrug. 'Abelia, I think. It's quite childish and definitely isn't Daniel or Michael's.'

Ryan nods, already moving into the hall. 'I'll call the local police.'

I nod. Every cell in my body is screaming at me to run to the car and chase after them, but that's what the note demands. And while I'll do as it says, I need a moment to think first.

Two, four, six – I count the stairs two at a time. Three

minutes later, I'm changed into jeans and a thick jumper, and I'm in Michael's study, staring at the row of red binders filled with every lead about Abigail from every private investigator Michael hired. I don't know what I'm looking for, or if there are answers here, only that what is happening now is connected to what happened thirteen years, ten months, and sixteen days ago. It has to be.

I take the first one from the shelf. It's heavy. There's a label on the binder that reads May–June 2009. They're the first notes Michael gathered, and I'm sure most of this is information I know.

The rest of the binders aren't labelled, so I pick one at random and pull it from the shelf. It's heavy like the first, but when I open it up, all I see is blank paper. Hundreds of pages, hole-punched and empty.

'What the—' I start to say, pulling down another binder and then another. They're all the same. All of them filled with blank paper.

'Sarah?' Ryan calls up the stairs.

I take a final glance at the folders, snatch up the first one again and make for the stairs. 'I'm coming.'

We run to the car together. 'Aldeburgh Police will send someone as soon as they can. They're dealing with a road traffic accident right now though and can't divert officers to the cottage. I called DC Swain too. She's already on her way and will meet us there. But even with the sirens, it'll take her a few hours to get to Suffolk.'

'We'll be there in less than an hour.' I glance at the sky as I clip in my seat belt. The sun has set in the minutes we've been inside the house. The sky no longer orange and dusky but dark blue and clear.

We pull away and minutes later we're on the main road heading for the one place I never thought I'd go back to. I stare down at the file on my lap. I never thought I'd open this folder either, but now it's here I wonder what, if any, answers it holds.

'Is that one of the PI files?' Ryan asks as he moves into the outside lane. The car jolts a little as he moves quickly up each gear.

'The only one,' I say. 'Michael told me he's been paying private detectives for years and collecting all the leads and interviews and putting them in a stack of red ring binders in his study. Except I just looked and this is the only folder with anything in it. All the others are empty. They're filled with blank paper. It doesn't make sense. Why would he tell me he's hiring investigators and pretending to put information in folders?'

'I don't know. What's in that one?'

My throat aches from the emotion building inside of me. We're speeding along the road now. Lights from the cars we pass blur into streams. My past is hurtling towards me, or I towards it, at the same pace. I've locked the past away, focused on the day to day. *Look forward not back.* I thought the motto had served me well, helped me survive, but now I'm not so sure.

My fingers peel back the hard plastic cover of the binder. 'I don't know where to start or what I'm looking for—' My voice catches as I see Abigail's photo. The one we took on holiday that Michael used in all of his campaigns, the same one the police gave to the media in those early days.

It was taken on the beach. Abigail is standing by the huge boulders, a bucket and spade in her hand. She's grinning at the camera, head tilted a little to one side, brown hair dancing in the breeze.

Her smiling face grins up at me, causing a bolt of lightning to hit my chest. I close my eyes until the pain passes and then I open them and turn the page to another photo. It's the CCTV still of the stranger with Abigail in the pushchair that the woman saw and called the police about. I keep turning. The next page is a newspaper article about Abigail's abduction and then another and another. There's nothing new to learn from them. I turn the page again and it's blank. Empty. And so is the next and the next. Just like the other binders I left behind.

Where are the details of the reported sightings? Where are the interviews the PI must have done?

I think back to a week ago and lying in bed beside Michael on that first night Abi came to the house. I even asked about the binders. He was so quick to tell me there were no leads. I should've pushed him. But he got so hurt when I called Abi 'that girl'. Was it all a deflection to stop me asking any more questions?

Then I wonder what Michael has been doing all these years. He clearly wasn't searching for Abigail. But of course that's not the question that matters, the question that turns my stomach and causes bile to burn the back of my throat: why has he spent nearly fourteen years lying?

# FORTY-FOUR

## SARAH

Friday, 7 p.m.

'It's empty. This folder. It's just blank pages like the others.' My voice sounds shrill and too loud in the quiet of the car.

Ryan glances down at the folder. The car swerves to the left for a split second before his eyes are back on the road. 'Could someone have swapped the contents and filled it with paper so you or Michael wouldn't notice?'

'I don't know. Michael keeps the cabinet locked. We didn't want the kids to see the files by accident. He keeps the key hidden in the drawer by his bed.'

Anger starts to pulse in my temples. What's going on? Why has he been lying to me?

I'm about to close the folder when my finger nudges against the round edge of a CD tucked in at the back.

'There's a CD here,' I say, pulling it free. 'Eleanor Geary interview.' I read the sharp letters written in black marker pen.

'Who's that? Do you know?' Ryan asks.

I nod. 'She's the woman who phoned the police in the first

few hours after Abigail's abduction. She reported seeing a man running down a beach with a pushchair and that's how the police found the CCTV footage of the stranger on the boat.'

'Play it,' Ryan says, tapping a space on the dashboard.

My eyes scan the car. 'It has a CD player?'

He huffs a laugh. 'It's a pool car. They're a little behind the times, but it's good for us now so don't knock it.'

I find the thin slot and push the CD inside. For a moment nothing happens, but then there's the crackle of air in a microphone and a deep male voice fills the car.

'Mrs Geary, thank you for taking the time to speak to me again. I'm recording our conversation so that myself and the Wicks can listen to it back at a later date.'

I picture the investigator sitting at Mrs Geary's kitchen table. He was a wiry man with thinning short brown hair. Ex-special forces, he told us during his first visit, when we'd still been at the cottage, when I'd still clung to hope. His firm had come recommended. He'd had success with another missing child case.

'Oh my!' Mrs Geary's shaking voice jumps out from the speakers. 'Will they hear this? I feel just terrible. I should have done something. We could have stopped him if we'd known, but Roy was wittering in my ear about minding my own business, so I didn't do enough. I'll have to live with that for rest of my days.'

I feel a pang of guilt. The elderly woman wrote to me not long after we'd gone home. Two handwritten pages on peach paper, pouring out her sadness for what she'd seen, wishing she'd seen more, done more. I'm sure she hoped for a letter back; a pardon of some kind. The 'it wasn't your fault' speech that so many people have tried to give me, but I never replied. Hearing the emotion in the woman's voice now makes me wish I had.

There's a clink of china on the CD then the investigator speaks. 'Can you tell me what happened please, Mrs Geary?

From the start, if you don't mind. Any and every detail matters now.'

'Call me Eleanor,' she replies. 'Well, we were sitting on the bench overlooking the sea on the little stretch of beach by the fort at Felixstowe. The restaurant had been full, so we'd got some takeaway chips and decided to watch the cargo ships come and go from the docks. We like to try and guess what might be inside.

'Roy had had his prostate out the year before, so he'd gone straight to the gents after the chips. It all goes straight through him now. It was after he'd gone that I saw the man.'

'Did you see a car?'

'No, just him, running flat out along the beach with that poor little girl in the pushchair, bouncing along inside it. He put a hand in the air to wave down the boat, and the pushchair almost toppled over. I remember thinking, *That little girl looks too big for a pushchair*. I could tell because of how far her knees stuck out, and those bright-red jelly shoes that my Tina used to wear, resting on the footrest. I knew by the way her legs were flopping around that she was asleep and I thought, *Blimey, that's a lot to sleep through*.'

'Jelly shoes?'

'Yes, you know, those plastic sandals kids love so much.'

'I believe in your statement to the police you referred to them as red shoes.'

'Oh my, I don't think I told the police they were jelly shoes. I didn't think it was important. But they definitely were the same as my Tina's. Should I call the police and tell them?'

'I'll be updating Mr and Mrs Wick. They can do that for you, and the police will be in touch,' he says.

'The men on the ferry were pulling up the ramp, but he shouted out to them to wait.'

'Did he use that word... wait?' the investigator asks.

'I'm not sure... I guess he could have. The men on the ferry shook their heads a bit as if they knew this man was going to make them late, but they lowered the ramp anyway and helped him get the pushchair onto the boat.'

'It could have been a dad and his daughter coming back from a day trip to the arcades. It was the last ferry of the day as I understand it,' the PI says.

She sniffs. 'That's what Roy said too. I almost didn't call. Can you imagine if I hadn't been there to see it? Those poor parents would've had nothing to go on.'

'What made you call the police?' the investigator prompts, steering the woman back on track.

'It was those legs. They were just too long for the pushchair. It gave me the heebie-jeebies. If I'd have known that a little girl had been taken, then I would have stopped him. I would have done anything to save little Abigail Wick.'

'Mrs Geary, forgive me for asking this, but I spoke with your neighbour and she mentioned that you have a habit of calling the police and reporting strange goings-on. She said you thought she was a prostitute.'

'That was an honest mistake.' Mrs Geary's voice rises, hurt and indignant. 'She had men coming and going at all hours. How was I to know she was a sports therapist, whatever that is? I'm a vigilant person, that's all. If I hadn't called the police when I did, then those parents wouldn't know anything...'

Mrs Geary is rambling now and crying and sniffing too, but I've stopped listening. My head is spinning again, but I don't know why. My heart is pounding in my chest. I watch the yellow streetlights flicker past and feel another wave of nausea. I press eject and the car is silent again.

'Are you OK?' Ryan steals a glance at me.

I shake my head. 'Something she said... it's not right.'

A second later it hits me. Shoes. Red jelly shoes. Not trainers.

The timing was tight to get from the holiday cottages to the docks. Almost implausible. But Mrs Geary phoned 999 just minutes after the bulletin went out to the police call centre. Four-year-old girl missing from holiday cottage in Thorpeness, Suffolk.

I throw open the binder and pull out the CCTV still of the man and the pushchair. The café on the beach only had one camera facing the car park. It wasn't a good angle. Someone – a police technician, I imagine – has tried to zoom in on the figure running with the pushchair. The quality is poor. I can see all the tiny square pixels.

In the early weeks, I watched the short clip over and over, staring at the man and hoping for any jolt of familiarity. Searching my memory for anyone I'd ever met, even for a second, who might have taken Abigail.

But I never looked at the pushchair. Not really. There'd been nothing to see but a pair of legs.

I hold the photo up to the light and stare at the legs and the shoes. They're a blur of red, and we thought they were Abigail's trainers, but Mrs Geary remembered they were jelly shoes because her Tina had had a pair.

My heart pounds against my chest. How could I have missed this?

'Sarah, what is it?' Ryan asks.

'Abigail's shoes. Mrs Geary said "red jelly shoes". The photo is blurry so we could only see the colour.'

'And?'

'Abigail was wearing red trainers that day, not jelly shoes.' Goosebumps march along my arms at the memory. The realisation.

'Are you sure?' he asks.

'I bought them especially for the holiday. They were a birthday present. Red and blue were Abigail's favourite colours. She loved the trainers so much that we had to bribe her with extra stories at bedtime just to get her to take them off every night.'

'Could the man have stopped somewhere and bought new shoes for her? Or maybe he'd had them in his car and swapped her shoes.'

'Maybe. But the timings were so tight to begin with. It's, what, just under an hour to get from the holiday cottage to Felixstowe. She hadn't been missing much more than that when Mrs Geary called 999. And why risk taking the boat anyway? He could have driven round to Harwich or any of the other stops on the ferry? It would've only taken another thirty minutes.'

'And you don't remember the PI telling you about the jelly shoes?'

'No. He must've told only Michael.'

My comment hangs in the air. The implication, the question, unspoken but still there. Did the PI tell Michael? Did he know that the little girl in the CCTV image wasn't wearing red trainers? Why didn't he tell me? Tell the police?

'The police suspected he had a boat docked somewhere,' Ryan says.

'I know,' I whisper. 'But what if...' I pause, struggling to find the words. I don't want to say them. I don't want to admit that everything I've believed for fourteen years was wrong and the proof was there all along. 'What if it wasn't her, Ryan? You heard that investigator. It's not the first time Mrs Geary has phoned the police.'

Ryan doesn't argue. He knows it's possible. More than possible in fact. There was never another sighting of the man and the pushchair, or of Abigail. The men who ran the ferry didn't remember which stop the man got off at. They barely remembered him at all. Whatever Mrs Geary saw in that moment that made her call the police and report it, the ferrymen didn't give him a second glance.

Ryan moves a hand from the wheel and places it over my own. 'Maybe it's time to talk about what happened? What do you remember about the day Abigail disappeared?'

The goosebumps return. I shiver, hugging my arms to my body and closing my eyes. 'I remember everything.'

# FORTY-FIVE

## SARAH

Then

A trickle of warm water runs under the sleeve of my jumper and down my arm as I balance another plate on the draining board. It's surprising how little I miss the dishwasher. Perhaps if washing up at home could be done standing by a window overlooking a garden with a white picket fence and a pebble beach beyond it, it wouldn't be so bad.

Although it's not the beach or the sea, glistening like a thousand mirror shards in the sunlight, that draws my eyes, but Daniel and Abigail again. They're playing in the garden with the buckets of pebbles they'd collected earlier. Janie is crouched down between them. Her long black braids are pulled into a bun at the nape of her neck as she examines the collection of rocks and pretends to eat one, making me laugh.

'It's been a good holiday, hasn't it?' Michael whispers, kissing my neck.

'Yes, it has. We should do it more often.'

'Now that the business is up and running, it'll be easier for me to take more time off.' He runs his hands over my hips.

'What's the plan now? If you and Janie want to head to the pub for some girly time, I can hold the fort here. Rebecca's got at least another hour of napping after all that sea air today.'

'What you mean is, don't involve me in the girl chat, right?'

Michael laughs. 'Busted. I can nip out and get us a Chinese later too, once you're back.'

'Let's decide after the kids are in bed. I'm still full from the fish and chips earlier. I wish I hadn't eaten so much now.' My stomach feels heavy. The extra weight from my pregnancy hasn't shifted as quickly as it did after the first two. The weight is all on my stomach and I'm sure the gossip columns will be speculating that I'm pregnant again by the end of the week.

'No one expects you to be perfect, honey.' Michael wraps his arms around me. 'The viewers love the fact you're normal. If you get back in front of the cameras all stick-thin and groomed, touting your own fitness DVD, then you know they'll hate you.'

He's right of course, but it wasn't quite what I'd wanted to hear.

'How about a run?' Janie asks from the open back door. You know you'll feel better afterwards. It'll be like old times but without the hangovers.' She grins, reminding me of the long runs we'd take along the Thames on Saturdays at uni, sweating out the wine and shots from a Friday night at whatever club we'd been invited to. It feels like a lifetime ago.

I laugh. 'You're on. As long as you don't mind going slow for me.'

'No way. You're the one running around after these beauties all day.' She nods to the window and the children outside. 'That takes some stamina.'

Her face falls and I can tell she's thinking of her own desperation to be a mother and the tough time she's had with Phil.

'Let's do it then,' I say, and five minutes later I'm in leggings and a T-shirt and slipping on my trainers. 'There are a few rolls left over for dinner for the kids,' I tell Michael. 'We might as well use them up rather than taking them home tomorrow.'

'Got it,' Michael says with a mock salute.

I step to the window and glance again at Daniel and Abigail's play. 'They're having a great time.'

'Yes.' Michael nods. 'This is what we wanted, isn't it? A technology-free week where the kids have no option but to play together.'

'Apart from the times I've seen you sneak back to the car to check your phone and call the office, you mean.'

'Busted again.' He holds up his hands in mock surrender. 'I promise, no more phone until we get home.'

'Are you sure you don't mind looking after things here?'

'They're my kids too, Sarah. Of course I don't mind,' he says.

'I know, it's just... Daniel—'

Michael sighs, making me wish I hadn't said anything. 'That whole anger thing was about his dyslexia and not being about to keep up with his classmates. He's good now. We found it early. He's getting the support he needs. Like you said, they're having a great time. There's nothing to worry about.'

They'd been having a great time in the park a few months ago too, I think but don't say. Until I'd told Abigail and Daniel that it was time to go. 'Rebecca needs her dinner.'

It had been a stick that day. He'd thrown it across the play-ground, missing the buggy by half a metre and hitting a tree instead. I don't think he'd aimed for the pushchair, but it had been close. But Michael is right. It was frustration at not seeing what his class could see with the words on the page. He's been so much better.

My eyes focus on Daniel's face as he turns towards me with cheeks red from the wind. He has his arm around Abigail's shoulder and they're both in giggling fits about something.

'Ready?' Janie asks.

'As I'll ever be.' I grin, glancing back to the window a final time. I hesitate for a second and consider saying goodbye to Daniel and Abigail, but I don't want to interrupt their game and they'll want to come too, no doubt.

So I turn away instead and head with Janie to the front door.

If I'd known in that second of hesitation that it was the last time I would see Abigail, I would've taken her in my arms and held her tight. I would never have let her go.

# FORTY-SIX

## SARAH

### Then

The cottage isn't particularly pretty. A single-storey block, painted white, with a red roof. It sits back from the road in a row of seven other seafront properties. Some are basic like ours, others are grander, with balconies overlooking the sea. Inside, the cottage is poky with a kitchen-living room, divided by a beige two-seater sofa. There is a single bathroom with a shower-head fixed over the bath, and a flimsy shower curtain that does little to shield the water spray from reaching the floor. Either side of the bathroom are two small bedrooms – a twin for Abigail and Daniel, and a double for Michael and me. With Rebecca's travel cot next to our bed, there's barely room to move.

The location and the garden make up for its lack of space. The garden, like the cottage, is raised higher than sea level. There's a white picket gate at the end of the garden with six wooden steps leading onto the beach. Janie and I skirt the side of the property towards the shore and the coastal footpath before falling into a jog, turning right on the path towards Aldeburgh. The sea is to our left, hidden by a mound of pebbles that requires a person to scramble up them before reaching the beach and the water's edge.

The wind is unrelenting. There are no gusts or interludes. It is constant. Both cold and warm, it pummels my face, blowing in my ears like low rumbling thunder, but we fall into a rhythm and it really does feel like old times, with just enough breath left to talk.

I start the chat. I share my guilt about my role on *This Morning* and how often I'm away from the children, relying on extra clubs at school and nursery, and our neighbour, Mrs Dillinger, more often than I'd like. But how, even though I feel that guilt, I want more too. I mention a Saturday night quiz show Don has put me forward for and Janie cheers.

'You'd be perfect for it,' she says.

Our trainers pound the well-trodden path and my eyes focus on the distance – the red roofs of Aldeburgh and the church tower standing taller than the rest. The path weaves away from the beach and onto open grassland. It dips down, causing a momentary break from the wind. All of a sudden, a whiff of cigarette smoke catches in my senses. My breathing is quick and heavy and I pull the scent into my lungs. I don't know much about cigarettes, but it smells stronger than the usual tobacco brands. Camels or something foreign, I guess. My eyes roam the path ahead of me, but it's empty.

We fall back into our stride and Janie talks this time. She tells me her and Phil aren't speaking. That he's cold and distant, blaming her, it feels like, for failing to give him a child. Before I know it, Janie and I are bickering. I've said the wrong thing, suggested she leaves Phil. I've overstepped.

'Don't,' Janie hisses at me. 'Just let me be angry.' She turns around and runs back towards Thorpeness, ignoring my shouted apology.

I stand for a moment, watching her run and knowing she

needs to cool off, so I carry on to Aldeburgh and the aroma of fresh fish in the air and the screech and gabble of seagulls above my head.

I loop around a small boating pond before turning back, the wind hitting me now, making every stride on my aching legs feel harder. I long for a hot shower and glass of wine and to see Janie and apologise again.

I'm twenty or so metres from the cottage when I see Michael standing on the mound of stones directly in front of the house. I smile and shout, 'Hey,' expecting him to turn and smile, but his eyes are wide, his expression fraught.

'Abigail!' He screams her name and spins in a full circle. The anguish in his voice sends a shiver through me.

'Michael, what's happened?' I shout, my aching legs forgotten as I close the distance between us, scrambling slightly as I race across the pebbled beach.

He stumbles down the ridge towards me. His eyes continue to scan the path around us as he talks. 'Abigail is gone.' His words are quick and shaky. 'She was in the garden. I only turned my back for a minute. Daniel cut his hand on a stone. I took him inside to get a plaster. When I got back, Abigail was gone.'

A noise leaves my mouth. A gasp-like laugh halfway between disbelief and panic. 'She'll be hiding under her bed again, that's all. Daniel will know where she is. I'll go ask him.'

I turn towards the cottage, but Michael grips my arm so tight it hurts. 'She's not, Sarah. I've checked everywhere.'

The realisation is painfully slow. I can see it, but I can't. I believe it and I don't. Abigail is gone. She was in the garden playing and now she's not.

'She'll be on the beach by the rocks she likes to climb over or collecting more pebbles.' The relief is instant. That's where she is – she has to be. I turn towards the beach and take a step.

'I've just come from there.' Michael is shouting now and

holding my arm tight. 'You look around the town. She might have walked to the park. I'm calling the police.'

'Daniel and Rebecca,' I say as we sprint together towards the cottage – me towards the town and Michael to his phone.

'They're fine. Just go, Sarah. Abigail has to be somewhere.'

She wasn't.

# FORTY-SEVEN

## SARAH

Friday, 8 p.m.

The ticking of the indicator pulls my thoughts back to the present. My mouth is dry from talking. My body aches as if it remembers how fast I raced the streets, shouting Abigail's name.

Ryan turns the car from the dual carriageway onto a single road with a line of traffic crawling in both directions. Holiday makers, weekend getaways, commuters on their way home – our speed is dictated by a row of headlights in the darkness.

'We'll be there soon. Fifteen minutes,' he says, perhaps reading my impatience as we drive through scattered villages, barely hitting anything above thirty miles an hour.

'Something isn't adding up,' I say, gnawing at my bottom lip.

'What do you mean?'

'I don't know. I'm trying to remember.'

For so long, I've kept the memories locked up, hidden. Now they're free and spinning in my head. I think of the fear on Michael's face on the beach. His insistence I search the town. He was taking control, I tell myself. And yet... It's on the edge of my thoughts...

'Michael told the police that he made tea for Abigail and Daniel. That they came in to eat it and then went back outside to play. He went into the bedroom to wake Rebecca when Daniel came in crying because he'd cut his hand on a stone. By the time Michael had found a plaster and calmed Daniel down, Abigail was gone.'

'Right,' Ryan says, flicking the briefest of glances at me. It's just a second but I feel his concern, his care in that one look. 'So what's bothering you?'

'I don't know.' Frustration, like a pressure cooker, builds inside me. 'It's like I can feel it, but I can't see it. I can't get to it. Tell me what you remember – maybe that will help.'

Ryan glances at me for a moment before he speaks. 'Er... it was about six thirty by the time I arrived. The police had shown you the CCTV footage of the man they believed had taken Abigail. You were shaking and almost hysterical, and I remember thinking I had to do something to help you. So I made some cheese rolls and put them on the table. I was nervous. It was my first assignment. No amount of training can prepare you for what it's like stepping—'

'The bread rolls.'

'What about them?'

'You made cheese rolls.' The words are quick. I have to get them out before they slip out of reach again. 'The rolls were still on the side. You used them. So how did Michael make them for Abigail and Daniel's tea? How did they eat them if they were still on the side when you came in later?'

It's a minor thing, I guess. Maybe Michael found them something else to eat that I'd forgotten was in the cupboard. Or maybe the timeline is off. But maybe he lied. Maybe Michael knows more about Abigail's abduction than he's ever let on.

Bread rolls, jelly shoes, DNA that doesn't lie. A girl who is a half-sister. Twenty-five per cent in common with Abigail's toothbrush fourteen years ago. Michael's daughter I knew nothing about. Empty binders. His lies are stacking up.

I don't know what happened to Abigail nearly fourteen years ago, but I sense I'm getting closer to answers, and that scares me to my core.

I stare out of the window into the blackness of the night and try without success to make the pieces fit. Despite the years since I last made this journey, the surroundings begin to feel familiar. There's a caravan forecourt on the right, with rows and rows of caravans lit by big blue security lights. A little further on is the blue petrol station, and then the roundabout. We're almost there. Trepidation burns like acid in my veins. Suddenly, I'm not so sure we should be rushing. I'm not so sure I want to know.

The holiday cottage sits on a single strip of road running parallel to the sea on the edge of Thorpeness. The road is just wide enough for two cars if they pass slowly, but we're alone on the stretch.

The headlights of Ryan's car pick up the flimsy picket fences that surround the properties on the shoreline. A grand glass house and several other new houses now fill many of the gaps that had once been empty space or gardens.

'The turning is just here.' I point to a dirt track, but Ryan is already pulling in.

Michael's car is parked outside the cottage. Something sinks inside of me and I realise that, despite the note and everything I now know, a tiny part of me was still clinging to the hope that this was all a mistake, a misunderstanding.

'Well, at least we know they're here,' Ryan says, switching off the engine.

The faint moon casts a spotlight on the properties, and I

know without moving closer that the cottage is empty and locked tight. The salt from the sea carries in the wind and brushes my skin through my clothes.

I shiver as much from seeing the cottage again as from the cold and the smell of the beach and the memories it unleashes.

'Where do you think they are?' he asks.

'They must be on the beach.' I step towards the cottage and the path along the side.

'Sarah, wait,' Ryan calls after me, voice low. 'We don't know what we're walking into.'

I shrug. 'What choice do I have?'

'Let me go around. They don't know I'm with you. If you're walking into something bad, then at least I can phone for back-up.'

He's right and yet I still find myself asking. 'Something bad?'

'Like you said, a lot of things aren't adding up and we know someone has been helping Abi. He could be with them too.'

The image of the man in the Underground trailing Abi flashes in my mind.

*Oh, he is with them.*

'Where's the nearest access point to the beach?' Ryan asks.

'I think it's a few minutes in that direction.' I point towards the town. 'There's a public car park and beach access from there.'

He nods and turns away, leaving me alone in the moonlight. A burst of adrenaline twists in my stomach as I hurry between the cottages.

Dark clouds drift across the sky over my head, threatening to swallow the glow of the moon, and I catch sight of a torch's light swinging back and forth directly in front of me. My feet crunch the stones, signalling my approach as well as if I was shouting at the top of my voice. The noise is so similar to the crunch of my wheels on the driveway, but there is no calm this time, no Pavlovian response. Every hair on my body tingles as I stumble up the mound of pebbles towards the answers I've been waiting fourteen years for.

# FORTY-EIGHT

## ABI

'Don't move.' His voice rings out across the beach. Loud and angry. The barrel of the rifle swings wildly between them, and every time it passes Abi, she can't stop herself flinching. Shrinking back.

Her body is shaking with the intensity of an electric current running through it. It's fear and the cold night air penetrating through her skin and rattling in her bones. There's an urgency to his movements now. The calm commands have disappeared. He's losing control, she thinks. The realisation sends a fresh, heart-pounding panic juddering through her. She can't tear her eyes away from the gun.

He's going to kill her. She's sure of it. Three bullets, he said when he'd marched them towards the rocks and forced them to sit. One of those bullets is for her.

Silent tears stream down her face. Her nose runs too. There's no warmth left from the day. Even scrunched inside the sleeves of her jumper, Abi's fingers are numb. An ache-like pain runs from her lower back down to her thighs. How long has she been sitting on this rock face? It feels like hours.

Where is Sarah? She should be here by now, and yet Abi prays she won't come. As soon as she arrives, it's over.

He paces back and forth before them in the torchlight. Long strides, furtive looks to them and to the houses. Abi follows his gaze. From where she's sitting beside the water's edge, it's impossible to see anything more than a few second-floor windows. The properties are black and lifeless. They are completely alone with only the rhythmic crash of the waves on the shore filling the silence.

Panic mounts another assault on her body, squeezing her heart and twisting blades in her gut. The reality of the situation feels slippery in her thoughts. How is it still Friday? The same day she was Abigail Wick, sitting with her family on the red sofa of *This Morning*, telling the world she was home.

Something changes. A noise in the distance. The crunch of pebbles. He spins around, rifle swinging with him, searching the horizon, then stopping as a lone figure moves quickly towards them.

Sarah is here.

Abi's airway shrinks. She's out of time. Dead. She wants to shout out, to warn Sarah to run while she still can, but fear has stolen her voice.

'Sarah,' he shouts, his voice shrill, almost unhuman. 'I'm so glad you could join us.'

'What's going on?' Sarah replies, looking between them all and then at the gun. 'Oh my God.' The final words are a whispered gasp.

'What's going on?' he shouts. 'What the hell does it look like?'

There's a moment where no one seems to know what to say. Sarah takes a final two steps to reach the rocks, her gaze darting from Michael to the gun, to Daniel, and then finally to her.

'You're not my daughter, are you?' The question has lost the accusing tone. It's just a question. A simple one.

Finally the roulette wheel stops turning in Abi's mind. She shakes her head. 'No. I'm not. I'm sorry.' Fresh tears brim in her eyes.

'I'm sorry,' she says again. 'I never meant... I didn't mean to hurt you.' His eyes are on her now too, but she doesn't care anymore. 'He told me you wouldn't want to know me. That you'd tell me to piss off if I told you the truth. I shouldn't have believed him, but I did.'

Abi draws in a breath, fighting to stop the emotion consuming her. 'I... I just... I wanted to see the life I could have had. To feel what it was like to have a family who cared about me. He... he knew it too. He told me if I pretended to be Abigail, I'd get everything I wanted.

'I didn't know he'd do this.' Abi looks at him then; a glance. If he feels anything – guilt, hate – it doesn't show. His eyes are wide but distant too, flat. 'He convinced me I'd be helping you by giving you your daughter back, and I... I knew it was wrong, but I was desperate. He gave me money and came up with this whole plan about pretending I'd been living in Colombia. I didn't think I had a choice. It was that or living on the streets. I... was wrong.'

'Enough,' he shouts.

There's a click, and it takes Abi a second to realise where the noise has come from – the gun. He's done something. He's getting ready. It's over.

'I'm sorry,' she stammers over and over. 'I'm so sorry.'

# FORTY-NINE

## SARAH

My heart thunders in my chest. My mouth is dry. My eyes keep being drawn back to the long thin rifle. I can't process it. Where did it come from? How did he get it? Stupid questions. The how doesn't matter. It's the why.

I force myself to look at Abelia and the girl she is. Lost. Alone. Confused. There's so much I don't know, but I have the answer, the truth about her. Her voice as she whispers her, 'Sorry,' no longer carrying the mix of America or Spanish in the accent, trails off.

I turn to Michael. His face in the torchlight is ashen. And despite the danger striking the air like lightning, the gun, the threat and the fear that chases through my blood, I still feel fury rise up from a deep well inside me.

'What did you do, Michael? What is all this?'

His head hangs, shaking from side to side, until his chin is almost resting on his chest and I want to scream at him to look at me. But I can't keep my eyes away from the rifle. I find myself reaching out, stepping forward to take it.

'No.' He steps back, pointing the barrel at me. 'Enough.'

I nod. I try to stay calm and be the person he needs – a

mother. I look from the barrel to the hands clutching it, up and up until I lock eyes with my son. There's a wildness to Daniel's expression, an anger I haven't seen in him for many, many years. I wonder again where he got a rifle and why we're here. Why did he bring Abelia into our lives and trick us into believing she was Abigail? Why would our son do this?

I knew of course. The second I saw the figure in the long black coat trailing behind Abi in the CCTV footage DC Swain showed me. I might not have seen his face, but I recognised the long, loping stride of my son, and I knew he was involved.

Michael may have lied about many things over the course of our marriage, but what's going on right now is about Daniel, and even though part of me is terrified of the gun and what he might do next, another part of me wants to take him in my arms and tell him it will be OK. But as Daniel's hands jerk, moving the rifle to point at Michael, I'm not sure it will be. I don't know how Daniel got a gun, but it won't have been easy. And the only reason I can think that he's done it is because he plans to use it.

'Tell me.' I move, my legs breaking into a run. I try to fly at him, but the stones shift beneath my feet and I slip. 'Daniel, what's this all about? Will you please tell me what's going on? How did you find Abelia?'

'Oh, Mum.' Daniel tries to sigh as though he has all the time in the world, but I am his mother and I can see that beneath the show of calm, he's as terrified as I am. 'Why don't we start at the beginning with your dutiful husband shagging around long before you stopped showing any interest? Isn't that right, Dad?'

Disdain laces Daniel's voice, and I gasp and stand back to look at my son.

'It was one time.' Michael lifts his head. 'A one-night thing with a woman in a pub when I was at a marketing conference in Birmingham. I got drunk. It was one time, I swear. Daniel was a baby and you were so focused on him.'

I laugh, a wailing ha from the shock and the pitiful excuse. Even now, after all these years, he's still justifying it in his head.

'You knew about Abelia, didn't you?' I ask.

He shakes his head. 'Not really. Caroline called me when she was pregnant. I must have given her my number at some point. She told me she was having my baby, but I didn't believe her. She was easy. I wasn't the only guy...' He shrugs. 'I told her to get lost.'

My mind races back over this week and Michael's behaviour. The gasp as he saw Abi's photo for the first time. It wasn't me he saw in that face, it was Caroline. I look at the man I've shared twenty-five years of my life with and see only a stranger.

'But that's not all you did, is it, Dad? You didn't just tell her to get lost, you threatened her. You told her that if she ever contacted you again, you'd kill her and the baby. Nice one, Dad. Way to get out of paying child support and giving a child of yours the life they deserved.'

Daniel's voice breaks at the end. It isn't just anger and fear I see in him now. It's hurt.

'Daniel...' I start, searching for words I don't have, 'whatever happened with your dad, this—'

'Stop,' he cuts in. 'It's time.'

'For what?' My eyes are drawn back to the rifle.

'To talk about what happened to Abigail.'

Everything stops. I can no longer hear the waves crashing to the shore or the crunch of stones beneath our feet. I see only Daniel. 'You know?' I gasp. 'You know what happened? Tell me.'

He sighs again and raises his eyebrows. 'Can we drop the act now please? Abi has reverted to being a Brummie, Michael's admitted to being *the* world's worst dad. Can't you be honest now, Sarah?'

I shake my head. The grief is closing in around me and I can feel the sting of tears burning the back of my eyes. 'Tell me, please, Daniel. Where's Abigail? What happened?'

'Wait... You really don't know?' Daniel's gaze darts to Michael, before moving back to me. 'Promise me you don't know?' The mocking tone is gone. His face falls slack and his Adam's apple rises high then falls. The gun shakes in his hands. He lowers it a fraction and then it's up again, pointing at me, but I don't care.

'Please tell me,' I cry out. Pleading.

'You—' Daniel starts to say, but there's a movement to one side and Ryan appears beside him.

'Put the gun down now, Daniel,' Ryan says, voice loud and calm. He steps around to the rocks and places himself between Abi, me and the barrel of the gun. 'You don't need it.'

Daniel jolts backwards; his eyes are wide. 'You shouldn't be here.' He pokes the gun at Ryan. 'Get back,' he screams. 'This has nothing to do with you.'

'OK, Daniel. I'm stepping back... see? Let's all stay calm. The police are on their way.'

A darkness crosses Daniel's face. A cloud. I recognise it from the outbursts he had as a child. That stick in the park. Those moments where nothing could penetrate his rage.

He turns to Michael. 'You didn't tell her?'

Michael's face is hidden behind his hands. His shoulders rise and fall.

'Stop crying!' Daniel's screech echoes across the beach. 'You have no right to cry. Be a man for once in your life.'

There's a moment of stillness. Abi whimpers beside me but all my focus is on Michael now.

He drops his hands to his side and lifts his face to look at Daniel. 'I was trying to protect you,' he says.

'Protect me? You ruined my life. You took everything from me. You made me live a lie.'

Daniel steps closer. The gun stops shaking. His finger

squeezes the trigger a little then releases it. I almost don't notice Ryan's slow sideways steps as he circles closer to Daniel.

'Michael, Daniel, please.' I look between them, willing Ryan to hold back. I have to know the truth. 'Tell me about Abigail.'

Daniel spins at me until the gun is level with my head. He's only a metre away. Close enough that even a bad aim will kill me. My heart lurches, but I don't flinch or cower. I have to know. His faces scrunches inwards and I see the child he once was.

'I killed her. I killed Abigail.'

# FIFTY

## SARAH

Daniel's words hit me with the same force as a bullet from his gun. The wind stops. The world stops. I'm no longer cold or scared.

'Daniel,' I say, 'what do you mean?'

He makes a noise, a howling sob, then a gasp and another sob. 'I fell over in the garden and she laughed at me. I... picked up one of the rocks we'd collected from the beach, and... I threw it. I was so mad and I wanted to kill her. It... it hit her on the head, and it did. It killed her. I killed her. I killed Abigail.'

Daniel's sobs are louder now, but I barely hear. My world folds inwards, collapsing. Abigail is dead. My beautiful girl. Dead. Killed not abducted. No stranger luring her from the garden. No pushchair, no ferry ride.

The pain stretches out from my chest, all the way across my body, and yet there's still more I need to know.

'But the police – why did—' I stop. I can't ask the question and I don't need to because Michael is already talking.

'I didn't know you knew she was dead,' he cries out at Daniel, dropping to his knees and falling at our son's feet.

Daniel leaps back, the rifle now pointing at Michael's head as he turns to look at me.

'Daniel came into the house with a cut on his hand. He was shaking and crying and he told me he'd thrown a rock at Abigail. I told him to wash his hand in the bathroom and I went outside.

'She was just lying there on the ground, her head on the paving stones. I thought she was pretending at first, but then...'

He stops, swallows and I bite back the scream lodged in my throat and the desire to cover my ears and not hear any more.

'I went closer and I saw her eyes were open. She was gone. I think the rock Daniel threw knocked her out and then she hit her head on the paving stones. There was nothing anyone could do, Sarah. It was instant. She wouldn't have felt a thing.'

I force out the question I have to ask, the one we've been building to. 'What happened next?'

Tears stream down Michael's face. 'I didn't want Daniel to know he'd killed her. I didn't want that hanging over him his whole life. It would've destroyed him. So I... I went back inside and I told him Abigail was fine, that she was still playing outside and everything would be OK. I decided I'd make it look like an accident happened after that, so that Daniel wouldn't carry the blame of his sister's death. I put the TV on for him and told him not to come outside—'

'Don't forget the part where you made me promise not to tell anyone about the rock I'd thrown. Remember that bit, Dad? Where you hissed in the face of your six-year-old son that if he ever spoke a word about what he'd done to anyone, even Mum – especially Mum – the police would come and he would go to prison for a really long time.'

I shake my head, unable to believe what I'm hearing. 'Michael?'

'I thought if he told anyone about the rock, they might

realise what had happened. The only way I could make it look like an accident was if no one ever found out what he'd done first.' He turns back to Daniel. 'I was trying to protect you.'

'But I came back out,' Daniel shouts. 'I saw you crying over Abigail's body. I saw her eyes. She wasn't moving. I saw what I'd done.'

'I didn't know that,' Michael sobs. 'I thought you still believed what I'd told you. All these years, I swear, I thought you didn't know the truth.'

I blink and all the pieces of the puzzle I couldn't look at are now staring me in the face. I see them, but I can't believe it. 'So... so...' I repeat the word, louder each time as I force my voice out and face the truth I've spent fourteen years hiding from. 'So you pretended she'd been abducted? You made me believe a man had stolen my child?'

'It wasn't supposed to be like that,' Michael croaks out the words. 'I wanted it to look like she'd wandered out of the garden and fallen and hit her head. A tragic accident. I was trying to protect our son.

'I talked to Daniel and made him promise not to tell anyone about the rock he'd thrown, then I made sure he was watching the TV, and then I... I picked up Abigail's body and carried her to the beach. Just here.' He waves a hand at the rocks. 'I was upset. I wasn't thinking straight, and then you came back from your run early.' Michael looks up at me for just a second before dropping his gaze to the beach. 'I panicked and said she was missing. I sent you looking for her and called the police. I knew they'd search the beach and find her body and it would look like she'd slipped.

'But then that woman called the police and they started talking about an abduction. No one searched the beach in time and the tide came in and... Abigail... she must have been swept out to sea.'

I close my eyes and fight to draw in one ragged breath after another.

All the time I screamed Abigail's name in the streets with Janie. All the time Michael and I had clung to each other, waiting for news. All that time and my little girl was less than a hundred metres away from me. Dead. Acid burns my throat. I taste it in my mouth and swallow hard.

'But you could've said something,' I say. 'All those hours we sat together waiting for news. You could have made them search the beach. You knew the tide would be coming in.'

'It was too late.' Michael shakes his head. 'They were already calling it an abduction. It would have looked suspicious if I'd told them to search the beach.'

I'm stunned. Frozen in this hell, but I force myself to speak. 'So you sent me off, convinced me Abigail was missing, and forced our six-year-old son to lie—'

'I'm sorry. I was grieving and panicking and I didn't know what to do.'

*Grieving.* The word stirs a hate in me more powerful than anything I've ever felt before. 'You were grieving,' I scream. The sound bounces across the beach. 'What about me? What about your family? You didn't give us the chance to grieve.'

The depth of his lies is pressing down on me. All the years I thought he was still searching for Abigail. The charity and the support groups were what – a cover? A way to appease his guilt. None of it was real. More pieces of the puzzle fall into place.

'That's why you didn't want the DNA test. It had nothing to do with your belief that she was our daughter, because you knew. YOU KNEW,' I shout again, 'that she wasn't. You knew Abigail was dead. How exactly did you think this would play out, Michael?' I wave my hands at Abi, still crouched on the pebbles, and Daniel standing over us. His face is ghostly, scrunched up with anger. The rifle is still pointing at Michael's head.

I look to the cottage where my daughter died, and at the sea that swept her away. I feel my legs weaken under me. I'm desperate to fall to the ground and give in to the grief – razor blades slashing and slicing at me from the inside out – but I won't. Not yet. 'What did you think would happen? Did you think I would accept this girl as Abigail and we'd all live happily ever after?'

Michael sniffs and raises his head. His eyes are watery in the torchlight and filled with pity, but all I can see is a man I hate with every fibre of my being.

'Yes. I'm sorry, but yes. I knew it wasn't Abigail, but after all the years I'd looked for her—'

'Pretended to look,' I yell. 'I saw the files.'

He nods, a broken man. 'I... I hired the first PI because I knew it was what everyone expected, but I panicked. I thought he might find out something—'

'Like the truth, you mean?'

Michael nods, his Adam's apple pushing up and then down. 'I couldn't tell you or anyone else that this girl wasn't Abigail. I thought she was some girl trying her luck and I knew the DNA test would prove she wasn't our daughter But then it came back as a match and I didn't know what to do. It was Abigail's death all over again. I couldn't tell anyone she wasn't Abigail without explaining how I knew. I guessed she must have been Caroline's daughter and that she'd found out I was her father. I thought she needed a home and I thought maybe she could... fix us.' He sobs, a gulping cough of a noise.

'Daniel,' I say. He looks ghostly pale and scared to death. Digging fingers squeeze my heart. The burden he's carried all this time rips me apart. 'You could've told me,' I say to him.

Daniel shakes his head from side to side but doesn't move his eyes from his father, now shuffling back until he's pressing himself against the rocks. Ryan is still beside Abi, but my focus is only on Daniel.

'Dad came to kiss me goodnight on the first night after Abigail was gone. He said, "I've told your mum that you threw a rock at Abigail. She's very cross with you, so don't say anything to her or she might tell one of these policemen and then you'll go to prison and we'll lose two children instead of one."'

'So you stopped speaking.' I shake my head, freeing tears that race down my cheeks.

'I thought you knew Abigail was dead,' Daniel says again, his voice just a squeak now. 'He told me not to tell anyone.'

The hurt drops from his face and all that's left is rage. He moves the gun, aiming it at Michael's face. 'I thought you'd both been lying to the world and to me and Rebecca for all these years. Pretending to be the people whose daughter was abducted.

'When she' – Daniel nods to Abi – 'got in touch with me, I saw a way to get back at you. A girl almost the same age as Abigail, same hair, similar looks. I wanted to see if you'd carry on pretending and you did. So I did too. I wanted you to pay for the pain you put me through. I got Abi to take your DNA sample,' he says and suddenly the gun is on me.

I shake my head, fighting to find my voice. 'Daniel, I would never have done that to you. I'm so sorry that I didn't know any of this and that I couldn't help you. I thought you were OK.'

'Well, I wasn't,' he cries out. 'I was pretending. Learned from the best.' He shoots me a look and then swings the gun back to Michael.

I cry out. 'Daniel, it wasn't your fault. None of this was your fault. Please don't do this.'

'It's too late.' His body shifts position, legs stepping apart, bracing himself. 'You, me and Dad. Three bullets.'

'No!'

My shout is lost to the noise of the gun exploding into the night. A crashing bang, a roar that reverberates through my body. Everything slows down and speeds up all at once.

Abi's hand is on my arm and she's dragging me down. I hit the stony beach with a hard thud. Ryan launches into the air, throwing himself at Daniel. I wait for the next bang, the next bullet, but it doesn't come.

A second passes and another. I look to Michael. He's slumped against the rock, cradling his ear. But there's no blood. His chest heaves. Daniel missed. On purpose? A mistake? I don't know.

Daniel is face down on the beach with Ryan on top of him. 'I'm sorry,' he sobs, releasing the gun from his grasp. 'I'm sorry, Mummy. I'm sorry, Mummy. I thought you knew. I wanted to hurt you both for lying and making me lie. I'm sorry, Mummy. I'm sorry.'

I pull away from Abi and scramble across the beach to Daniel. Ryan shakes his head, urging me to stay back, but I can't. I cradle my son in my arms, shushing his tears as my own drop onto his head.

I don't hear the police approach until they're upon us. A dozen uniforms and DC Swain. I wonder how much she heard.

All of it, I realise, as she hoists Michael from the ground.

'Michael Wick,' she says, 'I am arresting you for perverting the course of justice in the death of Abigail Wick. You do not have to say anything, but it may harm your defence if you do not mention when questioned something which you later rely on in court. Anything you do say may be given in evidence. Do you understand?'

He nods, and his eyes find mine. What I see in that look is not sorrow or regret; it's acceptance. The fury returns and I see the rifle on the beach; for a split second I want to reach for it and kill him for all he's put us through, for what he's done to Daniel and to Rebecca.

But I don't. Daniel needs me. Rebecca needs me. I think of Abi too, and everything she's been through. We're her family.

It's over.

I have the truth. My daughter died fourteen years ago. Her body is gone, washed out to sea. I stare out at the black waves. My grief is a riptide pulling me under.

*I'm sorry, sweet baby. I'm so sorry.*

# FIFTY-ONE

## ABI

Friday, 10 p.m.

Abi remembers the sound of the wind roaring in her ears. She remembers the gun swinging wildly between the three of them, and the this-is-it feeling of being about to die tearing through her body. She remembers the shift of pebbles beneath her as she reached up and pulled Sarah down, and the commotion of the officers rushing in.

But now that she's here, in another police-station waiting room, sitting on another row of blue plastic chairs, Abi can't recall how she made it from the beach to the beige-brick one-storey police station in Aldeburgh. The memory is gone, as though she blacked out, but she's sure she didn't.

Two chairs away, Sarah hunches forward, dropping her head into her hands and unleashing a rasping gasp that knots Abi's stomach so tight she longs to be back on the beach just to have the sound of the wind deafening her.

Abi tries to summon the crushing desperation she felt a year ago when Jhon died and the last living soul who cared about her, or even knew she existed, was gone. But the desperation is no longer there, nor the sense of righteousness Daniel instilled in her with all his 'it's time to get the life you're owed' speeches. The life she thought she deserved. But Abi sees the truth now, a fog clearing from her mind. All she deserves is prison.

She lied to the police. She broke the law. But it's for what she's done to Sarah and Rebecca that she really deserves to be punished. Abi hangs her head. The thick clumps of her tangled hair droop over her face, hiding the silent tears streaking down her cheeks.

The door leading into the police station opens, pulling Abi's thoughts back to the waiting room. She lifts her head a fraction.

'Ryan.' Sarah rushes forward and collapses into his arms; her petite frame seems fragile enough to snap beside the sturdiness of his body.

'What's happening? Where's Daniel? Is he OK?' Sarah pulls herself free, her expression frantic as she looks at Ryan.

'He's with an on-call doctor,' Ryan replies, guiding Sarah back to the chairs and sitting down beside her. 'He's agreed to have a sedative to help calm him down. He needs to be assessed by someone from the mental-health team. It's going to be a while before the police can talk to him.'

'I should be with him.' Sarah's gaze flicks from Ryan to the door. 'He needs me.'

Ryan takes Sarah's hand before he speaks. 'You can't, Sarah. Daniel is twenty. In the eyes of the law, he's an adult.'

'Can you be there at least then?' Sarah asks, tears pooling in her eyes. 'He needs someone beside him, just to check he's OK?'

'I'm too involved in this to be impartial. I was on the beach, remember? The best we can do is have a solicitor present, but right now Daniel is saying he doesn't want that.'

'Where the hell did he get a gun from?'

'It's an air rifle,' Ryan says. 'You can apply for a licence and get one if you're over eighteen. They're not as powerful as a real gun but they can do some damage. Certainly at close range, they can kill.'

'But—'

The front door of the police station opens, blasting the waiting room with cold salty air. A large man in a suit hefts his weight to the front desk. His shirt is crisp, his suit sharp, just like his eyes as he assesses Abi.

'Can I help you?' the desk sergeant asks from the counter.

'Freddie Adams,' the man replies, his voice deep and booming in the small space. 'Solicitor for Michael Wick.'

The desk sergeant presses a hidden button and motions to the grey door. 'This way please.'

Sarah draws in a shuddering breath. 'That bastard,' she whispers. 'That bastard has a solicitor already?'

Ryan nods and squeezes Sarah's hand. 'Try not to think about it right now.

'I have to get back to my report,' he continues. 'I just came to let you know Daniel is OK, and to see if either of you want a drink?'

Sarah shakes her head. 'I'm fine.'

'Abi?' he asks.

Sarah starts at the question as though only just realising Abi is there too.

Abi shakes her head and drops her gaze to the dark-blue floor. 'No thank you.'

'They're speaking to Michael first,' Ryan adds, his voice soft and low. 'Then, depending on how Daniel is feeling, they may speak to you next, Abi.'

Abi swallows back the mounting panic and nods again. She deserves this, she reminds herself.

'I'll check back with you soon.' Ryan disappears through the grey door, leaving Abi and Sarah alone once more.

Sarah steps back but instead of returning to her seat, she moves to sit beside Abi. 'Tell me everything,' she says.

'Everything?' Abi wipes her fingers across her cheeks and forces herself to look up.

Sarah's eyes are etched with red, her face stained with streaks where her tears have washed away the make-up, but there's the same determination and strength in her expression that Abi has seen in her all along.

'I want to understand what you did and maybe see if I can understand why. You said on the beach you didn't have a choice. Why not? The truth this time,' Sarah adds, her tone cutting into Abi's chest.

Abi thinks of the parallel life – the house with the courtyard at the edge of the city, the mother and father who loved her. The image disintegrates into sand in her mind.

'I grew up in a one-bedroom flat on the third floor of a fourteen-storey tower block in Birmingham,' Abi says. 'My mum was called Caroline. She was from America. I don't know whereabouts, and I don't know how she came to live in England. She suffered with depression and hated leaving the apartment. She was scared to be alone too, so she kept me with her. Every day she'd lie on the sofa and watch American movies and TV shows.

'I didn't go to school. The only visitor was my mum's boyfriend, a man called Hector. Caroline called him Jhon, so I did too. He stopped by once a week when I was really little and stayed the night. His name was on my birth certificate. Up until last year, I thought he was my father.

'I used to think when he wasn't with us that he was working. He always had really strong coffee and I thought he was a coffee salesman, travelling the world, but it was just in my head. He had another family. When he'd visit, he'd set me schoolwork and teach me Spanish. Then when I was about seven, Jhon started to visit less and less and stopped staying over, and my mum's depression got worse. I used to think he still visited because I was his daughter, but I don't know now.

Maybe it was just pity that kept him visiting my mum and paying the rent.

'I started going out by myself. Just to the shop and back because there was no food to eat. An old woman on the floor above gave me some clothes. Then Mum got sick. It was really quick, but I guess she'd been ill for a while. She used to complain about pain a lot.'

'So your mum died when you were twelve. That was true?' Sarah asks.

'Yes.' Abi nods. Her throat aches with the hurt of the truth she's now telling, but she doesn't stop. All she has left is the truth, and she owes Sarah that much. 'She really did die when I was twelve.'

'I'm sorry. That must have been very hard.'

'Thank you,' Abi says. 'After that, Jhon kept paying the rent and popping in from time to time. I thought... I thought I was free then. That without Mum holding me back I could have a life. Jhon helped me find a school and signed me up. I tried going for a bit, but I dunno' – Abi shrugs – 'it was a lot to take in. There was so much I didn't know and... I'm not stupid, but they had a way of doing maths that I didn't get. The teacher told me off for doing sums in my head. No one really spoke to me, and that was worse somehow than being in the flat all day by myself.

'I stopped going one day and no one cared. So I got a job washing pots in the kitchen of a café, and when I looked old enough, the owner let me waitress too. I earned enough to buy bits of food and some second-hand clothes, and with Jhon paying the rent on the apartment, I survived. Then he died too,' Abi whispers.

'Last year?' Sarah confirms.

Abi nods. 'Then I got a letter. He must've got someone else to post it because it arrived after he died. I knew he'd been ill, but he never told me how bad.'

Tears threaten at the back of her eyes and she wills them away. If she breaks down now, she'll never stop.

'It said that if I was reading it, then it meant he was dead. He said he loved me, but he wasn't my real father. That he was sorry for not telling me sooner, but Caroline had made him promise not to tell me who my real father was. The letter said my father was a man named Michael Wick. A marketing guy Caroline had met a few times. Jhon didn't know anything else about him, other than that Caroline had told Jhon that Michael had threatened to kill her and me if she ever contacted him again. Jhon wasn't sure if it was true or not, but he warned me to be careful.'

'So you reached out?'

Abi sniffs. 'Not at first. I didn't do anything at first. It just seemed so unreal. But then a rent-demand letter arrived and I panicked. Without Jhon's help I didn't have enough money to live anywhere. Jhon was all I had, and he was gone.'

'I did a Google search on Michael Wick and marketing, and only one name came up, but I was scared to contact him. I found out about Abigail and you and Rebecca and Daniel. I watched you on YouTube. I tried to find a number or email for you but there wasn't anything.'

'So you found Daniel?' Sarah rakes a hand through her hair before pushing it behind her ears.

'Yes, on Facebook. It was the only way I could think to contact any of you. I set up an account and I messaged him and told him everything. He replied straight away. He told me how broken you all were, that you'd never got over Abigail's abduction, and how you were so protective over Rebecca that you would never accept me. He said he was sorry, but there was nothing he could do. But then a few days later, he messaged me back, saying we should meet. He had an idea; a way for me to get the family and the life I wanted, and help you all too.'

'By pretending to be Abigail?'

A sob escapes Abi's mouth. She covers her mouth and nods. A mesh of relief and horror sit like a rock in her gut. 'I'm sorry.'

'What about Michael? Did he know any of this?'

Abi shakes her head. 'No. I caught him looking at me a couple of times and thought he might say something, but he never did. I had no idea about Abigail,' she says, the words coming fast. 'I swear. Daniel never told me his plan. I thought it was about me finding a home and you all getting a daughter and sister. By the time I realised it was about something more, it was too late.

'I tried to question him. I asked him over and over why I couldn't just turn up and be me, Michael's illegitimate daughter. That surely a father wouldn't turn their child away, but he laughed at me. He made me feel stupid. He said you'd never allow me to be part of your family. He told me I could be the one to heal you. I could be the one to be loved and I could have everything I ever wanted and the life I would've had if Michael hadn't turned his back on me when I was a baby. All I had to do was pretend to be Abigail.'

'I wouldn't have turned you away. I'm not saying I would've welcomed you with open arms, but—'

'I know that now,' Abi says. 'I know it's no excuse, but I had no money or family. No friends. Daniel gave me money and made me feel... important. Like I mattered. It was the first time anyone had made me feel that way.'

'What about your name? Is it really Abelia?'

'Yes. The old woman in the flat above shortened it to Abi and I liked it. It's just a coincidence that it's... that it's so like Abigail's.'

'After you contacted Daniel, what happened next?' Sarah asks. 'Why did you wait a year?'

'Daniel told me to leave my job and keep a low profile. I was so used to being on my own' – she shrugs – 'it wasn't a problem. I lost some weight and dyed my hair darker. Daniel came up to visit sometimes, bringing more money and telling me what to do. We did a DNA test just to be sure Caroline had been telling the truth.'

'So you never lived in Colombia?' Sarah shakes her head.

'No. I went there for a month. Daniel helped me get a passport here and took me to France in his car. I had to hide in the boot for hours. I was so scared someone would find me. He said it would be harder for them to track me through my passport if I flew out of a different country. We drove all the way to Spain and I flew to Buenaventura from there. I applied for a Colombian passport with my birth certificate because Jhon's name was on it and he was Colombian. And then I waited for it to be issued. I knew it was crazy, but Daniel said that no one would believe I was Abigail if I said I'd been living in Birmingham the whole time, and someone was bound to come forward and say they remembered me as a baby.'

'And the chicken-pox scar?' Sarah asks.

'Daniel told me about the scar on Abigail's chest.' Abi closes her eyes as a wave of nausea rises.

'I didn't realise he remembered,' Sarah sighs.

'I used a cigarette.'

Sarah gasps. 'You gave yourself a scar?'

'Daniel said... he said I should. He thought you might ask to see it.'

Abi bites her lip and waits for Sarah's next question. A minute passes in silence.

Abi turns her head and looks at Sarah. 'Deep down I knew it would all come crashing down. I knew they'd find out who Jhon was and that he lived in Birmingham, but Daniel said it didn't matter. He said they wouldn't check, that they'd believe me. He told me to stick as close to the truth as possible. Now I see it wasn't that they wouldn't look; it was that it didn't matter to Daniel if they did or didn't. He thought by the time the truth came out, his plan would be over. I think meeting on the beach was his plan all along,' she continues. 'He said earlier that he had three bullets and was going to use them all. I thought it was for me, you and Michael, but...'

'It was for me, Michael and for him,' Sarah finishes. Fresh tears fall down her face. 'He must have bottled Abigail's death up inside him all these years. He thought Michael and I were forcing him to lie. It's no wonder he wanted us to pay. I just... I wish I'd known.'

Sarah's face contorts with a hurt that Abi can feel knotting her own insides.

'I'm sorry about Abigail. About everything,' Abi whispers. 'You don't need to worry about me anymore. I won't cause you any problems. I'll probably be going to prison, but if I don't, then don't worry – you'll never have to see me again anyway.'

Sarah shakes her head. 'No.' She pulls in a deep breath and straightens her back before she turns to look at Abi. 'You're Michael's biological daughter, and like it or not, that makes you Rebecca and Daniel's half-sister, which means you'll always have a home with us.'

A lump balloons in Abi's throat as she takes in Sarah's words.

'I can't stop you from running away when we're done here, and I wouldn't blame you if you did, but I hope you won't. I hope you'll face up to the mistakes you've made. We've got some hard times ahead. Rebecca will need your support.'

Abi's vision blurs from the tears now swimming in her eyes. 'Thank you,' she whispers. The words aren't enough.

'Don't thank me yet. The British media will eat us alive when this news gets out, and that goes for you too.'

The grey door opens once more, but it isn't Ryan standing in the doorway this time, it's DC Swain. 'Abelia?'

Abi nods and stands up.

'We'd like to talk to you now,' DC Swain says, holding the door open for Abi to step through.

Sarah's voice echoes in Abi's head as she wipes a hand across her face and forces her feet forward. *I hope you'll face up to the mistakes you've made.*

Abi doesn't know if she'll ever be able to make up for what she's done, but if Sarah and Rebecca let her, then she's going to try. She did this because she wanted a home and a family, and even though it's gone wrong, she hopes one day she might still find those things.

THREE MONTHS LATER

# FIFTY-TWO

## SARAH

Tuesday, 2 p.m.

The dining hall is smaller than I expect. There's an oak table running down the middle, and, to one side, a silver trolley stacked with trays, standing beside a cubby-hole into a kitchen.

Dr Hall leads me to a chair and motions for me to sit down beside a tray of drinks. She's smaller than the woman I remember from years ago, when she first met Daniel. Thick grey hair hangs around her face, and every few minutes she pushes her glasses closer to her face.

'We have set mealtimes,' she says, sitting opposite Sarah. 'Breakfast, lunch and dinner. We encourage all of our guests to eat together, along with staff. We feel it fosters trust and brings a family feel to the place.'

Regret sears in my stomach. Why did we stop bringing Daniel to see Dr Hall? She helped him to speak again after a year of silence. Maybe if he'd kept talking to her, things would've turned out differently. It's another regret, another maybe to add to the growing pile in my mind.

'Coffee?' Dr Hall asks, picking up a silver jug.

I nod. 'Thank you.'

She pours me a cup before sliding the milk towards me. 'Daniel will be here in a few minutes, but I wanted to talk with you first.'

'How is he?' I ask, cradling the cup in my hands. The heat burns my fingers, but I don't move them away.

'My obligation is to Daniel, and confidentiality means I'm restricted on what I can tell you. I will say that he's talking very openly about recent events. There are a lot of layers to peel back before we can address the past. He's buried a lot of hurt and anger. The memory is a strange thing, Sarah. Sometimes young children block out things that have happened, and other times they remember every tiny detail. I think Daniel is the latter, but he's battling with a lot of guilt.'

The hurt tightens my throat, and questions crowd my mind. I draw in a breath and fight for control. This isn't the time for me to break down. My eyes are drawn to the planks of wood stretching across the floor and I start to count them.

Dr Hall places her hand over mine. 'He may not have had a choice in being sent here, but he's in the right place. It's going to take time. Agreeing to see you is a big step.'

I blink back the tears. It's been three months since the beach. Three months since I last saw my son. 'Is there anything I should or shouldn't say?'

'We restrict contact with the outside world as much as we can. No social media. No newspapers. No access to news channels. Titbits creep in from visitors, but we do what we can to shield our patients. It's especially important for Daniel that he feels able to address what he's done in his own time, through his own eyes, and not through those of others.'

I can tell by the set of her face that she's read the headlines, the ones calling him a monster. She wants to shield him from it.

I want that too. I wish there was a way to hide them from Rebecca. The truth about her father has hit her hard. She's upset and she's angry. She's no longer trying to make everyone happy, and often her anger is directed at me. I understand. She can't direct it at Michael, who's hiding himself away somewhere and won't see her.

I grit my teeth against the fresh wave of anger I feel towards Michael and focus my thoughts on Rebecca. She's angry at Abi too. She feels betrayed, although already I've seen her thaw a little towards her half-sister. One day, I think they'll be close again. Only Daniel has come away unscathed in Rebecca's anger. She's written him a letter. It's in my pocket to give to him.

It will take time for Rebecca to heal. I've asked her if she'd like to see a therapist. She's considering it. So is Abi. They're both strong. They'll be OK. I have to believe that.

'Daniel may ask you questions,' Dr Hall continues. 'Please be mindful not to tell him more than he needs to know, but don't lie either. He's only at the start of his journey to recovery. I've given him a notebook to write in. He's spoken a few times about wanting to write everything down in a story. I think it could be a good way for him to address the past.'

A door slams from the other side of the hall, the noise echoing around us. Dr Hall stands and smiles as Daniel steps towards us. His hair has been washed recently. It looks a shade lighter and is fluffy on the top. There's an outbreak of angry red spots on his forehead and dark circles under his eyes, but my heart lifts to see him.

I stand too, unsure whether I should hug him or whether he'll let me.

Daniel's shoulders hunch and his gaze remains fixed on the floor. One, two, three strides and he's in the chair Dr Hall has just vacated. I sit down and wrap my arms around myself instead.

'It's good to see you,' I say.

There's a pause before he speaks. 'You too,' he mumbles.

Dr Hall clears her throat. 'I'll leave you to it. You have a session in the gym soon, Daniel, so we'll keep this short today.'

Daniel nods and places Dr Hall's empty cup on the tray. He fiddles with the coffee pot and the cups, lining the handles up so that they all face the same way.

'The gym?' I raise my eyebrows. I'm not sure how or where to start. I search my thoughts for neutral territory but there isn't any.

He shakes his head, and I long for him to look up and meet my gaze. 'It's like a rec room. I have to knock a ball about on a table-tennis table with a therapist. They think if we're hitting a ball, we might not notice the questions they're asking.'

'Are you OK?' I blurt out. 'Is it OK in here?'

He shrugs and begins realigning the cups to face the other way. 'Where else is there for me to go?'

I open my mouth to reply but stop. I don't have an answer for him.

He reaches for one of the clean cups and pours himself a coffee. 'What's happening with Dad? They won't tell me anything.'

Dr Hall's warning runs through my mind, but I can't lie. Lies have all but destroyed us and I can't tell another one. Daniel has been forced to lie for most of his life. If anyone deserves the truth now, it's him.

'He's been charged with perverting the course of justice,' I say. 'He's out on police bail until a trial. I don't know where he is.' I pause, wondering whether to say more. 'I'm meeting my solicitor next week and filing for divorce.'

He says nothing. Like Rebecca, he accepts this as the inevitable next step.

'He's writing a book,' I continue. 'For real this time, I think. He's signed a book deal to tell his side of what happened.'

Daniel exhales, shaking his head. He stares at the coffee in his cup with such intensity it's as though he's trying to move it with the power of thought. 'Do you think he'll go to prison?'

'I don't know.' It's the truth. 'I hope so. He deserves to rot in a cell for the rest of his life for what he did to you, Daniel. To all of us.'

Daniel has lied and manipulated us, but it's the enormity of Michael's lies that press down on me, just as they do anytime I think about it. The hurt is back too, clawing at my insides. It isn't just the first lie he told about what happened to Abigail, or even what he said to Daniel – although they cut deep – but all that followed. Fourteen years of lies and pretending. He stole our chance to grieve for Abigail. What kind of person can do that to those he loves? I don't have an answer. I never will.

The pressure threatens to crush me, but I can't allow myself to think about it now.

Daniel picks at the skin around his thumb. It's red and looks sore, and I want to take his hands and hold them in my own, but I don't.

'The rifle. Where did you get it?' I ask.

'I joined a shooting range and got a gun licence. It was an air rifle, but they can still kill people.'

I want to ask him if he meant to miss Michael on the beach, but I don't know how. The question pesters my thoughts in the small hours of the night when I can't sleep, but now isn't the time. Perhaps it will never be the time. In my dreams, it is me that holds the gun. Me that pulls the trigger and I don't miss, and Michael is dead.

'Are you keeping busy?' I ask instead.

'Ryan came to see me yesterday,' Daniel mumbles by way of reply.

'I didn't know that.'

Ryan's name causes a flicker of something inside me, but it's buried so far under the hurt that I'm not sure what it means.

'He wanted to say sorry for grabbing me on the beach. Well, that's what he said, but he spent most of the time talking about you.'

Daniel's face is still dipped but I think I see the ghost of a smile tug on his lips. It's just a glimmer, but I see the cheeky boy in Daniel fighting to break free.

'He likes you.'

It's my turn to shrug. I don't tell Daniel about the tearful calls I've made to Ryan in the dead of night. Or the peace I've found in curling on the sofa and resting my head on his chest. If there is a future between Ryan and I, then it's a long way off.

'Is Abi being charged?' The question rushes out of him. His eyes flick left then right, looking everywhere it seems but up at me.

'No. After your statement... they've decided not to prosecute.'

He nods. 'Good. She had nothing to do with this. She was vulnerable and I manipulated her. I would like to say sorry. Do you... Do you know where she's staying?'

'She's with Becca now. I've left them to pack.'

'You can't kick her out, Mum. It wasn't her fault,' he says with an urgency that makes my chest ache. 'It was all me. She was about to be evicted and out on the street. She had no one else to turn to and I took advantage of that. She's got nowhere else to go. You can't—'

I reach out and place my hand over his. He tenses and falls silent but doesn't pull away.

'I know,' I say. 'Abi told me everything. They're both packing. We're moving out. I want to live somewhere smaller.' Somewhere without memories of Michael in every room. 'We won't be moving far. Somewhere with a bus route to Colchester for Rebecca's school, and Abi is starting at the college in a couple of months to study for her GCSEs.'

I don't tell him that I've quit *Loose Women* and my cookery segment. Quit before I was sacked. I don't tell Daniel that my career as a presenter is over. The tabloids, all of the newspapers in fact, have eaten Michael alive; Abi and Daniel too. But I haven't escaped either. Like Rebecca, people are struggling to understand how I didn't know what Michael did. I can't blame them. It's something I struggle with myself. How could I have been so blind?

'Are you mad at her?' he asks in quiet voice.

'Sometimes I am.'

I think of the police waiting room at Aldeburgh and sitting beside Abi. Sometimes I lie awake and try to picture what it must have been like to grow up with a depressed mother who kept her own daughter locked inside with her for weeks at a time. I try to imagine how lonely Abi's life must have been without school or friends or family. I don't know how she slipped off the radar of social services, but the only person she had looking out for her was a small-time criminal who popped in from time to time.

'She's had it tough,' I say. The lies Abi told, what she and Daniel did, I know it should bother me. Maybe one day it will. Daniel isn't the only one at the start of his recovery. But, for now, all I can think about is how their lies led me to the truth about Abigail, and the truth about Michael. I can't hate her like I do Michael. 'She's still Becca's sister – and yours. I'm not about to throw her out.'

'Would you mind letting me know the address when you move?' Daniel mumbles. 'I want to write to her.'

'Daniel, of course I'll tell you the address. I don't know what's going to happen to you next, but you'll always have a home with me. Always.' Tears break free and roll down my face.

I hate that Daniel is in here and Michael is free, living in London somewhere, I guess. Easier to blend in somewhere with lots of people. Too much of a coward to contact Rebecca directly. We've had messages through a solicitor. Half-baked apologies and explanations. Whining letters begging for a forgiveness he'll never get. At some point in the future, I will have to consider how I misunderstood Michael so badly and for so long.

Daniel pleaded guilty to the charge of threatening with an offensive weapon. They tried to get kidnap added but both Michael and Abelia said they got into the car with him willingly. It was a final act of kindness from Michael, but not enough to earn him any kind of forgiveness. And, with Daniel pleading guilty, the Crown Prosecution Service didn't push it.

Pleading guilty meant no drawn-out trial. A judge, under the advisement of doctors, sent him here. Section 37 of the Mental Health Act – a hospital instead of prison. No sentence though. I don't know how long he'll be here. Months or years. I don't know if he'll ever be free. It's up to his doctors to decide his fate now.

We sit in silence for a spell. The question builds inside me, and even though I know I shouldn't ask – and ultimately his answer won't change anything – I do it anyway. 'Did you always know the truth about Abigail? That Michael had lied about the abduction?'

Daniel shrugs. 'Sort of. It's like I knew but somehow stopped thinking about it. Like I just started accepting the lies even though I knew Abigail wasn't abducted. Then when I found out about Dad cheating on you with all those women, I got really angry and kind of woke up. I just sort of remembered what had happened. I thought you were both lying about Abigail and that's why you didn't leave him.' Daniel's voice breaks and his sentence trails off.

Tears blur my vision and it hurts to swallow. 'Sorry, I shouldn't have asked.'

'It's OK. Doc Hall and the other quacks say I shouldn't

avoid thinking about everything. She thinks I didn't process
what happened to Abigail when I was younger. What I did.'

'Daniel, it wasn't your fault.'

'Will you come back and see me again?' he asks suddenly.

'Yes,' I reply, trying to smile. 'Every day if you'll let me.'

Another silence.

'I'm sorry,' he whispers.

Pain grips my chest. I pull in a long breath before I speak.
'Daniel. There's something I have to say, and I really want to
make sure you listen and hear it, OK?'

He nods.

'What happened to Abigail wasn't your fault. You were
only a little boy.' My voice cracks, betraying the emotion I'm
bottling inside, but I carry on. 'It was a tragic accident. I can't
begin to comprehend why Michael did what he did afterwards,
but that isn't anything to do with you, OK?'

He nods and a single tear splashes on the table between us.

'Michael robbed us all of being able to grieve Abigail's death, or
to try to move on from it. I will never forgive him for all the things
he's done to you and to us, but especially not for that. When you're
ready, we'll have a service for Abigail and say a proper goodbye.'

Finally, Daniel lifts his head and his soft brown eyes are
heavy with water as they look into mine. Without a word, he
slips from the chair and moves around the table. I stand and
step towards him. We meet in the middle, and he throws his
arms around me, hugging me tight.

'You were just a little boy.' My voice comes out a whisper
through the hurt I can no longer hold back. 'I should have done
more to help you. I'm sorry, Daniel.'

His tears soak through my top and onto my shoulder. I
tighten my hold around his body and feel his pain, his grief, mix
with my own.

A bell sounds from somewhere in the building. A single

chime. I don't know what it means but Daniel stands and wipes his sleeves across his face. 'I have to go.'

I sit and watch my son walk away and all I can think is that I should have done more to help him. I promised myself I would protect my family no matter what, and I will never forgive myself for how badly I have failed.

---

*My name is Daniel Steven Wick. My parents are Sarah and Michael Wick, and when I was six years old, I killed my sister.*

*It was not an accident.*

*I remember the blinding heat of rage, and I remember her laughter – a mocking, stupid giggle.*

*I remember the way my hand tightened around the rock and how every muscle in my body willed me to throw it, to stop the laughter. To stop her. Dead.*

*The quacks here say I was too young, that I didn't mean it. But I am the only one that really knows what happened that day, who remembers that feeling of intent that haunts my every waking moment.*

*My mother knew nothing, she claims, but she turned a blind eye to me. She didn't see what must have been so obvious. I needed her and she wasn't there.*

*They say my father is the guilty one.*

*They say I'm not broken just damaged. They understand why I brought Abigail back the way I did.*

*I wanted to punish my parents. I wanted everyone to know the truth.*

*Sometimes I believe the quacks. Sometimes I believe the papers.*

*I'm innocent.*

*I'm a monster.*

*I killed my sister. It wasn't an accident, but I tell myself now that I didn't mean it.*

*I shot my father. The bullet missed by an inch. I should have taken another second to line up my aim. A mistake I regret. One I won't make again when they let me out of here. And they will let me out. I'll play along. I'm good at pretending. And then when I'm free, I'll find the three bullets I need and I'll try again.*

*Next time, I won't fail.*

# A LETTER FROM LAUREN

Dear Reader,

Thank you so much for reading *She Says She's My Daughter*. If you want to keep up to date with my latest releases and offers, you can sign up for my newsletter at the following link. Your email address will never be shared and you can unsubscribe at any time.

www.bookouture.com/lauren-north

Sometimes book ideas come into our heads as a whisper of a 'what if' that builds over time into an entire story. And sometimes, like *She Says She's My Daughter*, the book idea comes fully formed as a knock at the door. I opened the door and standing on my doorstep were the Wick family. They had a story to tell me. It was tragic and dark, but I hope I did it justice. I will always remember Sarah for her counting and her strength in surviving the worst thing that could happen to a person. And Abi, for wanting something else from her life and being desperate enough to do anything to get it.

I always love to hear from readers, either with reviews, tags in posts, or messages. My social-media links are below and I can be found most days hopping onto Twitter and Instagram. If you enjoyed *She Says She's My Daughter*, then I'd be so grateful if you would leave a review on either Amazon or Goodreads, or simply share the book love by telling a friend.

With love and gratitude,

Lauren x

www.Lauren-North.com

 facebook.com/LaurenNorthAuthor
twitter.com/Lauren_C_North
instagram.com/Lauren_C_North

# ACKNOWLEDGEMENTS

A huge thank you to you, lovely reader, for making it this far. I really hope you've enjoyed the story of the Wick family. I loved writing this book and delving into Sarah and Abi's worlds.

Massive thanks to Lucy Frederick for believing in this book and the amazing editorial suggestions. Special thanks to the entire Bookouture team as well for all your efforts. So much work goes on behind the scenes, and I'm so grateful to Jess Readett, Mandy Kullar, Donna Hillyer, Laura Kincaid and everyone who's part of my team at Bookouture. Thanks also to Emily Scorer and the Bolinda team, and Amanda Preston for her amazing support.

Thank you to all the bloggers and early readers who work tirelessly to spread the word about books and champion so many authors across social media. You guys truly are ace!

To Tanera Simons for always believing in this book! Seeing it published means so much to both of us. And to Laura Heathfield for being completely on the ball, always!

Laura Pearson, Nikki Smith and Zoe Lea – you're the best friends I could ever have in my corner for writing and non-writing support. Thank you!

To Maggie, Mel, Pauline, Kathryn and Andy for reading this book so long ago and seeing something in it. I'm eternally grateful.

Andy, I dedicated this book to you because 'the one with the stranger on the boat' has always been your favourite. Thank you for always believing in me! To Tommy and Lottie for simply being the best kids ever!

Every time I write a book, I create a document to list all the people I need to thank along the way so I don't forget to mention them in the acknowledgements. Obviously, I forget to ever use it. So if your name isn't here, please forgive me. I'm so grateful for the support!